WELLS OF GLORY

Nov. 15, 2005

To Max Nichols
with fond
memories of
Journal Record
Christmas parties
at your house —
Blessings,

Mary McReynolds

BOOK ONE
LEGACY OF THE LAND SERIES

WELLS OF GLORY

MARY McREYNOLDS

CROSSWAY BOOKS • WHEATON, ILLINOIS
A DIVISION OF GOOD NEWS PUBLISHERS

Wells of Glory

Copyright © 1996 by Mary McReynolds

Published by Crossway Books
        a division of Good News Publishers
        1300 Crescent Street
        Wheaton, Illinois 60187

Cover illustration: Chet Jezierski

First printing, 1996

Printed in the United States of America

Library of Congress Cataloging-in-Publication Data
McReynolds, Mary, 1947-
    Wells of glory / Mary McReynolds.
      p.   cm. — (Legacy of the land ; bk. 1)
    ISBN 0-89107-889-4
    I. Title.   II. Series: McReynolds, Mary, 1947-   Legacy of the
land ; bk. 1.
    PS3563.C78W4   1996
    813'.54—dc20   95-48801

04		03		02		01		00		99		98		97		96
15	14	13	12	11	10	9	8	7	6	5	4	3	2	1

*This book is gratefully dedicated to
the major wells from which my life has drawn:*

*Yeshua HaMashiach, Creator and Lord,
J. E., husband and friend,
Toby and Carolyn, father and mother*

PROLOGUE

———❦———

ONCE WAS A TIME WHEN FOLKS sat on the porch summer nights and listened to silence while contemplating the movement of the distant spheres. Prairie nights rested sticky and hot on the skin. If you were thirsty, you lowered a bucket into a well and heard its cool splash echoing up the deep shaft. The pull on the bucket was a good pull, hard on the muscles, heavy with the stars dancing their reflections in the clear and moving water. Up the water came from the dark earth. Down came the fires of distant suns, floating in the bucket, in the dipper, in your hands so that you drank their light and saw that the light was impossible to separate from the life of the water itself. Though resting far below the ground in subterranean pools, the waters could be channeled up and up, right up into the light. Some men coaxed the streams to come forth by means of a divining rod. Though the Word of God forbade this and other heathen things, still the act was possible. Wells were witched and dug.

Once was a time when the man and woman waited for their children to run afar chasing fireflies, waited till the wild whoops over the magic blink, blink coming from a bug became low and indistinct. The woman would slip away quietly, leaving the rocker to creak and creak till the man saw she had gone.

Love was made those nights: children cupping tiny flames in cautious little hands; parents warming to older, more familiar fires, mysterious and profound. Love was made those nights with sighs and tears as the elements of earth and air conspired to bring forth life again.

Babes were born on the far side of summertime: tiny, wriggling, helpless things, pink with life and covered with birth. Women died those days, died of birth and died of death.

The man would stand and question God, looking long from mother to babe. The woman there on those coarse sheets was she he'd courted long ago, the girl he picked wildflowers for. He'd touched and loved those silent breasts a thousand times, and now no more. No child would suck their milk again. No boy would bring an injured foot to those limp hands. The voice that lulled was silent now. The baby there on that cold breast seemed to reach for hidden things, her arms and legs but lifeless bands.

The man—he'd swallow hard, aged by years as yet unseen, then turn, and walk away.

ONE

———————————◆———————————

A T THE AGE OF TWENTY-NINE, in the spring of the year when rains come unannounced and slow, Lillian Maude Jenness Reuben was having her seventh baby. Married for thirteen years, she was accustomed to the ways of birth. Her husband, ten years her senior, had coached her through this lesson like he'd taught her sums, for he had been her teacher two years before they married. He called her Lillie when they were alone, and she called him Ben. Four of their children survived; the two who did not were infant sons and the first residents in the cemetery up the hill. Others would join their place of rest, in their own times and seasons.

Lillie never took childbirth lightly. Though she wore a cheerful countenance, still there was at her core a serious part made so by birth and death. She knew about the pains and fear, how both must be ridden out. Yet this most recent birth, this seventh one, was different from the others. Her confinement was more difficult, for one thing—slower, harder. She kept waiting for an old and familiar buoyancy to surface, yet the pregnancy would not cooperate with her expectations. It rested heavy and stagnant over her body, oppressing her spirit. It had not been like this with the others.

The first contractions were insistent waves of pain, far apart at first, having begun the day before and forcing her to bed. It was when they came closer together that she knew it was time to send for Rose. Rose was more than a midwife; she was Lillie's first cousin and beloved friend. Rose would know what to do, would take charge. Lillie had already prepared the room, had tied the sheets to the bedposts for holding on to when nothing else availed. She remembered former births and pain, but surely they had not been like this. The force of each contraction was a fearful thing indeed.

Lillie made her peace with God, the same peace she made every day. She finished her prayer even as her husband came in to reassure her one last time. He wore his hat and overcoat.

"Rose should be here soon," he said, his eyes betraying his concern. "I sent one of the men for her some time ago."

"Where you going?" she asked in a quivering voice. "Don't go. Stay with me, Ben."

"I'm going into town for the doctor, Lillie. Don't want to worry you none, but I'm not satisfied with the way this birth is going. I'll be back soon's I can. No offense against Rose neither. I want the doctor here—that's all."

Ben was dressed for a hard ride in the rain. She envied him. He could get away from the birth. She could not. She wanted not to blame him for what was happening to her. She turned such thoughts over to her Lord, for she loved her husband with all her soul. Yet Ben was far outside her pain. She reverted to being a schoolgirl all over again, chiding herself for not studying more, for not preparing for this test.

Her pain intensified so that she could hardly remember the day before, much less her other births. Everything was wiped clean in this new pain. Was this what the doctor had warned her about when he told her she'd better stay in bed? But that was early on, before her stomach even showed a little bulge. Absurd man! She had a family to tend to, work to do. Well, she was in bed now. La!

Lillie wanted Rose no matter what. Rose had been with her through the last four births. They knew each other as only women who attend births can know another woman. Lillie trusted her. She wished she had sent for her cousin the day before and wondered what she could have been thinking of in not doing so. It was twenty miles to Rose's farm and back in a buggy in the rain.

Now Ben was gone, and he had a farther distance still to ride. The sky was so dark with rain that both kerosene lamps were turned up high. One sat on the dresser, doubling its light in the mirror behind it. The other was on the table beside the bed.

I could have the baby before anyone gets here, she thought, trying not to feel sorry for herself. Another pain rose and fell, carrying her to jagged heights of keen awareness.

She would have to suffer the doctor's presence. She had no choice in the matter really. Ben had made up his mind on that. He rarely insisted and when he did, she always obeyed him. Still, she feared the doctor's vacant stare.

"He looks like an undertaker," she had often said, and such he was, a stern little man who plied his trade for the living and the dead. Lillie distrusted his bulging eyes; how they peered red and strange behind thick spectacles. The smell of alcohol and formaldehyde permeated his clothing, and his hands were limp and damp to touch. She shuddered to think of his hands upon any part of her, this grim mortician-dentist, this land's excuse for a doctor.

If only Rose would come and the baby be born now. Now! she thought.

The front door slammed downstairs, and Lillie heard gleeful

shrieks and laughter, though all four children had been warned not to make a sound this day. There was a light, quick step on the stairs, and then her cousin burst into the room.

"Lillie!" Rose cried, hurrying to the bed and embracing her at once. "That horse will never forgive me for driving him so hard and fast!"

"Thank God you're here!" Lillie cried, bracing for the contraction that followed. Rose's presence was comforting. Her efficient manner and white apron made Lillie glad.

Rose washed her hands in the china basin on the table by the door and motioned to Aunt Addie who was standing in the doorway.

"Addie dear, heat some water and boil four towels straightaway. We'll need more pillows and blankets, too. It's cold as ice in here! Here, Lillie, let's change that gown. It's soaked through."

Four faces peered in from the hall.

"Grace, I want you and Gertie to take the twins back downstairs," Rose said. "You children need to be very sensitive now and help by being quiet and good. Remember what I told you? You'll help your mother best by keeping out of the way."

The girls each took a brother by the hand and turned to go.

"When will you be done?" Grace, the oldest, asked.

Rose laughed a little. "Now that's a fine question, dear, and one I can't possibly answer. Babies come in their own good time. It was the same with each of you. Run along. I'll come down when I can and let you know how we're doing."

Lillie reached toward her children, though, and all came rushing into the room for the hugs she offered.

"Be good," she whispered to each, with separate little promises of what they would do together when all this was past. The children left quietly, satisfied.

"I still think I'll shut the door," Rose said before going to the bureau for a fresh nightgown.

Lillie lowered her head helplessly. "I look so awful," she said.

"I've seen you better, and that's a fact," Rose said. "Never can understand why every blessed birth has to be so different— some hard, some easy. We'll wash you up a bit and brush your hair." Her dark eyes held to Lillie's. "It's bad, isn't it?" she asked, her voice nearly breaking. "I wish I could take the pain for you."

Lillie nodded, fighting back her own tears. She sighed as Rose's capable hands took hold of her soiled gown and drew it over her head. A clean, starched fabric rustled over her swollen body quickly.

Lillie groaned and sat forward while Rose plumped up the pillows behind her. "It's bad," she said.

Rose pulled the sheets and quilts back. "Never knew your legs to swell so." She applied liniment to her hands and set to work rubbing Lillie's bloated ankles and calves with expert fingers. Lillie winced with pain and grabbed the knotted sheets as the next contraction began.

"Hold on!" Rose cried.

The mattress rose and fell; Lillie bit her lips to keep from crying out. She lay panting and trembling as Rose wiped her face with a moist towel.

"You want to have this baby before old sawbones gets here?" she asked. "Well, let him come. You and I know what to do. One old man underfoot won't make no difference to either one of us now, will it?"

Lillie managed a weak smile. "I'm powerful thirsty," she said. Rose poured a glass from the pitcher on the nightstand, mixed in a teaspoon of apple cider vinegar, and told her to drink it all. Lillie obeyed, making a face as she drank.

"Ugh! It's so sour!" she said. "That's one taste I'll never get used to. I hate having anyone see me this way, Rose. Even you, even Ben. But for that doctor to come in here and see my legs when he told me to stay off them, well, I'm in no mood for his scolding ways. Ben's gone for him, though, and there's nothing I can do but endure the humiliation. He's that worried about this birth."

"As if he wasn't with the others!" Rose said. "Don't I know? Some men take hold when their wives is underway, but that one of yours buckles and near faints every time a baby comes. And him no stranger to birthing either—not with all the livestock on this place!"

"He worries over them, too," Lillie said.

"I'm not criticizing—only saying. For all of that, he's a doing what he thinks best."

"You'll be getting used to a husband's ways before you know it, Rose, when you and George is married. Things change pretty fast, I can tell you that."

Rose frowned as Lillie bore another contraction. "Seeing you like this doesn't make me too eager," she said. "Here, leave this washcloth on your forehead and try not to talk anymore."

Lillie knew there was more to her present difficulty than met the eye. It was more than her legs being swollen, though that was bad enough. She had had swelling during the last two pregnancies. The thing was, she felt tired inside, worn out. The sight of her legs made her heart heavy and sad, like it had to work harder somehow. Her legs were puffed and stretched looking, like cheap fabric on a garment that's ready to tear because the person wearing it is way too fat. Her legs scared her when she saw them against the sheets, saw their hard roundness and unfamiliar size! La! They used to be trim little things, like the rest of her, not these stumps of wood, these marble blocks of skin. She was ashamed that Rose and Ben should see them, not to mention the bleary-eyed doctor!

Two hours passed, interspersed with thunder and harder rain. Lillie fainted twice. In between, when she felt the least bit conscious, she feared the expression on Rose's face. Only once did her cousin look hopeful, and that was when Ben and the doctor finally came in. They hadn't bothered to remove their coats and stood panting and dripping rain all over the floor.

Lillie groaned as the doctor drew the covers back.

"I knew it!" he exclaimed. "It's milk leg sure as shootin'. Just what I warned you would happen." He frowned and shook his head from side to side. She took his tone to heart in some dim part of her self, experiencing the inexplicable feelings of a scolded child, like the milk leg was her own fault. She lowered her gaze to the floor, thinking only that the thoughtless man's duster had dripped water all over the clean rug. "I told you to stay off your feet, didn't I, Mrs. Reuben?" He removed his coat and rolled up his sleeves angrily.

Lillie sighed. It was easy for him to say. He didn't have four children to tend to or Aunt Addie to fret over, much less the chores and washing and cooking. La! Didn't have the care of two growing girls and two little boys, God bless them. His idea of good medicine was plentiful doses of Chamberlain's Colic and Diarrhea Remedy and staying off your feet. Even so, she had made an effort to stay off her feet. She just couldn't do it for very long at a time.

When she was eight months along, she wrote to her older sister who lived in town. Lillie wrote two letters virtually pleading with her to come out to the farm and help during the last month of her confinement. Maureen was stronger, a woman who had given birth to all three of her children as easily as falling off a log. Perfect in her unruffled attitude toward life, she was efficient like

Rose but utterly lacking in the midwife's compassion. Maureen made excuses and would not come.

Ben told Lillie to give it up, but still she wrote one last time. "It isn't as if a pregnancy lasts forever," she said. Maureen wrote back that it was too far to leave her own family and that Lillie had Aunt Addie and two girls old enough to take hold and make do.

Lillie chafed, thinking of Maureen's Negro maid who lived with them in town and did all the cooking and housekeeping. Maureen, she felt, was being spiteful. The reason her sister wouldn't come was because of an argument they'd had years ago about whether to live in town or kill yourself working a farm. Maureen's husband was a banker with prospects. These prospects demanded a fancy house on a street with lawns and fences.

Not that the two sisters had ever been particularly close. Their upbringing had been fraught with conflicts from doting parents who each had their favorite child and didn't bother to deny it. Lillie had early sworn to raise her own children with no partiality, and to her knowledge, she had done so. There was a brief period of sibling peace when their husbands prepared to make the Run for Unassigned Lands. Absurd arguments sprang up over the merits of town versus farm life. How stupid it all seemed now. Still, Lillie had buried her ill will; Maureen never had.

So Maureen had not come, and Lillie had not stayed off her feet. She vainly hoped that her condition would somehow right itself. Now, the momentum of unseen truths brought her to an hour when she saw, and confessed, her folly. The realization rose in the form of a silent and private prayer asking God to forgive her for being so stubborn.

Rose placed steaming hot cloths on Lillie's abdomen and tried to reassure her. The doctor thumped and probed, suggested startling remedies, and coughed without covering his mouth.

Aunt Addie came and went, wringing her hands and herding the children downstairs for dinner and weekly baths. Ben paced the room on bare feet—he never wore his shoes inside—hands knotted in his pockets.

Lillie watched the smoke from the doctor's pipe wrap an airy wreath around the room. She watched it float and drift and wished it would change into ether like real doctors used in hospitals in towns where folks were civilized and knew what to do to silence pain. She longed to breathe herself into oblivion.

The phrase "a time and times and half a time" came to her on the sharp, somehow nostalgic smell of the tobacco. She couldn't recall where she'd read the words but thought they were Scripture. The circle of smoke was a fragile thread that bound the room's occupants in a common circumference till her pain broke through of its own accord, slicing her away from the others.

Lillie thought she knew why. She was a reader, after all. She and Ben taught their girls to read. She read whenever there was time, mostly at night, into the late hours, the pungent smell of kerosene outlining every word. Lillie was a reader and a delver. She read about Eve in Genesis and delved into the curse of having babies and having desire unto her husband that would make her have babies. She read about God setting before His people life and blessing, death and cursing. She understood that idolatry doesn't have to involve something made of stone, that the land itself could be worshiped, or even the stars. She saw this kind of adoration in her husband's eyes at times, saw his worshipful gaze turn to soil and sky and water. It scared her to tempt God so.

And, oh, but it was coming hard, this curse of birthing in sorrow. She couldn't help the screaming now, no longer cared that such startling sounds ripped from her throat, to the dismay of the twins who were downstairs howling through the house and the girls who stared in amazement and fear from behind the bed-room door at this stranger who was their mother, wailing like a banshee and thrashing so on the bed.

Seven births and this was the one all right. Lillie knew that some folks really never believed in death till it hit them. She wasn't that way. The death throes of each of her parents and many others she'd nursed through the years rose up in her memory, sharp with detail—individual testimonies of how folks made their exits from life. She knew that few thought about death at all until it made its insistent appearance, demanding one's undivided attention and not going anywhere until such attention was given.

Her husband believed in God, but he had told her he would never believe in being alone, had made her promise that she wouldn't go first and leave him—as if she could make such a promise in the first place. Lillie watched Ben now, felt a peaceful kind of sorrow for him that lasted only a moment. It was all she could spare. She could tell by his weeping that he was preparing himself, that death had asked for permission to speak and that it would have its way. She was sorry for Ben, but she had to go.

There was no one alive who could even begin to prepare her soul for the length and depth of the valley she had entered. A phrase from *Pilgrim's Progress* came and went, a passage about making death your company-keeper. It was downright peculiar! All her life she'd kept company with first her parents, then her sister, then her schoolmates, and lately her husband and their children. But all along, it was death walking right beside her.

Sometimes she had hints of it. She knew the Gospels were about overcoming death through her Lord. She knew she was dead to sin and alive to God through Jesus. She believed she had received the Lord's imparted life. And now she had to walk in the light of that belief. Now her own time had come to pass through the Cross in all its power.

Another pain pushed her deeper into the valley as her spirit prayed. She sensed that her Lord and death had been there her whole life long. All her practicing of holiness came forward to assist her, for she was far into the valley now, close to being swallowed whole. La, what a shadow it was, too, darker than moonless nights or storms on the prairie. They couldn't hold a patch to this. It was the valley of the shadow, all right.

Lillie heard someone's voice—Rose or Aunt Addie—she couldn't tell which. It was a woman's voice, comforting and low, uttering little bells of prayer. The words gave her a jolt. She was hearing a new sound, the silence of God's peace. She looked for her Shepherd, but it was powerfully dark and her body a solid trembling.

Delirium came and fled. There was no way for Lillie to know when it was that she sat bolt upright and cried, "Oh, save me, sweet Jesus!"

At that precise moment Ben bit his lips and read the time on his pocket watch. She, to her great surprise and relief, fell back upon the pillows stained with sweat and tears . . .

. . . ALL IN A MOMENT SHE WAS WALKING, a quiet, peaceful walk at twilight. Yes, it was so. Dusk had fallen. The yard was quiet and stiller than she'd ever seen it. It wasn't an ominous stillness but gentle with an all-encompassing quiet . . .

. . . There was a grove of orange trees. This was a peculiar thing. She had only seen trees like these in picture books, yet here they were, an orchard full. The fragrance of orange blossoms hung in the blissful air, its sweet citrus smell reminding her of

Christmas. White-plumed birds were starting to descend from a great and mighty place . . .

. . . The sky broke back—that's all she could tell. It just seemed to break away from itself. Clouds like jagged mountains lined the far horizon, majestic props waiting for the play to begin. Lillie gazed into the vaulted sky—large and white; the strange birds drifted down . . .

. . . "But I haven't got a wrap," she said out loud, straining all the while toward the lovely creatures. *Living creatures,* she thought, *with eyes like wheels of fire.* One looked at her, its burning gaze penetrating as it loomed huge and white just above the trees. It hovered patiently, beckoning in the language of silence to come . . .

. . . "Have no fear," the angel said. "His righteousness is all the robe you need." Lillie lifted her arms and was at once caught up with an awesome rush of wings . . .

. . . "Oh, my Lord," she cried. Peace like a river flooded over her and waves unspeakable, full of glory. She felt something like the push of when a baby is born and wondered for the barest instant what it could be, and then the burden was passing, gone, and now forgotten forever . . .

. . . In her arms was a lightness and joy to carry to His kingdom, for it was long decreed that Lillie would not enter that realm alone. There was no clash of thunder, no roll of drums or wind—only the incredible Light whose rays now filled the universe. Two souls were gloriously free in the place where there is no time. For Lillie, it was as if she had been waiting for this event all her life. For the other, infant soul, it was all she would ever need to know.

TWO

———◆———

THE RAIN POUNDED THE RED DIRT as Benjamin Franklin Reuben hitched his two best horses to the wagon. He cursed under his breath when his finger got caught in the cinch. The oath was a muffled sound that made the horses back up and look a little wild. Pulling a wagon in the rain was not their cup of tea. It was as if they knew they were carrying something sad and heavy. Ben had secured the coffin with two new ropes, though, and it would hold. He felt a sense of urgency about getting to the cemetery. He couldn't have said why. The family waited on the porch. For him, he guessed.

Lillie had been dead for nearly thirty hours. The tulips were blooming.

Ben wanted to keep the wagon in the barn until the last possible minute. He threw a tarp over the pine box and sniffed harder than usual. Tears made his nose run, and he was determined not to cry, not like this, not with the family looking on. He bit his lip and wiped his nose with his sleeve. As if to assure himself that he was Ben Reuben after all and that life would go on, he straddled his nose with a thumb and forefinger and blew hard, a habit he was known for. He checked the ropes again and shivered.

The rain let up, making a softer sound. Somewhere in the distance the song of a lone bird trilled over the morning air. Ben gazed long at Lillie's garden. The sight of the morning glories over the trellis brought fresh tears. The vibrant blue was the color of his wife's eyes.

He faced the coffin and laid a gloved hand there, as if the mere touch of his living flesh might somehow bring her back. He shook his head, knowing beyond all knowing that Lillie was gone. Her soul had fled the beauty and the pain of mortality. She was past the visits now, the secret things a corpse endures, all the weeping, the children hanging back with hollow eyes and hiccuping tears, scared of her silent body.

"La, look at that child," Aunt Addie had said. "Who's he think she is anyway? It's his own poor dead ma, that's who. Now kiss her, Herman Reuben, and shush those tears. Kiss your mama goodbye."

But Herman Reuben screamed when Aunt Addie held him up to the coffin. He grimaced and bowed his three-year-old back, refusing to kiss the lips of the dead woman. Ben told Addie to let him be.

Ben blamed himself all over again, seeing in the event something he could yet control or should have controlled. But what could he have done about milk leg? He blamed himself because he loved Lillie, had promised her a good life, and did his best to give it. He blamed himself because all his work had finally come to this.

Lillie wouldn't blame him, though, nor would she haunt his sleep. He had given her everything he had. He built her a proper house, not one of those sod shacks so common at the time. He cut the cottonwood logs and peeled the bark himself. He covered the roof with brush till he could finish it properly, and two years later he added the second floor. He built the barn with lumber bought in town. They were settled and took care of each other. He learned to like other people more than he'd ever done alone, and that, too, was a gift he'd given to Lillie, for she loved everyone.

He built her the chicken house and the milk house and the smokehouse and the root cellar. He put his mind to work studying how best to farm and do things right. The teacher had a teachable spirit so that the farm did well and prospered. He bought and sold horses and mules and knew how to break and train them. He learned how to use a horse-powered drill to find water and was known for his well-digging skills. Every night he came home to her, to Lillie, and told her stories of what he'd done and heard and seen. And she cared so much that she listened to him and was fond of his company and let him know.

They were spared many kinds of grief. They counted themselves blessed that no child of theirs had ever drowned in a bucket of slop or was gored to death by a bull. Such things happened to folks they knew. Storms had never torn house or barn from their foundations; floods had never taken their crops away. No fires had burned their land, nor thieves broken in to steal.

Now the rain changed its tune again, hammering the tin roof with a wet, metallic sound. Ben stared listlessly at the sacks of seed stacked along one wall, the tools of his drilling trade along another. Sowing seed had always been a ritual for him, a meaningful task he enjoyed. Drilling water wells was an essential gift in this raw land. Now both occupations seemed but a weariness to the flesh.

Planting and sowing. Seedtime and harvest. Birth and death. What had he read the night before? Something about a grain of wheat being alone until it is planted. At least Lillie wasn't alone. Ben thought of the infant beside his wife.

"She's a pretty little thing," Rose had said sorrowfully. Only

Rose could bring herself to wash the lifeless little body; no one else could bear the pitiful task.

They named the baby Elizabeth Caitlin because it seemed a worse thing than death to bury a baby without giving it a name. They laid her tiny body under Lillie's left arm, the doll-like head resting on Lillie's shoulder.

Aunt Addie read about the cloud of witnesses in the book of Hebrews and how you are to lay aside every weight, but Ben thought how Lillie had no weight at all and how he wasn't ready to lay her aside. He was tormented with the thought that God had judged him for loving Lillie so much.

Lillie had led him to God over the years. It happened over days and weeks and years of being with her and observing her chaste and loving character. One day he woke up believing in the God of the Bible and His Son. He repented of his sins and said that this must be what being born again was all about. Never once had Lillie pleaded with him to believe, yet always she had prayed. He didn't see as clearly as she did, though. Seeing through a glass darkly, like he read in 1 Corinthians 13, was what he experienced.

"It's the best I can do," he'd told her.

"It's enough," she'd answered.

Ben listened when Lillie read the Sermon on the Mount, something she did every Sunday in the front parlor, for, she said, "You can never hear Jesus' words too often." They would discuss the Lord's words candidly and how they applied to their own lives. Ben said he never saw anyone living the Sermon, except for Lillie and Aunt Addie some of the time. He said it was impossible to turn the other cheek. Lillie agreed. She added that it was impossible for man, but not for God, that all things were possible with God.

Ben became interested in prophecy and what was to come.

When the calendar turned on the new century, he reflected long on what the next hundred years would bring before the year 2000. Already there were wars and rumors of war. Even the ancient people of God, the Jews themselves, were stirring. He thought that most certainly the Zionist movement portended something for this day and age. There was a mystical side to Ben Reuben, else he wouldn't have repudiated his former reliance on reason. Ben studied Daniel's visions and the book of Ezekiel. He marveled at the descriptions of angelic beings as wheels of light. He bought Matthew Henry's commentaries and believed that mankind had entered the beginning of the latter days. Signs of the end abounded. He made notes from his studies every night. He started working on his own commentary on the book of Revelation and what the seven thunders might have uttered.

Thunder rolled on this April morning in the year of the Lord 1900, the year that Lillie died.

Ben struggled with his faith as the single word *corruption* came to him with shuddering truth. It would happen to him one day, this strange inertia and humility of the human body, this submission unto death. He wiped his eyes and got hold of his emotions. Thunderous reverberations shook the sky, the house, the barn, the whole world.

"Time to go," he whispered to the red mare. He climbed into the driver's seat and worked the reins, coaxing the mare and the stocking-footed gelding toward the house. Rain pattered on the canvas-covered box behind him, startling him anew.

His children stood on the porch and looked at him with the same forlorn expression on all four faces. Hiram and Herman wore sailor suits Lillie's sister had brought from town. Ben didn't want to accept the gifts, but Aunt Addie said it wasn't worth the fight. So let the twins wear their little sailor suits and those hats! It broke his heart to see them.

"Please, Papa, let us ride, too."

Someone had spoken to him, the first words he was aware of having heard that day. He looked down at his oldest child, who at twelve so resembled her mother.

Gertie, four years younger, also stared up at him, holding a bunch of damp daffodils in her tight, little fist. "Yes, Papa, please," she said softly.

Ben nodded and at once felt the weight of all four children settling into the wagon behind him. He urged the horses forward as the rain turned to a soft mist. He liked the weather itself, remembering that some of his best times with Lillie had been rainy days. When it was dry for a spell, he would get nervous and anxious to hear the thunder again, to see the lightning streak across the sky. The air would turn hot and strange with unseen lights and powers, like a strangely sanctioned lust. Lillie shared his passion for rain.

Once he called weather the wayward child of God's creation. He told Lillie that underground streams and pools were wild things, untamed till coaxed from the earth. How she had laughed with him, saying that he was himself a wayward child and wild as subterranean depths. This happened when they were picking cotton, their limbs aching, fingers sore and bleeding under an Indian summer sky. No, he thought, amending his memory. She had said it that year they had worried so about the rows of corn looking limp and dead from lack of rain. But there was always cotton, always corn. And then he did remember. She had called him the wayward child one October as they watched blades of wheat struggling through the soil. The wheat seemed kin to them, destined for hard times and adversity that neither could allay. Both of them knew what was coming; both of them dreaded the uncertain winter snows and summer heat that would follow.

Lillie's death spread over the world like rain.

Ben's thoughts brought him to the top of the hill and the cemetery. He drove the horses and wagon into the enclosed yard and immediately felt a new, more powerful sundering from his beloved. The event before him, the actual burial, took on its own life as the crowd of mourning friends and family parted. Someone touched his arm; someone said something comforting; others wept.

The horses lowered their heads in a transcendent moment that gentled their animal natures. Wildflowers of many colors bent over the darker green of the wet grass; clusters of white spirea cascaded in long, willowy strips along one stone fence. The rain tapped against the exposed coffin lid when the tarp was removed. Ben's eyes filled with tears when he saw the gaping hole, the shovels.

Grace and Gertrude helped the little boys out of the wagon while Ben and three other men carried the coffin to the grave site.

The preacher from town stepped forward and recited Psalm 23. "'The Lord is my shepherd,'" he began. He said that Jesus is the Resurrection and the Life, that Lillie and her baby were even now, at this moment, in the kingdom of heaven. All heads were bowed as someone sang, others joining in, "A Mighty Fortress Is Our God." The song seemed over too soon, the ensuing silence too harsh.

Aunt Addie raised her head. Looking for all the world like a stern prophetess come to rebuke the wind, she recited Proverbs 31 in its entirety.

"'Give her of the fruit of her hands, and let her own works praise her in the gates!'" the old woman cried at last, her heart and voice breaking. Feet shuffled on the grass; throats cleared. It was clearly time to get to the work at hand.

Six men came forward to lower the coffin into the ground.

Ben could only stand to one side and stare into the space below. He jumped involuntarily when the coffin touched the bottom with a dull thud. The sound made his heart skip, his stomach turn. The tall man wiped his eyes, unashamed at last, not caring who saw his tears. It didn't matter anymore. His wife and baby were laid to rest, and he had to grieve. He had to weep like he had to inhale. It was a requirement of the living.

"Dust to dust," the preacher said, "ashes to ashes." Friends and family picked up handfuls of dirt and dropped them over the coffin. The sound of falling earth dulled Ben's senses at last. He stared through a blur of tears, saw Rose hold back, shaking her head, saw Lillie's sister turn furious eyes on him. The truth was he could scarcely breathe and didn't care what anyone thought.

The grave was covered by the steady shoveling of other men's hands. The small mound was finished well after the close knot of humanity had loosened and dispersed. Folks simply went home.

Hiram and Herman walked around the cemetery in the aimless way of three-year-olds while Grace and Gertie wove wet flowers into bright but fading crowns.

Ben watched his children, remembering a story about a crazed man digging up his beloved's grave. The book was one of Lillie's favorites. It had a strange title, he thought, *Wuthering Heights*.

Ben stared at the ground, said nothing. Someone took the children home.

THREE

B EN'S MARRIAGE TO LILLIE WAS A BRIEF and blessed inter-
val between two desolate points. His life before her had
seen its share of grief. Born in 1861 to parents past their
prime, Ben had an older brother who fought in the Civil War.
This brother, whom he scarcely knew, died from head injuries
during a retreat. Not long afterward, Ben's mother succumbed
to the ravages of female trouble. His father held on for a few
years. Having done well as a merchant, the German immigrant
nursed his fondness for rich foods until his cravings gave him a
heart attack. At the age of eighteen, Ben found himself the sole
survivor of his family home and store. His father had left him
several thousand dollars in the bank.

Ben sold his father's business and continued to live frugally.
An avid reader, he continued his studies and earned a certificate
to teach school. He possessed an alert and curious mind and
asked questions of everyone. He learned about horses from
those who traded them, about money from those who made it
their business, about farming from farmers.

His great skill was digging wells, a talent he came to by much
trial and error. Though many town and country folks said their

wells were found by divination, Ben thought such claims little more than superstition. He witnessed several dowsings and was at a loss to explain how the Y-shaped willow branches turned and trembled in the diviners' hands. Once he had reached out to stop a shaking branch in a well-witcher's hands and felt a jolting vibration race up his arms.

"It was plain spooky," he told Lillie. "I decided then and there to have nothing more to do with witching wells."

Sometimes he was called in to dig wells that had already been witched, but half the time these turned out to be dry holes. He was amused at how well-witches had a short memory for failures.

Ben believed there was always water somewhere below the ground. The only magic involved was to keep on digging. Most wells went down a hundred feet. Shallower holes wouldn't hold up over a long span of time. His gift was prospecting and finding good spots where water was likely to be found, usually bottom land or places close to flowing streams.

His personal wells ran silent and deep. Ben didn't mix with wild men and was shy around women. Later he would tell people that this was not due to any strength of character on his part but to the grace of God alone. It was simply that a voice in his heart told him to wait, and he obeyed. He moved to a small town in the southern part of Kansas, a train stop along the route to the Indian Territory. Here, where his life changed forever, he plied his well-digging trade and taught grades one through eight in a one-room schoolhouse.

Lillian Maude Jenness was his best pupil, a stunning girl of fifteen. She came from what folks called a good family, and her older sister was already married.

It didn't take the discerning schoolmaster long to appreciate the young girl's unassuming beauty and bright intelligence. Though he tried not to single her out for special attention, he nonetheless fell in love with her. The voice in his heart told him that she was the one. There she sat, day in and day out, listening so seriously and with such grace to his every word and helping others with their lessons. She could be quiet and reflective on the one hand and then laugh joyously, ringing the world with light. Everyone loved her. She was wholesome in thought and deed, and when anyone asked her why she was so happy, she would say it was because God loved her and made her want to please Him.

Ben started going to church so he could see Lillie outside the school environment. When he heard the minister read a passage in the Gospel about Jesus describing a man in whom there was no guile, he reflected that Lillie was like this, too. She had no affectation at all. He sought her parents' permission to court her, and when she was sixteen, after a time of observing the most circumspect of behavior, Ben proposed to her. She surprised him no end by accepting. Both were virgins.

They were married in the schoolhouse in the spring of the year, Lillie wearing a white gown and Ben a new suit. They were young and elegant and much in love, undaunted by the way Lillie's sister held back. Mr. Jenness praised his new son-in-law, saying that he was both bright and enterprising.

Ben worked hard. He managed his inheritance well and turned it to profit, but more than money, he wanted land. He wanted a farm. He read about the farming opportunities in the Indian Territory where the Five Civilized Tribes were settled. Though the tribes occupied much of the area, observers wrote, there was one vast unsettled portion that any citizen, white or black, would be allowed to own and farm. Ben joined hundreds of people who wrote letters to the president of the United States asking him to open the Unassigned Lands for settlement. Ben quoted such concepts as Manifest Destiny. He said that the Indians' tribal way of life was over, especially for those tribes who had turned Confederate, hoping to save their plantations and slaves. A Union supporter, he had no patience with and felt no pity for anyone who had rebelled against his government.

One year later, when Ben and Lillie's first child was born, Manifest Destiny was unleashed in an announcement from Washington, D.C. The two and a half million acres of Unassigned Lands would be opened for public settlement.

The Reubens named their baby girl Grace and made bold plans.

The year was 1889, the twentieth century only eleven years away, when Ben Reuben applied to stake a claim in Oklahoma Territory. Throughout the country, traveling revivalists proclaimed that the second coming of the Lord Jesus Christ was at hand. Ben hoped there would be enough time to stake his claim and start his farm before prophecy unleashed its torrent of latter-day events.

"Stay Your hand, oh Lord," Ben prayed. "Delay Your coming this little while."

Fifty thousand others applied to stake their claims, and many prayed the same prayer. They came from everywhere in all manner of vehicle and dress. Profit, adventure, and the life force beckoned. They waited in the dusty tents of makeshift camps, rowdies with rough manners rubbing shoulders with gentlemen from the East, getting into fistfights with mild-spoken dreamers. Fired by a collective lust, they pitched their tents beside campfires and drank strong coffee and liquor, too, talking into the night of what they would do when they had their land and how it would all play out in politics and the economy of the nation. Men, women, children, babies at the breast—they slept in the back of wagons, under soiled canvas, beneath scraggly trees and brush. Those who could afford it rented rooms in hotels and boarding houses.

These were the children and grandchildren of immigrants who had followed earlier dreams. Recessive genes were at work to vouchsafe their wildly hybrid claims. It was their right, they declared, their divine and manifest right to own land. Never mind that for millennia the land had belonged to no one. Though roaming bands of humanity gleaned its treasure and beauty, the Indians had never presumed to lay claim to it. Can a man own the air, or land, or rushing waters? the red men asked.

The latter-day Americans said yes, and Ben Reuben's voice was one of the loudest. Why, even the president of the United States said it was so.

Thus Benjamin Franklin Reuben concluded his teaching duties and moved his family to yet another town along the Kansas border, so close to Indian Territory, he joked, that you could just about spit and hit the Unassigned Lands. He spent his time gathering information and purchasing the tools and supplies they would need, about two wagons full. He read every pamphlet printed that described the topographical features of the Oklahoma Territory.

It was good land, everyone agreed, with abundance of water and game, and it was simply waiting to turn into fields of cotton, grain, and pasture grass. Black river soil held the promise of corn, wheat, and sorghum. Ben had no illusions, of course. Spring storms could trigger a prairie fire and summer's heat smother like a wool coat. After the sweet relief of fall and Indian summer, the harsh winters would work to break whatever human spirit remained. Five years of endurance, though, was all it took. Anyone could endure five years. Then the land would be his and Lillie's, all 160 acres of it.

Ben left nothing to chance in selecting the horse that he would ride to stake his claim. After several days, he found what he was looking for—a russet-colored stallion with a stout chest and strong legs. Already named Steeler, the horse was trained to run and cost, as Ben told his wife, "a pretty penny but worth every bit of it." Ben rode him every day until man and horse knew each other well. Leaving Lillie and Grace in a boarding-house, he rode south to scout the most favorable quarter sections of land. His plan was to ride in two days before the scheduled run and prepare to race from the Pottawatomie Line. After he had staked and filed, he would return for Lillie and Grace, their wagons, and livestock.

On the morning of April 20, 1889, Ben packed a small tent, dried food, a hatchet, a gun, and his claim flag. He checked on his wagons and livestock, paid the stable owner an extra five dollars to keep an eye on everything till he came back, and had a last cup of coffee with Lillie.

"I wish you didn't have that gun," Lillie said while he bounced Grace on his knee. "I can't help feel anxious knowing you may have to use it." Lillie was busy keeping her mind off the dangers of the land run by ironing every article of clothing they owned. She hadn't been able to sleep well since moving to the border town and was glad to be seeing their last days of living there. The air outside was always charged with noise and restless folks, like the undercurrent before an electrical storm. It made her nervous.

Ben had been through this with her before. He spoke gently and reassuringly. "I know what to do," he said. "I know my way around guns and those that use them. Remember that I've been to the Territory and know the way. We'll have our claim as long as I can avoid those thieving Sooners who try to get in before it's right and legal. That's where the gun comes in."

Lillie sighed. "Well, you do have the fastest horse money could buy," she said, but her frown said more.

Ben knew she was thinking of the Run itself. She could brood over tragedies real and imagined for days. Lillie took gruesome newspaper accounts to heart, as if they were written for her private musings alone. She couldn't be stopped once she started reading them either. Tales of horses rearing and stomping a man's head in, of guns misfiring and bullets striking innocent bystanders dead on the spot, of snakebites with no remedy, of quicksand along rivers and streams sucking wagons and entire families to an awful death kept her reading in a frightened monotone. He knew such stories kept her awake nights.

"Those writers have some imagination!" he'd say, but Lillie would roll her eyes and tell him to "listen to this." She'd be off again recounting still another tale of woe.

"I have no intention of leaving you a rich, young widow," Ben said. "If you think I'm foolish enough to do that by not knowing one end of a gun from the other, then you've got the wrong sow by the ear is all I can say." Still, he smiled at her so she would know he was partly teasing.

"'Course you have sense," Lillie said, pouting prettily. "It's other folks that can have mean ways, Ben Reuben." She pressed a shirt collar with one of two irons; the second heated on top of the woodstove. "But that's not the only thing I'm worried about," she said. "What if it doesn't happen, Ben? What if you can't stake a claim in the first place?" She set the iron on the stove and took up its hot replacement. "They say there's close to forty thousand people doing this Run, and they all want the same thing, and they can't all get it, can they? Someone has to lose."

"Now, Lillie, where's your faith? We've prayed about this already."

"I know," she said. "It's wicked of me to doubt and fear. It's just that it would be so much safer if we staked a town claim, like my sister and her husband are doing. You know about running a store. We could be merchants as easily as farmers. Then we could buy us a farm later, one that's already been started."

Ben shook his head. "I didn't come this far to stake out a town site," he said. "I'm not saying it isn't all right for your sister and her banker-husband. Someone's got to settle the towns, to be sure. But I've no interest in being the butcher, the baker, or the candlestick maker, for that matter. And I sure don't want to go back to teaching and such while you wait for us to do what we really want to do—to farm, to have our own place, and everyone else getting a good start ahead of us. We're doing this thing together, side by side. That's what our money is for—to build up a farm, to work the land proper."

He put Grace in her buggy as Lillie set the ironing aside and sat beside him on the bed. Ben took his wife's hand and stroked the smooth skin with his finger. "You'll be glad, Lillie," he said. "It's what we've waited for, a real beginning, and all it takes is the willingness to stay and do what has to be done. Think about our plans for the house, the barn. Remember the drawings we've made and where you said you wanted to plant the flowers and the garden? It'll be everything you want it to be. And what difference does it make if there's forty or even fifty thousand people in the Run? I know we're going to win."

She sighed. "You know what, Ben Reuben? I believe you. Yes, I do. But more than that, God's will be done. That's what I rest on. His will is all that matters."

Lillie was still enthusiastic when he left the next morning. She turned hopeful eyes up to him and kissed him fervently on the mouth. He was glad for that kiss, drawing her youth and joy from it. He secured his saddle one last time, swung over Steeler's back, and took little Grace up in his arms. The baby laughed and cooed, banging on the saddle horn with her dimpled fist.

"Now I'm ready," he said, handing Grace back to her mother. Lillie watched him all the way down the road and didn't care who saw or heard her as she called after him, "Ben Reuben, you are a handsome man!"

MONDAY, APRIL 22, DAWNED FINE AND CLEAR. Ben had never seen so many people gathered in one place, creating a new and solid thing, a moving snake of humanity. His heart beat faster at the sight of hundreds of wagons and buggies, of men and women on horseback, of men and women on foot. When he later tried to recount the event for Lillie, he confessed that he was at a loss to describe all the bizarre impressions: people on bicycles and unicycles, people hanging onto the sides of train cars, ugly faces, pretty faces, wild faces—every one of them intent on one thing, to win a race for a piece of land.

"It was just a roar," he said. "Like the Judgment Day of God Almighty."

Ben held onto his horse with every sinew, wondering how any force in the world could control this heaving line of humanity. He felt for his stake flag again, making sure it was still tied securely to his saddle, right behind him where he could grab it and pound it into the ground in seconds.

The starting gun fired, its staccato report suspended for one split second before the earth moved and roared. The man and horse flew over the ground as the land rolled beneath them like a moving thing.

He guided his horse in and out and away from the hordes of other runners. Great clods of dirt fanned over and around him, and many times he held up a gloved hand to protect his face.

The plains absorbed the thunderous shock and echoed back

in protest with the groaning of all creation. Babel had come to stampede in a moment of time while the remnants of eighty tribes watched.

The country began to look more familiar to him. There was a ravine Ben recognized—there the clear stream winding below through a stand of trees. Fields of ripened grain already danced in his imagination; his house and barn took form there, too. He and Steeler cleared the ravine easily, but the horse came down hard on the other side. Ben leaped off as the animal stumbled and fell. All in a moment, the stake was pounded, the exchange of flags made and secured. But it was a bitter victory when he turned and saw Steeler thrashing on the ground. Cursing and brushing back the tears, he took out his pistol and fired a bullet into the stallion's magnificent forehead. Ben walked several miles to file his claim and to purchase another horse. He set up camp for a week, dug his first well in the Oklahoma Territory, and went for his wife and child.

Ben brought his young family to their new home, along with everything they owned in the world. Within the month they were putting together the materials for their house on the plains. By late summer they were on their way to being regular settlers, and by fall the soil turned under his hands and plow like it understood it had a new master, that a real, live man had come to tend it in obedience to the commandment to subdue the earth. There were sweat and tears, briars and thorns in abundance. Ben found that the earth was a grudging giver of its hidden bounty and that joy of ownership cost much. It could be found somewhere between the heartbreak of disappointed hopes and the triumph of harvest, a tenuous balance of mind and soul.

As for the body itself, it was always tired. Dawn came with relentless demands; dusk fell on unfinished tasks. Yet they stayed and thanked God for their tiny portion of Manifest Destiny.

They planted and built. They harvested and stored. They shared what they had with those who had nothing. They loved one another and bore their children. They watched the sky for every possible sign and promise. They grew strong and then older. It was the life they wanted. It was the life they got.

Grace thrived, and then Gertrude was born, a calm and healthy baby. It seemed for a time that all Ben and Lillie touched turned to their good. Adversity was not far behind, however. There were crop failures, setbacks. The next two pregnancies resulted in stillbirths. Lillie despaired over each lost baby as her faith was shaped anew. Strengthened by resources beyond herself, she loved her husband and daughters all the more. She was still beautiful, adorned as her biblical counterparts, the patriarchs' wives, with a meek and quiet spirit. When the twins were born, Herman and Hiram, her joy was complete. Lillie turned her love of God to new charities, her heart and hands going out to those in need. She prayed daily, judged none harshly.

They planted orchards and gardens. They went into town on Fridays for store-bought goods. They were frugal and wise. Every year they planted something new, and sometimes made mistakes. They tithed whatever they earned, giving the tenth to those in need without being asked or seeking thanks.

These unspoken lessons were not lost on their children. Thus were taught the merits of hard work and honest words, of faith in God and kindness to one's fellow man.

Lillie was the quiet force, the hidden stream that tapped into the source of God's rich love and grace. Many an hour Ben found her waiting through the night, her heart inclined in prayer. Beyond all men, he counted himself among the blessed.

"WELL, NOW, THAT'S IT THEN," Ben said under his breath. The cemetery was empty. Only he remained with the wagon and horses. He was soaked through. He stared at the reins in his hands and saw how they were connected to the horses and how he was connected to them. He was responsible for them. If one of them leaped a ten-foot ravine as old Steeler had done and broke its leg, he would have to shoot it. If they were hungry, they had to be fed. It would always be so. What remained was to farm and take care of his children.

His eyes bored a hole down the hill, away from the cemetery. There was work to do. He climbed onto the buckboard and let his mind follow the living signposts of his soul back to his home. Still, he took a long time getting there.

By dusk the rain had cleared. The sun hung like a million crowns set on fire. Ben thought of a time when he had considered the sky eternal, the sun forever. He no longer believed this, yet his eyes raced to the heavens. Lillie would be there, part of the vast clouds of witnesses. He could not see her, though, and lowered his gaze. What he saw was his house, and it looked the same as ever. It always seemed so one-dimensional from a distance, filling out the closer he got. The downstairs were all lit up, and only two buggies remained in the yard. One was hitched to a stamping horse that pawed the ground, impatient to be down the road and kicking up the mud.

Ben unhitched his horses, fed, and watered them. He closed up the barn and pulled his coat closer. It was chilly and getting darker by the moment. He had observed this many times before, that sometimes he would come in at twilight and only turn around twice before night fell. He walked into the house, took in the parlor with a dismal glance, saw who was sitting where and who was nowhere to be seen. Addie set her embroidery aside and looked at him kindly. Rose and the doctor sat on the sofa drinking coffee. There was no sign of the twins or Grace.

For one reckless moment, he wondered where Lillie was and if she had supper ready for him. The first of death's realizations settled over him.

Gertie sat at his desk, dwarfed by its immense size. Intent upon her drawing, she sat with one leg curled under her and the other touching the floor. She held the paper down with her left hand and wielded a charcoal pencil in the other; sometimes she made long, sweeping lines. Ben looked over her shoulder as he stroked her wild little curls. Gertie looked up.

"What are you drawing?" he asked.

"Mama," she said. "It's a picture of Mama in the clouds of heaven." And she held up the picture for everyone to see.

"It's very like," Addie said, dabbing at her eyes with a lace handkerchief. "That's a gift from God to draw so, Gertrude. Thank Him for it every day."

Ben stared at the picture with numb wonder. When had this child become so apt? He had no abilities in art, and Lillie, for all her reading and love of music, had never drawn with such detail and power. Granted, it was a child's work, but the sketch not only looked like Lillie, it revealed some part of Lillie's personality that was private and well-known to Gertie. How she knew her mother was pictured here. The sketch overstepped its crude boundaries and touched the hem of life itself. Lillie gazed from the page with luminous eyes and that smile, that way of hers.

"Is it good, Papa?" Gertie asked, placing her hand on his.

"Yes, Gertie," he said thickly. The effort to control his emotions had been attacked by this tiny giant and overthrown. He was exhausted. He took off his boots and went up to his room on silent feet.

"Someone remember to wind the clock," he said from the top of the stairs.

Gertie looked at her drawing with the critical eye of an eight-year-old.

"But is it good?" she asked. Rose and Addie and the doctor, who had his hat on now and was ready to leave, all assured her that the sketch was not only good but very good indeed.

FOUR

———◆———

THE NEXT DAY WAS TERRIBLE, everyone trying to adjust in his or her own way to Lillie's death. When Ben came down for breakfast, the children were unnaturally quiet, like a spell had been cast over them. Rose cooked at the stove, turning thick slabs of bacon in one skillet and frying eggs in another. She acknowledged him with a sad smile.

"Where're the men?" Ben asked. The two hired hands usually hung around after an earlier breakfast to get their orders for the day.

"Said they had plenty to do and reckoned they wouldn't bother you today," Rose answered. "They're mending a section of fence in the east forty."

Ben poured himself a cup of coffee and took his seat at the head of the table. He observed his children one by one. Aunt Addie had not yet come to the table.

Grace's eyes were red, framed by dark circles of grief. Ben reached over and patted her hair awkwardly. Gertie was drawing again, a different picture today, a picture of an old iron stove complete with steaming pots and pans and a cat curled up asleep under one of the legs. The little artist's mouth was set firmly, her lips pressed tightly together. Hiram amused himself by poking his twin with a fork until Herman finally set up a howl of protest.

"Stop it, Hiram." The tone of his father's voice was evidently enough to instill obedience. Hiram dutifully set his fork on the table and swung his little legs against his chair in a nonchalant manner. Ben never knew how to read the older boy, older by three minutes than Herman, and so utterly different from his twin.

Rose brought warmed plates to the table, serving first the children and then Ben. She put a heaping platter of biscuits and two large bowls of gravy on the table before taking her place where Lillie used to sit.

"Guess Addie'll be here when she's ready," Rose said.

Ben kept looking up, amazed that he was still looking for Lillie to come into the room. Why was Rose sitting in his wife's chair? Why was she buttering the twins' biscuits? He looked around the room, observing its shape and contents as if for the first time. It was Lillie's kitchen surely. Her touch was everywhere, from the arrangements on the shelves to the gingham curtains she had sewn. He remembered the day she bought the blue-checked cotton at the general store in town. He remembered the nights she spent embroidering the pictures on the walls, farm scenes she had designed. It was a working kitchen, planned with an economy of space and storage. Dishes, pots, pans, mixing bowls, measuring cups—all were where they should be—handy, ready for use. Now these familiar things remained for other hands to use, to wash, to put away.

He sighed, trying to eat and tasting little. His gaze went over every square inch of the table as he searched for something that could not be found. Again he knew beyond hope that his wife would never sit there again. How they had loved that table, the two of them! Big enough to handle the family and then some—custom made by a carpenter in town who traded it out for produce.

The chairs came from Lillie's grandpa's chair factory in Baltimore, Maryland. Ben remembered when they got those chairs, twenty-two of them to be exact, a wedding gift from Lillie's parents. The chairs filled one wagon alone. They comprised most of the furniture in Lillie's dowry, leftover inventory from a Confederate contract gone awry.

Baltimore. What if Lillie had been born there, had never come west to Kansas, to Indian Territory? He answered his own questions. She would still have died at some point in time.

Rose took another pan of biscuits from the oven.

"I'm obliged to you," he said as she put them on the table. "But I want the children to help you, Rose. We can't expect you and others to carry the load for us. Hiram and Herman can fetch firewood and put it in the stove box. And the girls know they're supposed to clean up the table and wash these dishes. Hard as it is, we got to go on. I don't want the kids to get spoiled. Lillie taught them well, and I won't have it wasted."

"'Course she did," Rose said. "Things is still fresh and hurtful, though. It's been such a little while. I want to help out however I can, that's all."

"Gertie, take your things into the other room now and come back and eat what's been put before you," Ben said. Gertie had not touched her food. She looked up with a dazed expression, pushed away from the table, and obeyed him.

"We got plenty to do today to clean up from all the company," he continued. "I want every window open and the whole house aired out. Can't stand whatever it is that's smelling up the place." Ben stopped himself. He felt like he was rambling and not making any sense. "You children thank Rose for cooking your breakfast," he said, wanting to change the subject.

"And thank God for giving it," Aunt Addie said. The old woman stood rather ceremoniously in the doorway, as if she were taking in the entire company and expecting them to notice her at the same time. She wore a white scarf on her head and adjusted it self-consciously before taking her chair between Grace and Gertie. She rested her tired and rheumy eyes on everyone in turn before folding her hands, bowing her head, closing her eyes, and praying right out loud.

"We thank Thee, Lord, for these Thy bountiful gifts, and help us in our time of grief. Amen."

Gertie stared at Aunt Addie and asked between mouthfuls of hot biscuit, "What you wearing that scarf for, Auntie Addie? You going somewhere after breakfast? Can I go, too?"

Addie turned her head this way and that so everyone could see that she was indeed wearing a scarf.

"It's a sight on earth, it is," she said and then added solemnly, "I'm wearing it for the angels."

Ben kept his eyes on his food and said nothing.

"For the angels?" Gertie asked incredulously. "What do you mean, for the angels?"

"Angels, angels," Herman cried. "Mama's with the angels now."

"Shut up, Herman!" Grace snapped. "What do angels care if you wear a scarf or not?" she asked impatiently.

Addie sniffed. "The Bible says plain as day that women are to keep their heads covered. It says so in a letter from Saint Paul to the church at Corinth, and I think if it was so important for him to tell the Corinthians, why, it must be important enough for me to obey today. It's a sign to the angels that woman is under submission to man. To think of all the years I have not done this is a shame and a sorrow to me, but no more. I can start doing it today, and I have." She sighed deeply and turned her full attention to her meal.

"Here's coffee, Addie," Rose said. Aunt Addie smiled briefly and took the cup and saucer with trembling hands.

"Eat your breakfast, Grace." Ben said. He was in no mood to let Addie's eccentricity nettle him this morning and ordered everyone to quit talking and finish their breakfast.

Ben looked out the window and frowned. It was already an hour past dawn, yet the sky was dark with thunderheads. Lightning flashed in the distance—east. Ben thought the hired hands should look for other tasks besides trying to repair fences in such weather. Never one to quite curse the rain, he still thought this season's showers were too much of a good thing. The humid air was suffocating. He wanted the sun to shine on his wife's grave, wanted the flowers to glory in such light.

There would be no sun today and no consolation for Grace either, it appeared. She pushed a clump of cold gravy around the plate with a fork while stealing hurtful looks at Rose, looks that Rose was obviously at pains to understand. Gertie coughed and asked to be excused.

"You can be excused to do your chores," Ben said. He turned to Aunt Addie. "I'm counting on you to see that the girls keep up with their work, Addie. I won't have you taking the butter and milk to the cistern like I know you did the last couple of days. I know you meant well, and I don't mean to hurt your feelings, especially at a time like this, which is understandably hard on all of us, but that's Gertie's job. And when Grace is finished making the beds, there's churning to do—"

"And bread to bake," Addie interjected.

"Enough to keep everyone busy," Ben said in a tone that settled the matter once and for all.

The girls started clearing the table and filled a pan in the sink with boiling water from the stove.

"Aren't we ever going to talk about Mama again?" Grace

asked mournfully. Gertie covered her face with a towel, choking back her tears.

Ben inhaled deeply, feeling yet another knot rise up in his throat. "There's a time and place, Grace, and this isn't it."

He got up abruptly and left the room.

The twins cleaned their plates. Hiram finally managed to bring Herman to brief and bitter tears before Rose comforted the younger twin with honey on a biscuit and sent both to the back porch to play with the new kittens.

"Addie," Ben said from the front room, "I expect you to make the twins mind you, too. Switch them if they don't."

"Whatever you say, Ben. I'm under your authority and the Almighty's." She finished eating, slowly, while the girls washed up the dishes.

Rose removed her apron, folded it deliberately, and took her time following Ben. She watched him as he stood indecisively at the front door. *So unlike him to hesitate,* she thought, and felt shy approaching his back this way.

"I've been wanting to tell you something," she said softly.

"We may as well go out on the porch then," he said, opening the door for her. Rose reached for her woolen shawl on the hall tree and draped it around her shoulders. The sound of her boots on the porch seemed loud to her; she tried to step more quietly and only succeeded in feeling clumsier than ever. The damp air chilled her through, but she wanted to be outside for what she had to say. She felt a strong need to clear her lungs. Ben leaned against the porch rail with one boot and rocked back and forth.

"I'm asked to marry someone," Rose said.

"Jumping the broomstick, are you?" he asked, staring into the darkening sky. "George Luther, isn't it?"

"Yes, it is," she said.

"You seem surprised that I know. Lillie told me," Ben said.

He was silent for several moments. "George Luther and I were Masons together," he continued. "'Course I don't go for that stuff now, but he's a good man all the same. Lost his wife a few years back. Haven't seen him for a spell, though."

Rose heard Ben's voice as if it were coming from some far and distant place—he was that unemotional. She sighed. What else could she expect?

Ben looked off toward the barn. The subject of Rose's impending engagement was something Lillie had told him, all right. It was, in fact, about the last serious conversation they'd had together. He resented it that Rose had been the subject of that talk. He wished they had discussed something more enduring and personal to them both. There it was again, that catch in his heart. When would the reminders of her death stop attacking him like this, breaking, taking his reveries captive to new levels of grief and pain?

"He is a good man," Rose agreed.

"You said yes, didn't you?"

She shrugged her shoulders and pulled her wrap closer. "I told him I'd think about it. And now, well, I thought it would depend."

"On what?"

Rose at thirty-one was two years older than Lillie. She had been passed over by former beaux more times than she cared to recall. Though she was no beauty, there was a serenity about her that was pleasant enough, or so folks said. She was a hard worker and a faithful friend. She knew she was plain.

"It depends on whether I'm needed somewhere else," Rose said, and her look told him all he needed to know about what it was that held her back.

Ben's response was quick and sharper than he intended. "Well, you needn't feel obligated to me and the kids." While he had no intention of marrying Rose or anyone else for that matter, he wanted to be gentle with her, for Lillie's sake.

"Please don't misunderstand what I'm going to say, Rose. You're a fine woman, and we appreciate all you've done for Lillie, and how you always come when you can do it, and how you never complain. That's a good thing about you, a real good thing. But I don't expect you to give up George Luther to help me and Addie with the children. We'll manage. Folks do. I talked to Aunt Hannah and asked her to come live with us for a while." He cleared his throat and wiped his eyes.

"She said she would," he continued, shaking his head like someone was arguing with him. "I can't ask you to do any more for us than what you've already done. It wouldn't be fair in any case to you, Rose, since George Luther proposed to you. He's a fine man. I'm thinking it'd be best for you to say yes and get on with things and not be thinking about this business here anymore."

From his first words, Rose recognized the tone Ben was taking with her. It was one that made her call upon long habits of dealing with rejection to arrange her body, her eyes, the set of her mouth, even her hands so it would appear that she was accepting everything said.

"I see," Rose said and then, as an afterthought, almost strangely, "George is a good person. I'm a good person. So is Aunt Hannah. We're all good people, aren't we, Ben?"

He looked up quickly.

"Aren't we?" she repeated.

Ben leaned on his leg, continuing to rock. He nodded gravely, choosing not to pursue her train of conversation. "When's the wedding?" he asked.

Rose looked up at the sky. A pearl of light shone behind the storm clouds creating a halo of almost blinding beauty. The song of a lone bird drifted over the gently falling rain. The notes of unknown praise filled the woman with a yearning pathos. It was a feeling she knew would never be satisfied this side of the grave. The bird's song was followed by the crowing of roosters, the lowing of cattle, the song of the living, of those needing tended to.

"Soon," she said vaguely. "Next month more than likely. It'll be a simple service. One thing about George I do like is that he doesn't want any fuss, and I feel the same."

Ben reached toward her in an uncharacteristic gesture, one she found her entire self straining towards. They embraced briefly, awkwardly.

"We'll be there," he said thickly, surprised at the texture of her face against his cheek. "We'll always be there, Rose."

She eased away and nodded. "I'll be going home this afternoon," she said.

"Yes," Ben said. "I expect you will."

"I'll help get supper started and show Grace what to do."

"You're a good woman," Ben said. "If that man of yours doesn't treat you right, I expect to hear about it. Not that I think he won't."

"I'll be all right," Rose answered.

"And don't think I didn't see how Grace acted toward you this morning," Ben said. "I'm sorry for it. It's more than Lillie's dying working on that one. Grace has been in a state for some time now, and I don't know what to do. She's too big to thrash, and I never liked that way of dealing with children in the first place."

"She's growing up, is all," Rose said. "We all got to go easy on her. It's hard being the oldest and going through the changes she's feeling now. Leave her be, Ben. She'll come around and be better for it."

"She's been moody a good while," Ben said. "She's got

sullen ways and frowns like no one can do anything to please or suit her. Lillie saw it, too, and tried to talk to her. She's strong-willed, that Grace. Always has been."

Tears filled Rose's eyes. "I understand," she said. "I'll pray, Ben, for Grace and for you and for everyone . . ."

The tears had been bottled up too long. They burst with such force that Rose felt wracked throughout her entire body. Here came all the feelings for Lillie and Ben, all the horror of Lillie's death. Rose had tried so hard to ease her cousin's labor and pain. She and the doctor did everything humanly possible, she knew that, and it hadn't been enough. Rose had midwived before this, many times, without a doctor. But her experience did nothing to prepare her for complications. That's what Doc said they were, these connected events that led so inevitably to a soul finally taking leave.

She felt Ben's arms around her and knew that this, too, would never last. They had gotten carried away once, long ago when Lillie was bedridden after Gertie was born. Carried almost clean away. Rose got a hold of herself back then, and she did the same now. It would be too easy to give in to the passion of grief and then wake up hating herself and Ben for giving way to the flesh. No, it was time to marry. George Luther was a good man. He was not Ben, but he was a good man, and he wanted her where Ben did not and never could. George Luther told her she had the prettiest eyes he'd ever seen. George Luther loved her, she guessed. He said he did.

She would have George Luther and maybe a child or two and do the things that housewives do before another person dies, and the cycle of life winds its way once more. One day, Rose knew, one day she, too, would join her cousin and all the other sleeping folks on cemetery hill.

"It'll be all right, Ben," she said at last. She laid her hand on his arm to let him know it really was all right, that her life would go on with no grudge against him and, hopefully, with no regrets. It had been a pure flight of fancy to think this man of thirty-nine with three working farms and money in the bank would ever want her. Where had she got the notion? She turned slowly and went back into the house, leaving him there framed against the dark sky.

BEN WAITED TILL HE HEARD the door close behind Rose. He walked to the barn and went inside. Everything appeared clean and orderly. All his tools for drilling waited undisturbed and ready for use. There were folks who needed wells dug, and the rain wouldn't let him. He checked the sections of wooden derrick, the long steel beam with its much-used drilling bit on the end. The manila rope would have to be replaced before too long. He wondered at the danger he put himself in all the times he'd dug wells for himself and others. The only thing he really feared was running into a pocket of damp gas—deadly, invisible, odorless. One minute you're working away deep in the well, installing metal casing or what have you, and the next, you faint and die. Lillie saved him once. He had passed out, and she sent Grace for help while she herself raised and lowered a canvas sheet on the bailer bucket for thirty minutes. The fresh influx of moving oxygen saved his life.

Ben wept.

FIVE

BENJAMIN FRANKLIN REUBEN didn't want another wife. He had had the best, and she was gone. What remained were his land and children, and this was much. His farms were among the best in the district. He ran thirty head of cattle and an ever-changing number of horses. In addition, he had four mules, six milk cows, forty hens, two roosters, six sows and one hog, tame and wild ducks on three ponds, and two hunting dogs. He had a large cistern and a good well.

His house was a two-story log cabin with a brick chimney and a spacious porch on the southeast. The parlor had three walls with two windows each and a fireplace tall enough for a child to stand in. The parlor opened into a kitchen where twenty people could sit at a long table. There were two bedrooms downstairs—one shared by the girls and Aunt Addie and one for the twins. There were two rooms upstairs, one for Ben and Lillie and one extra—"to grow on," Lillie had said.

Ben built a one-room frame house behind the barn for the hired hands. It had a porch with benches for sitting on and hooks for hanging tools. There were ample shelves and wooden boxes for storage. As many as six men could live there during threshing and harvest, though usually there were only two or three the rest of the year. The room had three bunkbeds, a good-sized table, and a few of the Maryland factory-made chairs. A fireplace and iron stove heated the space in winter with meals served in the big house. The privy was located behind the barn down a path the children raked every day.

Ben Reuben had the start of a good apple orchard, a row of peach trees, and a pecan grove. He knew how to graft to produce the best fruit. He kept several beehives that produced honey he sold in town. He planted his vegetable garden every year on Good Friday, and from this produce fed the family throughout the year. They needed few store-bought foods—mostly salt, flour, spices, and some sugar, though they made their own sorghum and used it to sweeten cookies and cakes. Ben treated his kids to a sack of assorted candies once each month. He planted tomatoes, squash, okra, cucumbers, beans, and potatoes. He planted onions, radishes, lettuce, carrots, and pumpkins. In May he planted sweet potatoes.

There was a root cellar, a smokehouse, and a milk house for straining milk and separating cream. The screened-in back porch had shelves full of canned fruit and jellies and all the vegetables they grew. Washtubs in three sizes hung on big hooks hammered into the wall alongside assorted scrub boards, household tools, mops, brooms, and laundry baskets.

There was a medicine cabinet with homemade and store-bought remedies for everything from stomach complaint to pink eye. Lillie used chamberlye for earache, catnip tea for hives, goose oil to rub on the feet and armpits for a cold, and Groves Tasteless Chill Tonic for numerous conditions. They drank apple cider vinegar in water every day.

It was a well-planned and well-ordered house that he and Lillie managed with firm efficiency. There were times for baking, churning, cleaning, beating out the rugs; times for making soap and doing laundry; times for weekly baths.

"A time for every purpose under heaven," Lillie said. She liked the verse from Ecclesiastes so much that she embroidered it and hung it in the kitchen.

Slaughtering came in late fall or early winter and could last a week or two. Lillie worked side by side with Ben, scarcely flinching when he cut the hogs' throats and hung them up to bleed. She said she didn't know who squealed the loudest, the pigs or the children watching the goings on. She helped him lower the pigs' bloated bodies into scalding hot water and then scrubbed their carcasses before skinning. She handled the slippery organs deftly, washing out the balloonlike bladders for the kids to play with and saving the kidneys and livers for boiling.

She had Ben string up thick wire between two trees in the backyard so the house rugs could be cleaned properly and aired at regular intervals when the weather permitted. The same wire was used to hang the clothes on wash days. She was a hard worker and expected the same of the children, even the twins.

Now Ben faced that time most feared by men who love their wives. He was that most dreaded of words, a *widower*. The nights were terrible. He would lie in bed trying not to touch the empty space beside him and then roll over the feather mattress to bury his face in Lillie's pillow. It astonished him that he was still able to smell her there, the human scent of her, fresh as rain, elusive as air. Yet when he looked up, only a cold darkness met him. He saw the years of solitude lined up ahead of him as tiny, separate moments. While the endearing habits of their life together had ceased, the familiarity of memory was ever present. And the irony was that there was no Lillie to tell these things to, no softness to embrace to bring forgetfulness of mortality.

He prided himself that he had not taken advantage of Rose at a time like this, now when he needed a woman more than ever.

———————•———————

A MONTH PASSED, DAY FOLLOWING DAY with a regularity that wearied Ben and his family. The twins, still unable to grasp that their lives had been changed forever, had to be told again and again that their mother was not coming back. This sad task fell not only to Ben and Aunt Addie but to Grace and Gertie as well. Through each telling, Lillie's death was relived and confirmed, but with little comfort.

One morning after breakfast when the hired hands had cleaned their plates and excused themselves, Ben made an announcement that would work still more changes for the Reuben family.

"I made an important decision after your mother died," he said, "and you may as well be getting used to the idea now." Hiram and Herman fidgeted, wide awake and ready to get into trouble any minute. Grace got up and poured her father a cup of coffee with the air of a grown-up who didn't need any more lectures or explanations. Gertie licked some charcoal off her right thumb and smeared her pinafore in the process.

"I asked Aunt Hannah to come and stay with us awhile," Ben said.

The girls groaned at the same time.

"She snores," Grace said flatly.

"She falls asleep sitting up and then sits there and drools!" Gertie added.

Ben held his hands up for silence. "Those are petty complaints about a woman who loves you children and cares enough about the family to come live with us. We've all had to work together the last few weeks, and you've done well. But we need another woman here. Aunt Addie can't be expected to carry all the load, even with your help. Aunt Hannah may not be your favorite relative, but she's the only one who can come, and I expect you to show her respect and to obey her when I'm not here."

"Where'll she sleep?" Grace asked.

"She'll have the other room upstairs."

"Least ways we won't hear her snoring," Gertie said. "Only she does fuss so. I'd rather have Rose come live with us."

"Wose, Wose," Herman cried gleefully. "Wose come!"

"No, Rose isn't going to come," Ben said. "Rose is a married woman now and has her husband to think of. Aunt Hannah is a widow woman with grown sons. She's able to come and agrees to do it."

"Oh, she'll be concerned about us all right," Grace said dismally. "She'll boss us around like she owns us or something. You wait and see if she doesn't."

"Don't pull a long face," Ben said. "She's coming, and that's the end of it. How long she stays depends on how well you kids do. I can't be worrying about you all the time, and with her and Aunt Addie together I won't. You've all got to buckle down and do what your mama would expect if she was still here."

Aunt Addie sipped her coffee and adjusted the scarf on her head. "I know that Lillie would approve of Aunt Hannah coming to us in our time of deepest need," she said. "The good Lord knows I can't take care of you children by myself. He's heard my pleas and has provided a way for us in this wilderness. We should be grateful—yes, we should, and we will be, too."

"Thank you, Addie," Ben said. "There's more than enough for two grown women to manage with this bunch. Maybe you've all forgotten what a good cook Hannah is."

Ben stood and looked seriously at each child. Grace appeared to be the most upset by the news.

"I'm depending on all of you," he said. "And especially you, Grace. You're the oldest, and I want you to set a good example to the others. No pouting. This isn't what anyone asked for or wanted, but it's what God has decreed."

"God's will be done," Aunt Addie said.

"She better not try to be our ma—that's all I've got to say!" Grace said, bursting into tears.

Herman started crying at once. Hiram responded to all the commotion by screaming and hitting his twin in the face.

Gertie put her hands over her ears and closed her eyes tightly. "It never will get better! Never will!" she cried, running out of the room to sob alone in the parlor.

"Now see what you've done, Grace! Set them all off again! I ought to . . ." Ben stopped himself. He was trembling with anger and had come close to striking her. How could this girl twist his feelings into such a knot of conflict, this little slip of a thing who looked like Lillie but would never be Lillie?

Grace stared, brushing away her tears defiantly.

"Go to your room," Ben said to her. "Don't you think of looking at me that way ever again, and don't you dare talk back or say a single, solitary thing!" He pointed his finger at her as she slowly stood up and walked to her room.

Hiram kicked his brother savagely under the table. "Daddddyyy!" Herman Corban cried, holding out his chubby arms to his father. Ben picked up both his sons and held them tightly. Herman hugged his neck, but Hiram squirmed away and ran to the back porch where he immediately set to work kicking a washtub.

Herman patted his father's cheek. "Anna come?" he asked, blinking through his tears and wiping his nose.

"It's Hannah, Herman, not Anna," Ben said. "Gertrude, please come in here and take care of your little brother."

Gertie, choking back her tears, obeyed. She led Herman by the hand out to the backyard.

Aunt Addie looked out the kitchen window at the children, shaking her head all the while. "I'm plumb wore out from all that!" she said. "When did you say Hannah's coming?"

"Next week," Ben answered impatiently. He had told her at least twice before, and she kept forgetting. If he had any doubts about Hannah coming to live with them, they were silenced now. There was no way he could feel comfortable about ever leaving Aunt Addie in charge when he was gone. Even if she looked and acted all right some of the time, there were more than enough other times when she didn't seem to pay attention, a serious matter when there were little ones to look after. Besides that, she often got on Ben's nerves.

GRACE COVERED HER HEAD with her pillow to drown out the voices in the kitchen. She didn't want to hear the adults or the muffled cries of Gertie yelling at the twins. It gave her a headache. Everything gave her a headache these days. It was hard being the oldest in this family of children, and it didn't look like things were going to get any better. She had never liked Aunt Hannah and had told her mother so many times. Why couldn't her father let her be the grown-up? Why did he have to get Aunt Hannah to come in, spoiling everything and poking her nose into everyone's business?

On an impulse and perhaps childishly for such a grown-up girl, Grace bounced out of bed and went over to the mirror on the dresser. She stared at herself in it for a long time, thinking of all the changes that she'd gone through in the last month. They seemed enough to age her with at least one wrinkle. But what she saw looking back at her was a smooth, unblemished face. Only her eyes betrayed her suffering.

Grace was well-favored in a fragile way, not like the girls she went to school with, all tomboys with scarred legs, matted hair, and overalls. She had a pretty face, and she kept her hair nice, too. She even wore dresses in the fields, old ones with aprons. Her two good dresses were always starched and ironed. Her little body was trim and round in the places where women are supposed to curve in and out. She loved being this age and longed to stay twelve forever, even though she knew it wouldn't happen. She was becoming a woman whether she liked it or not, and mostly she did not.

Her mother used to say that pretty is as pretty does, so Grace tried to do pretty things. The pretty thing she did now was to pick up a brush and stroke her hair, counting to one hundred and then doing it again. Her hair was like her mother's. Light ran through its auburn highlights like a fluid, moving thing; outside, when it was sunny, her hair looked almost red. She wore it pulled back with ribbons or the tortoise-shell pins that once adorned her mother's hair. Her father had given them to Grace less than a week after the funeral when he went through all Lillie's things.

"She would want you girls to have these," he said, handing them one article after another. He had not given them her rings or necklaces, however.

Grace wound up with three pairs of earrings that screwed into her ear lobes and pinched if she wasn't careful. Gertie was given three pairs also, and Addie took the last two that neither of the girls wanted anyway. There were also scarves and blouses. Gertrude was given her mother's brush and comb because Grace already had a set.

Lillie had four pairs of shoes and two pairs of boots. They were too grown-up for the girls to wear, and Lillie's feet had been tiny, too. Out came the quilts stored in one of the bedroom trunks. Ben put all her shoes and boots inside, along with her dresses and petticoats and gowns. Her wedding gown remained undisturbed in the second trunk. It was folded in papers and took up a lot of room, along with a pair of elegant button-down shoes and a parasol with pink ribbons wound in and out of its lace trim. Grace knew better than to ask to see the wedding gown. She also hesitated to ask for any of her mother's books, though she wanted them badly. Ben told them the books were for the whole family to use and would stay on the bookshelves in the parlor.

"Mind you kids don't bend their backs or tear any pages," he said. "Those books were your mother's pride and joy, and I won't have anyone treat them carelessly."

It angered Grace to be treated like a child. Why, she had started menstruating the night Lillie died. That made her as good as grown-up. Aunt Addie was the only one who knew. She had to be told because Grace had to tell someone. Grace would never have told Rose. She was jealous of Rose and didn't know why.

"Do you know what's happening to you?" Addie had asked her sympathetically.

"'Course I do." Grace felt humiliated. "Mama told me all about it last fall." It was true. Lillie had explained that certain changes would take place, that she would have an issue of blood every month except when she got married and was in the family way. Lillie told her she needed to know these things to prepare her for life.

"I don't want either you or Gertie to wake up in the middle of the night and not know what's happening to you," she had said. "My mother never told me anything. I was scared to death and just naturally thought I was dying."

What Lillie hadn't told Grace was that her stomach would feel full and bloated and hurt in such an aching way or that she might burst into tears over the least little thing. All Grace knew was that special linens had to be worn inside her underwear and that she was responsible for washing them and keeping herself clean and fresh. She never dreamed she would have to experience the horror alone, though. She would die of mortification if anyone besides Aunt Addie knew!

Grace had longed to tell her mother what was happening, but Lillie was having a baby and couldn't be disturbed once Rose and the doctor came. Then her mother had become delirious and didn't even know her own children! So Grace had to take care of herself. Filled with self-pity, she did her best. Now even the memory of the whole thing made her cry. She had felt so light-headed that she threw up; that was when Aunt Addie had spoken to her and put her to bed. The next morning Lillie and the dead baby were laid out for company to see. Grace stayed in her room in bed, keeping her awful secret to herself and crying for her mother.

Her father thought it was grief that kept her away from the others, so he left her alone. Grace didn't want to see her mother laid out in that ghastly box, but the time came when she had to leave her room and pay her respects like everyone else. Her stomach was cramped with pain, and every nerve was on edge. But when Grace saw her mother, her heart broke. There in the coffin, she saw her own childhood laid to rest forever with only a shell of memory remaining. She wanted desperately to believe in the resurrection.

"I can't . . ." She'd started to say she couldn't stand it anymore, but the words never came out.

"Poor child has fainted," Aunt Addie said, and someone—her father, she guessed—picked her up and carried her back to her bed.

The horrible day passed somehow, but that night, the one before the burial, Grace couldn't sleep. She tossed in the bed, groaning with pain and clutching at her stomach. She had heard of children dying from a burst appendix and wondered if that was what was happening to her. Aunt Addie came in and stroked her forehead and gave her a cup of warm milk. Aunt Addie told her that she wasn't going to die at all, that it was too soon for her to join her mother and Elizabeth Caitlin in heaven. After she left, Grace felt sorry for herself and knew for certain that she would first lead a tragic life and then die. Her fantasies rolled with the pain until she felt a new and pressing need. She had to use a chamber pot but not the one in their room; Gertie had gotten sick in it earlier. Grace would have to find another one, a search that would entail stumbling over who knows who in the dark. The house was full of people.

There was nothing else to do but go outside to the privy in the rain. She made her way through the house, hearing the telltale sounds of sleeping bodies all around her. Even the women sitting up with the coffin, Mrs. Dean and Mrs. Coonrod, had fallen asleep right where they sat. The coffin straddled four chairs, its grotesque shape casting shadows from the kerosene lamp's pale light; the lamp sat on top of the piano and was about empty. Grace shuddered and kept her eyes fixed on the back porch.

The rain had become a light drizzle, leaving the path to the privy all wet and spongy. She was glad that she and Gertie had raked the ground three days earlier. She remembered that her mother had reminded them to do it and that they had not particularly wanted to. She would give anything to hear her mother remind her to do a task now.

Her mother had told them to rake the path on the morning that her labor started. Lillie said it looked like it was going to rain hard, and they needed to get the job done before it started. Sure enough, it started raining before they were even through. Lillie had fixed breakfast that morning, a special breakfast of pancakes and eggs and bacon. She said the baby must be coming soon because she just wanted to cook and cook. That was before she complained about her legs hurting her and went on up to bed. No one was worried or scared, though.

Later that afternoon, someone went to get Rose, and her father had gone to fetch Doc Pierson. Her mother talked to the children before her pains got worse, sometimes laughing in that wonderful way she had. She talked about the baby and asked them if they thought it was a girl or a boy and how long it would take to be born. She made little jokes with Grace and Gertie and put Herman's hand on her tummy so he could feel the baby kicking. She had even read a story to them.

Lillie had been careful to keep her legs under the covers when she was in bed. Grace looked away when they were accidentally exposed. The sight of them frightened her; they had become so ugly and lumpy, big and white, like the distended belly of a frog.

Childbirth always came on a schedule unknown to Grace, and, as the oldest girl, she had been through many with her mother. Each was a huge and separate event, a monumental occurrence outside of space and time that demanded everyone's attention at once. There was never any choice but to obey its peculiar summons. Childbirth forced its way into her thinking so that she had to imagine the unthinkable. Each baby emerged from her mother's body, even as she had done, and there was only one place that could happen, as any goose knows. It made Grace shudder with fear and loathing.

When Lillie first started screaming with the pain, Grace internalized two indelible facts: the terror of giving birth and the knowledge that her mother was going to die. The two facts stood like pillars of stone. Grace had read that the pillars of Solomon's temple were named Jachin and Boaz. But Grace's pillars bore no such names, these messengers of birth and death. They stood at the temple of her mother's body as if passing judgment on all things mortal. Grace was numbed by the knowledge that she could do nothing to dissuade such fearful angels.

Her fear came again as she walked through the dark rain to the privy. Grace made her visit as brief as possible and walked back to the house; the rain slackened and then picked up again. A thin streak of light threaded along the horizon, peeking under the rain clouds. People would be waking up soon; there would be noise and breakfast and movement and sadness all over again. They would have the funeral on a day that would last forever.

Grace pumped water into a bucket and started rinsing her clothes. She poured out the soiled water and pumped fresh. Her body trembled with a sense of being violated by forces beyond her control. She was still wringing out the fabric when she saw her father watching her from the back porch. He opened the screen door and came outside, pulling his suspenders over his shirt. As he walked over, she hoped it wasn't light enough for him to see that her face was burning with shame.

"Do you need any help, Grace?" he asked in a kind voice. She hated to see him looking so sad and beaten down.

"No," she said, more emphatically than she had intended. Her lips quivered as she replied in a softer tone, "I'll be all right."

They stood side by side in the misting dawn, sentinels guarding a subject that would never be mentioned again.

GERTIE HEARD HER SISTER CRYING when she came back in the room to get her bonnet. She was going to take Herman for a walk. She heard the bedsprings creak as Grace sat up, apparently trying to act nonchalant about the earlier scene in the kitchen. Gertie was sensitive to her sister's feelings. It seemed too awful to compound her sadness by dealing the double blow of staring. She didn't like sadness to be expressed out loud, though she herself felt things deeply. She overheard her mother once tell Aunt Addie that she, Gertie, felt things in a private way.

"You can see it in what she draws," Lillie said.

Gertie didn't know if her sad feelings came out on paper or not. She had not yet learned to be objective about such matters. She only knew that her hands responded on a given signal that started somewhere in her heart and worked its way into what she saw pictured in her mind.

Oh, but there'd been so much weeping since her mother's death. Gertie's entire being had been wounded in a fundamental way that nothing human could heal. She couldn't even think of her dead baby sister without shuddering. The whole thing broke her heart so thoroughly that tears were redundant. She would never get over it, not like people who cry and heave and make such a to-do. She would grieve through the elements of charcoal and paper.

That's why she told Grace to stop crying. "Won't do you any good," Gertie said. "You'll get sick, that's all, and throw up like last night, and then you'll get sick all over again and not be able to clean the pot, and I'll have to. So don't, that's all. Just don't do it. I'm not going to clean it up again." Gertie sounded to herself like she really meant it this time.

"You threw up, too!" Grace cried. She could silence her sister with a single look or word, and she used both to such effect now. Her tone warned Gertie not to cross her again with emotion or logic, and her steady gaze finally made her sister look away.

"Anyway, Papa says you're to help Aunt Addie now."

Grace left the room in a storm of silent fury. Gertie thought that her sister looked beautiful in her anger. She was able to step back and observe such emotion like a detached little judge intent upon weighing all the evidence. The facts of the case would be stored in her memory and later revealed in a drawing.

Gertie grabbed her bonnet and took one huge sigh as her bulwark against the day ahead. It fell to her as it usually did, in an unspoken passing of duties and endless tasks, to look after the twins.

Hiram was the more difficult; he hated being touched by anyone but his father. The only other person he ever submitted to was their mother, and that was because she knew how to cajole the willful child. Hiram was the spitting image of his father and independent in the same way. Where he always yanked his stubborn little fists away, Herman, the compliant one, suffered himself to be led about by the hand. She could lead Herman anywhere; he never fussed or complained.

Gertie couldn't help but love Herman best. He made it easy with his bright blue eyes always looking so hopeful, so ready to widen with surprise or laughter. She was his friend first and his sister second. What she felt for him was a breaking flood that would pour itself endlessly on behalf of the beloved. It was as if she saw some future sadness in Herman, something in how he looked at the world around him. He didn't seem to understand that their mother was never going to come back. Sometimes he asked where she was.

But for now Gertie had to deal with the fact that Hiram had squirmed away and made himself scarce. "He most likely went to see the puppies in the barn," she said.

Herman held onto her finger tightly with one hand and used the other to point. "Swing! Swing!" he cried.

"Let's go see," Gertie said. They went behind the barn to the oak tree where their father had made two rope swings for them to play on. The sun rising over the hill cast a rosy light over a little tousle-haired boy climbing onto one of the wooden seats. Hiram completely ignored them.

"Let him alone," she said to Herman. "We have better things to do." And she led Herman down the trail that she and Grace had cleared after the last snow. The trail was one they worked on when everything else was done, when all the chores were out of the way; improving it was their labor of love. She took her time with Herman, pleasing him with a cold biscuit she had hidden in her apron pocket. Gertie laughed as Herman ate it greedily and called him a little pig. She saw Hiram a few feet behind them, darting across the path and hiding behind the trees. She ignored him. "Come along now," she said to Herman, and she proceeded to show him all her secret hiding places along the trail, the holes where creeping things burrowed, the hollows in the trunks of trees where she kept pretty rocks hidden away. At one point, she took him to a thicket where wildflowers grew.

"This is where we found that mother quail last year," she said, "Grace and I. The mother bird pretended to have a broken wing to get us away from her eggs."

"In tree?" Herman asked thoughtfully.

"No, on the ground. Quails have nests on the ground. 'Course they're all hidden and covered up with stuff. But you could step on them easy if you wasn't looking or didn't know they were there."

Herman picked up his feet and set them down carefully, rolling his eyes all the while.

They walked away from the thicket and followed the stream that flowed through the woods behind the pasture. It wound through trees and between rocks; at places it was quite wide, too wide to cross without stepping stones. At other places it was easy to leap over.

"This stream cuts through our place and starts way back, back at the Dean farm and farther still," Gertie said. She showed him the waterfall where the stream poured over red rocks and made a curtain of water.

"We'll head back now," Gertie said after they had sat a long while. They picked a handful of flowers growing on one side of the little pool and started back. Before they reached the house, Hiram ran into the back of her legs, hugging them furiously and howling with delight.

"Let's go back now, boys," she said, trying to get a hold on her attacker. "Aunt Addie has work for us, and we'll get in trouble if we don't help her."

Hiram raced away.

"What gets into him?" Gertie asked.

"Chickens," Herman said. "Gone to chickens."

"Maybe he did at that. We might as well go and gather the eggs then."

Herman pulled on her hand and pointed at the grass.

"Oh, all right," Gertie said. "We'll stay a little while longer. But then we've got to get to work. You don't want Daddy getting mad, do you?"

Herman shook his head and waited for her to smooth her skirt before sitting on her lap. He reached into her apron pocket in search of another biscuit, and when he didn't find one, he started tickling her. Gertie hugged him tightly and laughed.

"You ate all the biscuits, silly," she said, stroking his hair. "We'll get some more at dinner." Her fingers lingered in the short curls; she was glad his hair was growing back. Their father had cut it on the twins' third birthday two months earlier. He said he didn't want them to look like sissies anymore. Their mother had cried a little, picked up some of the fallen ringlets and put them in a book. Gertie had comforted her mother by giving her a drawing she'd made of Hiram and Herman with their hair still down to their shoulders. How her mother had smiled then! Gertie's eyes filled with tears as she remembered that pure maternal gaze of one who loved all her children best.

Gertie hoped to paint everything she remembered someday. She wanted to paint the picture she and Herman made together as they sat there in the grass. She hoped to get it all, how they held a delicate bloom with its purple petals all unfurled, how she gazed at Herman's upturned face, him clutching her long skirt as his curls danced in the early morning breeze. She wanted to capture how his eyes looked now, how they spoke of a loss forever searched for and of wonder ever new.

She shifted Herman to his feet and stood up behind him. "Hermy," she said, announcing her heart's desire to her attentive little companion, "someday if I've the things to do it with, I'll paint us in this meadow here and those clouds, too."

Herman nodded his head fiercely, hardly understanding what she said but approving of her tone anyway. He chuckled when she called him Shorty Britches and stayed close to her as they walked back to the house. It touched her heart.

"Look at us, wouldn't you, Herman," she said. "If we don't be careful, we'll turn into a couple of old crybabies!"

"Bye babies!" Herman echoed to his sister's delight.

***

ANGER. HARD, HOT ANGER BURNED INSIDE the older twin's wound-up little body. He wanted to be with the others, and then, just as strongly, he wanted to break away. He couldn't say what it was that he wanted in the first place, but he had to keep moving. Hiram was born with a restlessness that drove him and everyone else to distraction. Lillie loved him as much as she could, but she was often at her wit's end with him. She confided to Ben that she knew which baby had kicked her hardest inside the womb.

Hiram didn't like to be held for long or cuddled. He'd bow his back and yell his head off if anyone tried. He frowned if anyone looked at him or talked to him. But he wanted attention all the same. He wanted his mother more fiercely than ever Herman did. Herman was compliant, easy as a branch that bends. But Hiram even felt heavier, his mother said. Yet she had nursed him the same, sang to him the same, stroked his little head, marveled at his tiny hands and feet.

It was never enough. Whatever he wanted was not to be found; his need was so insatiable. When his mother died, when the source of his only desperate joy was gone, he withdrew like a wounded inhuman thing, torn by inarticulate grief and fear. Who would love such a child?

Gertie and Herman went off without him. If she tried to hold Hiram, he wouldn't let her. Grace avoided him, and Aunt Addie said everyone should let him be.

His father favored him, and that was his salvation. Hiram rested in the strength of the man who made him be still when he picked him up, made him mind and obey. He rested inside that safe place and nursed his baby pain while the rest of him fought to get stronger, to grow up.

HANNAH ZILPAH PAYNE WAS LILLIE'S AUNT and therefore the great aunt of the Reuben children. Her arrival and establishment in the household marked a line of demarcation separating past from future, an appearance set in stone and as intractable as the visitation on Mount Sinai. She was indeed a lesser deity who must be appeased and obeyed.

Aunt Hannah had always favored Lillie and said to diverse people on several occasions that Ben Reuben was not nearly good enough for her niece. The heavy peace occasioned by Lillie's death had softened the old woman's querulous opinions and pronouncements. When she saw Ben Reuben weeping at the funeral, she knew he was not only worthy of Lillie but tragically so.

"Their marriage was too good for this world," she now said to all and sundry. She said it was providential that her nephew-in-law had asked her help and that she was unencumbered to provide it. Inspired, she determined to mend the rift between Ben and Lillie's sister as well.

"Blessed are the peacemakers," she said often, reading from the very Bible that survived the battle of Gettysburg and returned with her wounded husband after the Civil War. She was a stout, matronly widow now, a woman who planned on surviving everything.

The time had come for her to survive taking care of the Reuben family. So it was that she stood in the open door on a fair evening in May, her huge arms folded in the stern manner that would become increasingly familiar to those greeting her. Her gestures affirmed there could be no compromise when she once made up her mind and that she made it up often.

Within minutes Aunt Hannah removed a handkerchief from the cuff of her sleeve like a conquering flag and spat into it. She wiped first Herman's and then Hiram's smudgy little mouth, talking all the while and issuing orders and directions to children and adults in the same tone of voice. All attempts to escape the giantess were thwarted and futile. The boys squealed in protest like baby pigs being rushed to the slaughter. Grace and Gertie steeled themselves for the worst.

"Now, Grace, come over here and let me have a good, long look at you," Aunt Hannah demanded in a tone that precluded negotiation. It happened that Grace came under Aunt Hannah's line of fire on the occasion of the young girl's second and somewhat irregular menstrual period. She didn't feel at all well and would have preferred this meeting, first, never to have happened, and failing that, to occur tomorrow.

Aunt Hannah's eyelids creased open and shut like wrinkled accordions while she pored over every feature on Grace's reluctantly upturned face.

"You have bags under your eyes, missy," she said—an assessment that Grace thought could only have dire consequences. "This can only mean one thing." Aunt Hannah launched into a long-winded diatribe condemning Ben Reuben for neglecting his children's health. She began to lecture on the merits of going to bed early, washing properly, and eating the kind of food conducive to not having bags under the eyes, which food should be supplemented, she affirmed, with nightly doses of castor oil.

Throughout this speech, most of which had been directed at her, Grace kept her head lowered and said nothing. She was determined not to take her eyes off the scrolling pattern in the faded rug and under no circumstances to give her Great Aunt Hannah the satisfaction of either her attention or her fear. She felt grimly glad that her great aunt carried about her person a certain unpleasant odor.

An exasperated Ben Reuben finally interrupted, "While I respect your wisdom in such matters, Aunt Hannah, and will yield on certain points, still I am in charge of this family." These somewhat faltering words were answered by one look from the formidable lady, a look so silencing that Ben subsequently amended himself humbly, even abjectly, "Yes, Aunt Hannah, we'll try . . ."

Encouraged, Aunt Hannah continued with her next appraisal, turning a keen gaze on Gertie. "I do not approve of nicknames whatsoever. You are Gertrude to me, and I hope others follow suit." Aunt Hannah's eyes then quite inexplicably moistened with tears. "Our little artist," she said, smothering Gertie in a sweaty, voluptuous hug.

Gertie yielded to the ferocious favor because it was the line of least resistance. She had not the combative nature of Hiram nor the mock compliance of Grace. Aunt Hannah's stop in mid-stride, so to speak, was a blessing for the rest of the family. Having sounded her boundaries, she settled her skirts over the one chair large enough to accommodate her undefined bulk and announced that she was thirsty. There followed a rapid-fire account of all the incidents that had beset her on the train and the subsequent wagon ride from town. "It should be a wonder to everyone," she said as Aunt Addie came into the room with a glass of water and a plate of shortbread, "that I arrived in one piece with no broken bones." Her chair creaked under the weight of each exclamation.

Addie adjusted the scarf that she wore for the angels. "Hmmpf. Well, I haven't battled inconsiderate train passengers all day, but making shortbread and bathing the twins took all the attention and patience I could muster."

"I should say so!" Aunt Hannah agreed. "Oh, you're a deep one, you are!"

An hour later the tide of activity receded, and everyone went to bed.

AUNT ADDIE CONSIDERED WHAT Hannah's being there meant. For one thing, it meant less work for her. She already performed so many services that she lost track of them, and she wasn't getting any younger. Oh, she once had a use for much speech, but as she got older, no one listened anymore. It took too much effort to raise one's voice, and it was simply easier to remain silent. It might not be so easy to be silent with Hannah Payne, however.

There was much for Addie to ponder. Now she would share the household with another woman, share its tasks, share its people. She loved the children and Ben; her feelings for Lillie could not be articulated, they ran so deep. Still, day followed day, and the work was never finished. You'd get the dishes done, and there was the next meal to prepare. You'd get the laundry washed, and there was the ironing. You'd get the floor mopped, and here was another mess. It wore a body out.

The house had its own life, too. That was something Hannah Zilpah Payne would discover for herself. The house breathed a separate entity into being every morning, one composed of pent-up this and pent-up that, a wild energy that poured from bodies and minds more youthful than hers, racing to a future beyond her mortal reach. Sometimes the children teased her and called her "Aunt Addled" when they thought she couldn't hear them. It hurt her feelings.

"I can endure all things through Christ who strengtheneth me," she would say to herself. Her Lord told her so through His Word. She would wear her holy scarf and pray and receive the strength she needed every day. She would labor in the vineyard till her time on earth was done. She would prepare meals, wash the laundry, help the children, and now get to know Hannah. When she needed peace and quiet and the solace of green pastures, there was the cemetery to go visit, to take flowers to. It was enough. Her life was full.

The house was sleeping now, all its energy laid to rest.

Hannah was in her own room, and Ben was out on the front porch, sitting as he did every night for however long it was.

Addie was grateful for her life, thankful that she had a home with the Reubens. She had worked side by side with Lillie for many years, never complaining, always helping. She had no place else to go.

She had almost married once, a long time ago. Her intended was a young man of delicate health, a poet. He wrote her many sheets of verse with lovely rhyming words and stanzas properly laid out. He couldn't be satisfied if there was a single smudge of ink on the page and would write and write until perfection was achieved. His name was Allen Dale, and he had the softest hands, never raised in anger against any living soul. Allen Dale's only fault was his poor health. He'd lose his breath over the least thing, the way consumptives did. Even the time he spent in a sanatorium was to no avail. Addie said, after her beloved's death, that his heart was too weak for this old world and that she would never love another.

She pulled the covers over her shoulders and burrowed into the pillow. "I can do all things through Christ who strengtheneth me," she said. She smiled as she remembered how the twins had gobbled up their shortbread.

SIX

———————◆———————

OT ALL FARM FAMILIES FARED AS WELL as the Reubens.
Ben's neighbors to the west hardly fared at all. About
the only thing that Roy and Pearl Dean produced that
thrived was their own offspring, and they had quite a few of
those. The oldest was their prize, though neither had the grace
or wit to know it.

May Dean's was the kind of beauty discovered slowly by
most folks. It was strangely insistent, though, like the seed of
an unknown flower that has drifted in from somewhere to
bloom in an ugly place. She didn't impress people immediately
with any particular or memorable feature, but she was always
spoken of as a "real pretty thing." Her eyes were larger than
her face seemed to warrant, resting over fine cheekbones. Her
mouth was small and well formed with straight teeth that presented a slight and not unattractive overbite. She had small
feet and small hands, hands that were never idle. There was
no time for idleness in the Dean family. May was busy from
early childhood wiping the noses and rear ends of her younger
brothers and sisters, all four of them. There were also dishes,
cooking, sweeping, hauling water—not much time to so much

as mind an unruly curl on her own head, and she had an abundance of those.

It was her hair that people noticed first. Thick with jet-black ringlets, it danced about her shoulders and down her back. Even when she was sitting still, which wasn't often, her hair had a life of its own. It crowned three dazzling points of reference—her mouth and her darkly exotic eyes.

May Dean's brothers and sisters, nuisances every one of them, demanded her time and chipped away at her youthful energy. There was never any question but that she would take care of them. The word *slothful* would have been mild in describing her mother. Pearl expected her to do just about everything.

"It's enough that I got to bring them into this world," Pearl would say. "Not like I can do all the rest of it, too—taking care of every blessed thing."

May had few memories of ever being alone. Her infancy was over before the second baby was born, and then came the others, rapid-fire, her pa said, in their times and seasons. Four children had died—two of summer complaint and two of pure neglect, or there would have been still more work for May Dean. At age sixteen it seemed to her that she had always been grown up.

There was one memory that haunted her with its brevity. It was of a quiet time before any of her siblings appeared, a pleasant time when her parents still laughed and could be happy. Things changed. May didn't know when her pa took to drink, still less, what demon goaded him. Life became a series of uprootings, a jolt of wagons and sleeping on the ground in makeshift tents, of rough men hanging about and card games and fights. There was always noise and hunger.

Roy Dean made the Run for the Unassigned Lands on foot; that he was able to stake a claim at all used up about all the luck he ever had. He soon discovered and had the lesson repeated many times that getting the land wasn't the same as working it.

When May Dean was five years old, her family lived in a one-room sod house. Though many such dwellings were done up in as nice and civilized a manner as the circumstances would allow, even to the whitewashing of the tightly packed dirt walls, the Dean soddy afforded no such comforts. It was a mud hut. May's parents argued all the time. May learned early on to stay out of their reach to avoid getting hit.

Pearl was no help. Everything she did was with sighs and groaning. Cooking was her one concession to work, and this was only because she was fond of eating. She cooked everything in grease, even vegetables. Her favorite dish was fried possum; this she cooked, fur and skin and head and all, in a skillet of boiling lard.

Sometimes Lillie Reuben came to call, and then the Deans had fresh bread, jam, and cookies. Lillie offered Pearl the Gospel in words and deeds. Pearl took the deeds readily; for the rest, her husband told her not to go getting religion, and she didn't.

It was as settled as the Dean family ever got. May Dean didn't know but what everyone in the world lived as she did. There was never enough, and even that didn't last long. She longed for a house like the one Lillie Reuben lived in. That would be grand enough for her. She loved to go there on those rare occasions when Pearl paid a call, usually begging for something. That part was humiliating, of course, but going inside to the good smells and clean rooms was worth the shame. Lillie Reuben never seemed to mind. She was generous and even gave things Pearl didn't ask for.

"It's not charity," Lillie would say. "You'd do the same if you had it to spare."

"If you put it that there way, then I guess it's all right," Pearl would answer with a heavy sigh. "We been having hard times, Missus Lillie."

Roy Dean worked as hard as any man in the county—when he worked. He was a good neighbor, when he wasn't drinking, but he drank every day. He was charitable, if he had anything to give, which wasn't much and wasn't often.

Sometimes Pearl confided in Lillie, "Roy Dean will never amount to nothing. There's a man what never finishes nothing he sets out to do."

"We must pray often for him," Lillie would reply.

May listened to the two women and took what Lillie said to heart. The words seemed true when she heard them at the Reubens' place, but when May was back inside her own filthy sod house, when she heard her folks screaming all over again, she forgot everything in the heat of the moment. She concluded that prayer only worked for some folks, not for hers.

She learned early on that it did no good for anyone to voice an opinion contrary to what her pa said. Roy Dean would do what he wanted, and that was the end of it. No discussion, no planning. Just up and do whatever came into his head at that exact moment, and woe to whoever got in his way.

Adversity was the only thing stronger than Roy Dean; setbacks of any kind unnerved the man. When the rains didn't come that first April and May of 1890, when he saw his green fields fold up around the corners like brown paper scorched on the edges, he took to serious drink. He cursed and said that God was against him. He didn't seem to notice that other farms were also suffering or that their owners made the most of the situation by planting turnips that season. He whined and bemoaned his fate, yet somehow he managed to find enough money to buy whiskey. He let the word out that he'd gladly trade his whole quarter section for a good horse.

Ben Reuben offered him more than that. He offered him a fair price for his farm, and Roy Dean sold it to him.

"We're moving to Russellville," Roy told Pearl one morning. He had spent the night at a saloon in town arguing the merits of Arkansas farming with a persuasive peddler passing through. The stranger's swarthy looks and convincing words impressed Roy Dean; that and the liquor consumed made up his mind. "I didn't come here to be no turnip farmer," Roy said.

"Who said a word about turnips?" Pearl shot back. She was disgusted with his drunken behavior and forgot herself. The slap across her face reminded her smartly, throwing her off balance so that she dropped the child she was holding and fell hard against the kitchen table. Roy Dean glowered at her, giving her reason to remember all over again that, in the absence of assent, silence was her best response and the only one he would accept.

May was old enough to know that the move from the farm, pitiful as it was, was a desperate thing. She shared her mother's shame over this and despised her father for forcing them to go. Right up to the last day, neighbors tried to talk Roy Dean out of his foolhardiness. He only waved a despairing hand at his unfruitful fields and shook his head.

"What have I got here?" he asked. "A man's got to take care of his wife and young'uns, don't he?" Pearl had given birth to their second baby two months before.

May Dean felt the full import of the neighbors' sympathetic looks. She was learning the same lessons as her mother with regard to her pa's anger. It always started with a simple word spoken out of turn that became twisted into the most incredible ugliness. Roy Dean carried every little thing all the way to screaming and bruises and tears.

They moved to Russellville. They went in a buckboard wagon drawn by two oxen and loaded with all their worldly goods. Roy Dean rode the only horse they owned, while May Dean sat in the wagon with her mother and baby brother. The trip was unremarkable in its hot misery. The few travelers they met along the way seemed unearthly apparitions, rising like phantoms out of the distance and receding the same way behind them. No one had much good to say about prospects going or coming.

Crossing the Arkansas state line did not improve their prospects or their luck. A card game in a dark saloon reduced their livestock by one ox. Roy Dean traded the remaining ox for a mule and to replace various items that he gambled away. They were desperately poor and ended up renting a place spread over the rocky soil of a steep hill, the only land available to them for the price. The owner let Roy Dean have it cheap on the condition that he fence the property.

There was no stall for the work mule, and the animal had to be tethered to a long rope till a place was fenced off for him. Roy went on a drinking spree and delayed the fencing. Thus it was that he found the mule stiff and dead one morning; the poor beast had broken its neck fighting against the rope trying to get to some water. Now Roy had to harness his mare to a rusty plow to break up the hard soil. The work was too much for him, and he was too proud to ask for help. He wanted nothing to do with the few Quakers and Baptists who lived nearby.

"Don't need their religion or their charity," he told Pearl. A year later he acknowledged defeat and returned to Oklahoma with a smaller wagon and one horse and another baby.

"It was all just lies and deceit," Roy whined to Ben Reuben. Ben took pity on Pearl and the three children. He rented their place back to them in exchange for a percentage of what they grew that first year. He gave them a milk cow and some chickens so Pearl could trade eggs and butter. He told Roy about new ways to make money. "You know these buffalo bones all over the prairie? Folks gather them up and sell them for fertilizer," Ben said. "A few dollars here and there comes in mighty handy, and you've got your family to think of, Roy. It'll go better this time around, you wait and see. Turnips do good here, and there's other things as well. You can catch fish and sell them in town. I've got fifty pounds of salted fish stored for the winter myself."

"But I've lost my land," Roy Dean said miserably.

"I'll sell it back to you when you're able."

As the years passed, it seemed Roy Dean would never be able. Ben let his neighbor's accounts carry over from season to season. He had witnessed Roy's drunken rages in town, saw him get into any number of fights and arguments over the least thing.

May grew up; another baby sister was born. Ben and Lillie both noticed how the young girl changed in her appearance and her personality. She was strikingly pretty but so somber. The once-friendly child now withdrew from simple conversation. She kept her eyes on the ground and scarcely had a word to say. She listened all right, but she watched everyone with furtive eyes, flinching if a sudden movement surprised her.

Roy told Ben that his family needed more room. "Can't live like animals no more in no hole in the ground," he said. Ben assessed the situation and provided building materials to frame in a two-room house, a modest beginning to get the family out of the soddy. He and his hired hands helped with the construction when Roy was sober. Roy seemed ready to explode into anger over the least provocation. Pearl started avoiding Ben and Lillie, too. She would turn her bruised face away and go someplace out of sight so no one could see her.

Ben stumbled onto quantities of empty whiskey bottles around the place, some jammed into the dirt, others stuffed in the crooks of trees. But in spite of Roy's drinking, the small house was finished. Time passed and the year came that Lillie died.

"I can't do what Lillie done to help them out," Aunt Addie told Ben. "They steal you blind, and it's no wonder 'cause poor folks got poor ways."

Ben tried to think of ways to protect the Dean children from their father's rages. There was always school during part of the year, but Mount Vernon's last schoolteacher quit before the term was over. If only he could find other places for them to live, on the pretext of getting them employment. Most of them were too young, of course, but not May Dean. She could surely find work as a maid somewhere, maybe in town. Ben made inquiries, knowing that Roy Dean would never refuse the prospect of hard cash. He figured that hard cash would one day buy the last bottle of liquor that would kill the pathetic man. There seemed to be no other way.

———————◆———————

BEN REUBEN COULDN'T KNOW that May Dean was biding her time in her own way, that she longed for moments when she could be alone in the Deans' small house. Such times were few and far between, but there was one such day a couple of months after Lillie Reuben's death, a day that settled in on summer's heat. Pearl was sitting on the front porch swing, the one that Ben Reuben had bought for them; her stained blouse was open so she could nurse Nellie, the youngest. The other three children had gone into town with Roy.

It was Saturday, and May would have gone, too, but for two things. One was, and this was a big reason, that she didn't like the way the town girls looked at her. She heard them say that she and her family were white trash. Even if it were so, she didn't want to hear it from strangers. The other thing was that she was sick to her stomach. The pain was almost worse than when the doctor had to take her appendix out the year before. These cramps were the kind that rolled around every few seconds or so, increasing with tempo and intensity. It was awful, and then there was the fear that she would throw up and make a mess.

May cleaned up the kitchen, hearing the creaking of the porch swing outside and the feisty grunts of her little sister. She felt a fleeting moment of tenderness and then caught sight of herself in the mirror on the other side of the room.

"Ugh," she said, thinking she looked as terrible as she felt. The glass had a long diagonal crack where her pa had thrown something at it. Besides that, the frame hung crooked on the wall. The mirror showed the reflection of a young girl with fierce eyes and a resisting kind of beauty that was determined to get on with the business of life. In the meantime, it was just too hot to stay inside.

"You ain't gonna die of the cramps," Pearl told her when she joined her on the front porch. "And you're later getting them than I was. I had you when I was fifteen. I used to be pretty, too. You ain't gonna die of cramps!" she repeated.

The air was like a furnace. May sat on a step near her mother, holding her head in her hands.

"What else's ailing you then?" Pearl asked, shifting Nellie to her other sagging breast.

"Nothing," May said sullenly.

"Whyn't you go off with your pa like the others?"

May's mouth went hard. "Didn't feel like," she said. "Mama, my stomach hurts so bad! What can I do?"

"Nothing. You can't do nothing for it. It's the curse of God Almighty on womankind, and you got to endure it is all." The grumbling woman frowned and then made a little "ow" sound herself; Nellie's teeth had come down hard on her breast. Pearl smacked the startled child's face, which set her to kicking and screaming.

"Don't you think Nellie's getting too big to nurse?" May asked in a disgusted tone. Nellie was two years old.

"You mind your own business, girl!" Pearl said. "What I do with Nellie is up to me, I guess. You're a-being saucy 'cause you can't be alone. I know why you didn't go! You was wanting to be alone here to the house, wasn't you?"

It seemed to May Dean that her mother was always looking for a way to needle her.

"You got yourself a fella hid off somewhere," Pearl said in a singsong voice. "Don't I know? Lots of boys—too many strings to your bow, missy. You think I'm stupid, but I ain't. You keep company and think we're too ignorant to know. Pull a long face like that! You look a-here and listen good. You keep yourself pure around these here boys, or you'll get into trouble! There ain't enough room for no more babies in this house!"

"Mama!" May cried in exasperation. "I got no boys hid off someplace, and I ain't keeping company neither!"

Pearl sniffed indignantly. "Ha!" she cried. "You think your ma's stupid 'cause she's not a fine lady like some I could name if I wanted to or cared, which I don't. I know some things, May Dean. I was pretty once. You watch out, or you'll get the beating of your life—see if you don't!"

"I got work to do," May said abruptly. Not even Nellie's smiles could keep her there another minute.

When she got around the house and out of sight, May fell down on the grass and sobbed quietly. Her slight body heaved for several minutes, and then it was over, like always. She wiped her eyes and stood up to face the sweltering July morning; it was already hot enough for her clothes to be soaking wet, and it wasn't even nine o'clock. She went to the back porch and picked up a tub full of dirty laundry, nearly tripping over the gray cat sprawled out on the steps. She carried the load out to the well and set it down under the mouth of the iron pump. The pump arm was rusted, and it took several tries with both hands before the water finally gurgled over the pile of soiled clothes. May went back to the house for the soap and scrub board, taking her time. The task was one she didn't look forward to; it would take her most of the morning.

She scrubbed steadily for several minutes, stopping only when she saw her ma's rumpled form at the side of the house. Nellie stood barefooted beside her mother. "We're heading over to Coonrods'," Pearl said.

May said nothing. All she could do was eye the mountainous pile before her.

"See you do a good job," Pearl said. "I expect to find things picked up inside, too, when we get back."

May smiled when her mother turned to go. It seemed amazing to her that within a few moments a rare peace settled over the place. "At least I'll be alone," she said to the sleeping cat on the step. "You hear that, old snaggle tooth?" The cat opened one eye; the other was missing. Its lean body bore bitter reminders of many feline wars; the torn ears and matted fur blended well with the squalid surroundings. He stretched, lost his balance, and nonchalantly set about recovering his dignity.

May got a second tub for rinsing. The sun climbed moment by moment until she figured she'd been at the wash for about an hour. The wet work helped take her mind off the heat. She was thorough at her work because she had to be; she wrung out every piece by hand, for there was no wringer. It was a hard, heavy business draping the wash over the clotheslines—two ropes tied from the back porch posts over to corresponding trees some forty feet away. May was fearful every time she hung clothes out to dry; if the ropes snapped, she'd have to do the laundry all over again. The weight of the wash caused the ropes to droop alarmingly; the sheets nearly touched the ground.

"Well, that part's done," she said to the cat. May Dean stretched her muscles, basking in the silence of the empty yard. It seemed as if every bone in her body was either sore or out of joint. Her back especially hurt from all the lifting and straining. She groaned, felt a powerful thirst, and drank a whole dipperful of well water before going back inside.

"Phew!" she exclaimed, carrying the last basket of dirty clothes to the sudsy tub. This was the nastiest part of all, doing the children's underwear. Two of the youngest went bare-bottomed at home, but not the others.

Half an hour later, she was done. She hung the limp clothes and told herself that she would have to get a new rope before the next wash for sure. May emptied the dirty water over the grass, carried the washtubs back to the house, and put the soap and scrub board away. She tidied the inside of the house as best she could and went to the well again. She pumped a gushing flow of fresh water and stuck her upturned face under it. It felt so good that she did it again and nearly bumped her head when she heard someone laughing.

"Careful you don't drown yourself," a familiar voice warned. "Doesn't look like there's anyone around to save you if you did." It was Jasper Knight, a boy she'd gone to school with the year before. May was embarrassed for him to see her looking like a drowned rat.

"Ma's gone to Coonrods' with Nellie," she said, trying to scowl and finding it impossible. Jasper had such a nice smile. "Everyone else went to town with Pa."

"Last time I was here, you had to pull the water out of the

well," Jasper said. He was taller than her pa now and had filled out some, too.

"Mr. Reuben, he put us in this hand pump," she said. "Sure is a good thing, too. Makes washing lots faster." She wrung the water out of her hair, flinging droplets at him.

"That feels good," Jasper said. "Makes a fella almost comfortable on a hot day like this. 'Course there's better things to do to cool off."

May looked at him. One thing that hadn't changed was that tangle of brown hair that kept falling over his eyes.

"Like a swim in the pond," he continued. "Yes, sir, a nice swim in this heat would feel mighty good. Seems like we used to do that a lot last summer."

May blushed, remembering. Jasper's blue eyes danced with an assumption that seemed to tickle him. "You will go, won't you, May Dean?"

"It sure is hot, all right." She jumped aside gracefully to let a grass snake pass. "But I don't know, Jasper."

"You've done it before," he said.

"Yes, but that was last summer. I'm older now, and so are you."

"There's no one home," Jasper said with a self-assured tone. "You said so."

"What brings you here anyway?" May asked, as if the thought had only now occurred to her. "I haven't seen you all these months, and suddenly here you are."

"I've been to my uncle's, helping him over to the Samuel house."

"The mansion?" May asked incredulously. "You been inside it?" The huge house was the talk of the whole county and had been for three years or more. There were no farmhouses in those parts to compare with it, nor houses in town, for that matter. No one had ever seen anything like it, a Victorian palace rising out of the prairie.

Jasper nodded proudly. "Done built some of it. Worked on the roof and painted some of the rooms, too. I hope to build my own place when I get more money saved up and start me a proper farm." He looked around the cluttered yard.

"Not like this place," May said, following his gaze. "'Course you won't be building nothing like that Mr. Samuel's mansion neither. Unless you found gold somewheres."

"No one could build what Mr. Samuel's done built. You'd have to be rich as Midas, which some say he is. I'll settle for a small, decent place with the right woman. How about that swim, May Dean?"

"Sounds like you're pretty sure I'll say yes," she answered. "But really, Jasper, I don't feel good. I wouldn't be much company for you."

"Let me be the judge of that," he said. "Can't you at least feed a hungry fella something and then decide?"

"Not much to eat," she said. "I can give you a slice of bread, though."

They went into the house quietly, as though afraid of disturbing the cramped little rooms. Dusty heat hung in the dark kitchen with a heaviness that made them both want to get back outside. Jasper's face revealed a momentary pity that May Dean hated to see. She knew how poor her family was, and she did not like to be reminded. She took a loaf of bread that she had made herself and cut him off two slices.

"There's no butter," she said. "The cow's sick, and we haven't been able to do any churning."

"Got any jam?" he asked.

"Some of this," May answered and handed him a jar that Lillie Reuben had given the family the previous fall.

"You make this?"

"No, it's from Mrs. Reuben. I made the bread, though."

"She died."

"Mrs. Reuben? Yes. Her and her baby girl, too. Ma sat up with their corpses."

"I'm glad I was over to the Samuel job, or I'd have had to dig their graves sure."

"Well, you'd only have had to dig one," May said sadly. "They done buried them together."

"Ugh! How'd you like to dig up a grave and find two skeletons instead of one?"

"Don't!" May Dean cried. "I don't want to think about them like that! They've died and gone to heaven—that's what Aunt Addie says."

Jasper shrugged and smeared the bread with strawberry jam before chomping into it.

"Let's go back outside," May urged. "It's too hot, and I don't like what we're talking about anyway."

"You don't want anyone to come in and find us here alone."

"That's right," she said, swinging the back door open. "You don't know what Pa does when he gets an idea in his head."

"What kind of idea?"

"Like I'm doing something I shouldn't," May said. "He asks me all sorts of things. And I tell him I'm not doing anything bad, and he beats me anyway!"

Jasper's surprised look turned to one of concern. "I hear he does have a temper. Why do you hang around anyway? You're old enough to leave."

"And where would I go? Hadn't thought of that, had you?"

"I'm thinking now," he said. "You could get married, you know."

"Who to? You maybe?"

"Maybe not me," Jasper said. "But I'm not such a bad sort, and I wouldn't go around beating no wife of mine. My folks don't do that way. You could do a whole lot worse than marry me, May Dean."

"Well, if this is your idea of a proposal, you may as well forget it." She shrugged her shoulders and wiped her forehead with a kitchen rag. "Whew! Wish it would rain!"

"That does it!" he said. "We're going swimming! Come on." She found herself walking eagerly beside him across the yard to the unplowed fields behind the house. Past this empty stretch of dirt were the woods; gangly trees shot straight up into the hot sky, their leaves a dull green that seemed weighted down by the noonday sun. No breeze stirred, not the faintest hint. A bumblebee flew by, buzzing low over a thick bed of clover.

They followed a rough path through the trees. Here the underbrush was rough and wild; thorny vines sprang up like untamed things to lash unsuspecting legs. The shade made the heart of the wood darker but not cooler; there was no respite here. The air was close and dank with smells of earth and moss and dirt. What animals there were stayed hidden away.

The unmistakable sound of a running stream suddenly broke the silence. Its clear waters cascaded over a shallow bed, picking up what little speed the dry weather permitted and leaving a thin residue of moisture along its edges. The faded green shafts of wild iris, bereft of flowers for months now, grew along one side, tattered and torn with a wild transparency.

The two young people followed the stream through the trees and around several miniature cliffs. It hadn't rained for days; the water took its time winding through the haphazard group of red rocks. At last the stream poured into a murky little pool before picking up speed and rushing on its ever-descending way. The rocks jutted out over the pool and created a small overhang for the thin waterfall. It was a quiet, secluded place, imminently inviting.

Jasper broke their shy silence after they both jumped in, clothes and all, standing up to their necks in the muddy water. "Why wouldn't you?" he asked.

"Why wouldn't I what?" May pulled her dark hair away from her face and let it trail in the water.

"Marry me."

May blushed. "Don't know why. Aunt Addie over to the Reubens' says it's wrong not to marry, though she never did herself. I seen how Mr. and Mrs. Reuben was, though—before Mrs. Reuben died, I mean. They acted like they enjoyed each other's company, not like my folks. My folks is always fighting and carrying on."

Jasper treaded the water, his hands brushing against May's arms every once in a while.

"Not everyone fights and carries on," he said. "What're you so jumpy for?"

"My pa would kill me if he saw us here," she explained nervously.

"For swimming?" His leg touched hers.

"No," she said, moving away. "For being alone like this. You look away now, and let me get out, and don't you stare neither. I mean it, Jasper. I'm getting out."

"Oh, don't go getting on your high horse," he said. "Just wait a little while. You haven't even cooled off yet. Look at how you're sweating, May."

"That's just water, silly."

"No, I mean there," he said, touching her neck with his fingers. His mouth was close and smelled like strawberries—not like her pa's sour whiskey breath.

May shivered, and then his arms were around her, and he

was holding her tightly right there in the water with the trees shading them. She pushed him away.

"Marry me," Jasper urged, his voice richly possessive.

"I got to get home. Pa could come back any time."

"I'll ask him then."

"Don't you dare!" May cried. "Promise me you won't!"

She swam away from him and climbed out of the pond, shaking the water out of her hair and wringing her skirt.

"I love you, May Dean."

She turned away. "Promise me you won't say nothing to Pa," she pleaded. "And don't follow me back to the house neither."

"When will you see me again?"

May smiled hesitantly. "Can't say. But I want to, Jasper. Leave it at that for now."

"I'll wait," he said. "Something'll happen so's we can be together again."

May hated leaving the pond and her earnest young man. The water had been so refreshing to her aching body—refreshing, too, to her lagging spirit. What she wouldn't give for a whole afternoon like this one, a time when she wouldn't have to worry about getting back to the house to take in the laundry and fold it and put it all away, a time when she wouldn't have to think about what her family was going to eat that night. In no time at all Zeke and Abe and Molly would be home again, her ma would come back with Nellie, and pandemonium would break loose. Saturday night stretched ahead with no relief in sight. She'd have to get her brothers and sisters ready for their weekly baths and put up with all their rowdy, ruckusy noise and shenanigans.

Afterwards, when everyone had wound down like little tops, she might steal a few moments for herself out on the porch, but not if Pearl was sitting there, pouting like she did when Roy was gone. Such times with her mother always ended in senseless wrangling and arguments. May Dean would have no recourse but to go back inside the stifling house with all its restless little bodies and try to sleep in the bed she shared with Molly, whose sharp little feet kicked her all night long. She would lay there fending off those feet, hoping beyond hope that she would be asleep before Roy Dean came in at whatever hour it would be, reeking with the smell of sour whiskey and puking all over the floor.

As she made her way back through the woods, she kept saying, "Let me leave here real soon, dear God," over and over to herself.

SEVEN

B EN RODE HIS HORSE PENNY over the last hill to Isaac Samuel's place. The newcomer had hired him to drill a well, and his wagon carrying the well derrick and drilling tools had gone on to the Samuel house the night before. All that business would be set up as soon as he found a likely spot for a well. Isaac Samuel had contacted him for the job two weeks earlier and hadn't batted an eye when Ben told him his fee would be $2.50 a foot and that the well should be dug no less than a hundred feet. Ben was thankful there were no well-witchers involved. Isaac Samuel came from the East, was more sophisticated than any of the settlers in those parts, and was rich. What Ben couldn't understand was why the man from St. Louis was building a mansion on the prairie. No one else could figure it out either.

The new rope he'd bought thumped against Penny's shoulder as she cantered along. The temperamental little mare didn't like the way the rough fibers felt and tossed her head every once in a while to let her rider know. Ben ignored her remonstrances, prodding her with his heels and holding the reins tightly; he was well acquainted with horses and never let his guard down for a minute, not even with Penny.

It was a clear Friday morning with no hint of a breeze. The air would be stifling in another hour or two. Ben preferred cooler days for this kind of work. The road he traveled was wide enough for a good-sized wagon, its dirt surface packed firm by all the traffic going to and coming from the Samuel estate. That's what folks in town called the country mansion.

As Ben approached the house, he saw scaffolding along the mansion's east side and heard men calling out indistinct orders. Their words were punctuated by the sounds of hammering and of wagons and equipment moving. The din of a busy construction site seemed out of place this far out in the country. Here was no working farm but a miniature version of a tent city. More than a score of carpenters and craftsmen were employed in building the house and barn. They lived in temporary dwellings— sturdy canvas tents with wood floors, bunks, stoves—all the comforts of home. Meals were prepared and served in a combination kitchen and dining hall tent with long tables and many folding chairs.

Isaac Samuel had stunned the entire community when he paid cash for two adjacent farms three years before, farms that had never been remarkable except for a crystal-clear creek that flowed through them. Work on his Victorian mansion began a year later, a project both admired and ridiculed throughout the region. None complained about the influx of money that came with him, though.

"Why, he don't even live there himself!" critics said. When Isaac made periodic trips from St. Louis to visit, he stayed in the previous owner's farmhouse where a foreman and a cook lived year round.

Ben Reuben's reputation for well digging provided his introduction to all this enterprise. When Isaac made his permanent move to Oklahoma that June, he determined that at least one new well was needed to service the big house. As Ben rode into the yard, he saw the tall man sitting in a straight-backed chair on the front porch of the smaller farmhouse. Isaac was going over some plans, and he looked up and waved.

"Glad to see you," Isaac said as Ben tied Penny to a watering trough and came up the steps. The two men shook hands. "Have some coffee before we start?" A plump Scandinavian girl came out on the porch with a silver serving tray. "Thank you, Helga," Isaac said. "Just set it on the table here."

"I'd be obliged for some coffee," Ben answered, tipping his hat to the young woman. He and Isaac sat down, watching the hive of activity going on less than a hundred feet away. The mansion stood on a slight rise and except for the scaffolding looked about finished.

"You've made a heap of progress since I was here last week," Ben said approvingly.

"She's nearly complete," Isaac responded. "I could go ahead and move me and the staff in, what staff there is. Helga will be plenty glad to see this crew finish up, I can tell you. It's been a lot of work for her cooking three meals a day for all these men."

"You'll be hiring other folks to keep the house then?" Ben asked.

"Have to. And I haven't had any luck getting someone from St. Louis either. They all think there are wild Indians and such in Oklahoma. I keep thinking there must be a local woman who would be glad for the work and a place to live."

"'Spect so," Ben said. "I may have one in mind for you to consider. We'll talk about it later. Need to get going if we're serious about drilling you a well or at least getting it started."

Isaac finished his coffee. "I've picked out a few men to help. They all said I was crazy not to get a dowser to find the water first. What do you think?"

"I've dealt with water-witchers before," Ben said evenly. "Don't do much harm or good, if you ask me. 'Course I take a more scientific approach to the whole business of well digging. And even then, most of it's pure luck and guesswork."

"A good number of wells in these parts have been witched, though, haven't they?"

Ben nodded. "A fair few. You got to remember that not all water that's dug is fit to drink. You got to find the right kind in the first place. Could be you drill into brackish water. It's got a puckery sort of sweet taste and acts like a pure physic—no good for regular use."

"I was hoping for a sweet water well," Isaac said.

Ben shook his head. "Now that's just what you don't want. Sweet water isn't good water like you'd think, and it sure doesn't quench the thirst. The best water has what I call sort of a bitter taste—nothing you can really detect but in comparison to sweet, it's bitter, all right. That's what you want. That's what I'm prospecting for."

The two men made their way toward the mansion, winding in and out of stacks of unused lumber, bricks, carts, and copper pipes. Long tables loaded with tools and hardware were set up in the grass; boxes of stained glass and lighting fixtures were tucked safely under these. Sunlight glanced off a huge copper tub sitting under an oak tree.

"Where do you do this prospecting?" Isaac asked.

"All over." Ben waved his arms. He was impressed with his neighbor's meticulous plans and the fact that Isaac's wealth seemed deliberately understated, almost incidental. Isaac Samuel's appearance and dress revealed a disciplined life and someone accustomed to good quality. He was refined and well spoken. "Sometimes I look for low-lying places, bottom land. You nearly always find a good source close to flowing streams and creeks, too. When do you plan on being all finished, did you say?"

"Next week," Isaac answered. "That's when most of these men will return to their homes, though a few of the single ones will stay on and live in the farmhouse. I'm anxious to get the ground ready for next season's planting and will need all the help I can hire."

Ben nodded. "Last folks who owned this place didn't take their farming here too seriously. Reckon you'll do a sight better."

"There's landscaping, too, and the well or wells pretty much determine how all this is going to be laid out. I have specifications for gardens, orchards, and a greenhouse."

"Enough to keep quite a few men employed," Ben said, shaking his head in amazement. "I never saw anything like what you're building here, not even in town. 'Course I've never been to any big cities to speak of. This place of yours is already the talk of the whole Territory."

Isaac smiled. "I know. I've heard what they say, too—that I'm crazy."

"That bother you?"

"No, I can't say it does. I'm too old to let other people's opinions shake my resolve. The way I see it, anyone can build a big house in a city where there are dozens more just like it. But how many architects would dare to raise a mansion in the wilderness?"

"So you're aiming to make a name for yourself?"

"In a way. And I appreciate the incongruity of it all, the challenge."

Ben laughed. "That's a mighty big word, *incongruity*. Don't expect I've ever heard it used in polite company. We sure got us a challenge, though, to find you some water that's fit to drink and from such depths as will keep you wet for years to come. Hold on now." Ben stopped and sat down on the ground.

"You said at least a hundred feet, and folks around here say you're the best driller around. I trust your judgment on this. What are you doing?"

"This isn't divination, if that's what you're thinking," Ben said. "Nor superstition. No clairvoyant work, no second-sight stuff, no trance-mediums, no seventh daughter or son nonsense, no searching by cards, water rods, or palms."

"You sound like a man of science or faith."

"I hope I'm a little of both. The desire to know hidden things is part of our race, Isaac. But Moses condemned the whole system of looking for magic signs and charms."

"I know. I've studied Moses."

"You a Christian?"

Isaac shook his head. "I'm Jewish, Ben. My grandfather taught me the Scriptures."

Ben slapped his hand on his thigh. "I heard you were. Never knew any Jews before you. So here's one of the chosen ones right here in Oklahoma."

"There are a few of us that have settled here," Isaac said. "What were you getting ready to say?"

"Only that superstition is found everywhere, even in these parts. And the result is always the same."

"Which is?"

Ben removed his boots and socks. "A certain loss of judgment. Purity and piety go right out the window. No sir, what I'm doing is simply taking off my boots. I do my prospecting barefoot."

Isaac laughed. "Now that takes real faith, what with all the glass and nails around this place."

"Best way," Ben said, glancing around at the ground. "Can't

say it's the only way to prospect, but it's been my way since I started. That'd be over twenty years now. Never failed me yet. There's water everywhere. Key is to find it."

"Have you observed well-witchers much?" Isaac asked as Ben stood and walked to a low-lying part of the backyard.

"Sure have. They each have their favorite tree branch to use—some willows, some peach, some apple. The branch has to fork into a shape like the letter Y. Idea is to hold on to the two splits and let the leg stick straight up in the air. They say that the water pulls the leg part down toward the ground. I've seen it happen before—felt it, too. But I won't have anything to do with it. It's forbidden in the Good Book, along with all heathen things."

"That's why I asked for your help," Isaac said.

"You see, I believe the Lord blesses our efforts when we ask Him directly," explained Ben. "No need for any mumbo jumbo either. Just think of all the water on this here earth. Why, I guess she's mostly water when you get right down to it. A big, old ball of water floating in space. And all the water that's ever been or ever will be is right here. Where's it going to go? Out into the universe? I don't reckon so."

"Now you sound like a philosopher."

Ben laughed. "Don't know about that, but I do know we got work ahead. It's already seven," he said, looking at his pocket watch. "Let's see what we can find around here. Good creek, good stream—flows down toward the back of your house—twenty, thirty feet away, I'd say." Ben walked back and forth, his steps now halting, now erratically tripping over some undefined trail. His face was a study of concentration. The workmen in the immediate area paused, observing.

"Would you look at that?" a couple of men said, laughing. "Trying to find water without no rods!" Others who knew

Ben Reuben told the scoffers to just wait—they'd see something, all right.

Ben stared ahead. "This is pretty straightforward," he said, ignoring the men's comments. He knelt down, felt the ground with his hands, looked away across the fields, up the incline at the rapidly flowing stream. They were perhaps thirty feet from the mansion's back porch.

"I think this is a good spot to drill," Ben said thoughtfully.

"You want me to have my men set the derrick up here then?" Isaac asked.

Ben told Isaac to stay there and went back to where he'd left his boots. "Yep, that's the place. Mark it with a big rock. I need me a drink of water." He wiped his face with his bandana before putting his socks and boots back on.

"Here you go, Ben." Someone in the work crew handed him a canteen. Others slapped him on the back, offering loud congratulations.

Ben held up his hands. "Better wait till we dig the well."

Isaac instructed his crew to erect the derrick while Ben attached the steel cable with its drilling bit. A horse was hitched to a connecting drive shaft and made to walk in circles, driving the drill up and down, up and down. The repetitive motion of the tumbling rod hitting the ground opened a small hole that grew to about twelve inches in diameter. Down and down the work progressed as the huge tool beat and punched its way into the ground.

"How's it work?" Isaac asked Ben over the pounding noise.

"It's a hard hit that frees up water in the rock below. We just keep doing it till we find a good supply."

The horse plodded along all that afternoon. Cool, clear water was found some hundred and ten feet below the surface of Isaac Samuel's backyard. Galvanized sheet metal casing would line the deep shaft; a pulley and bailer brought up a sampling for Isaac's first taste.

"Couldn't be any better," Ben said after he drank deeply. "This well should hold up for a good many years. 'Course now, a well isn't eternal. Things start to rust and cave in. You can replace sections of casing through the years as a precaution."

They discussed guttering and saving rainwater.

"I expect she's big enough," Ben said of the huge cistern by the house. The underground space was twice the size of most cisterns in the territory and made of concrete. Rainwater flowed through the gutters and was funneled through layers of charcoal before resting in the deep receptacle. Hand pumps in the kitchen and water closets would draw the clean water for household use.

Ben returned the next day to check on the well's progress. Brickwork was underway to enclose the opening. It would be a round well with a well-defined rim several bricks thick. After Ben and Isaac drank some of the new water, they set out prospecting far away from the mansion and barn. Ben selected two additional sites for windmills, spots they marked with piles of red rocks. "Look like altars," Ben remarked.

The two men took their time, enjoying the aspect of the meandering creek, the maturing oaks on either side. During the course of the day, they discussed everything from farming to the care of livestock. Ben decided he liked Isaac Samuel right well. It was good to have a serious man of means in the community, someone who could help a lot of folks, a householder who would need a good-sized staff to keep that three-story mansion of his going.

By the end of the day, Ben had persuaded Isaac to hire May Dean as a maid for three dollars a week and to provide her room and board. "Consider it a favor to me," he said, "in exchange for me helping you with these here wells. If May Dean doesn't work out, no harm done. You can let her go."

All the same, Isaac pressed him to take his standard fee for the well already dug, and Ben did not refuse.

PERSUADING ROY AND PEARL to let May Dean work at the Samuel house took some talking. Ben put the matter to them squarely, knowing they would feel obligated to at least listen because of everything he had done for them.

"Your daughter is of an age when she can take care of herself and contribute to her family's needs," Ben said. "Mr. Samuel is willing to pay her to be a maid in his house. It's a fine house, too. I've been there. A fine place for May Dean to live."

"She's our little girl," Roy whined, though the prospect of getting three dollars a week that he didn't have to lift a finger for was enticing.

"You've got three other children who're old enough to help Pearl," Ben said. "Zeke and Abe are both big boys now, and Molly's shooting up, too. May Dean's had as much schooling as most girls get around here and more than some. All she needs is a good place to start, and I can tell you, the Samuel house is that place."

"How much you say that crazy man's willing to pay her?"

"Three dollars a week and room and board. You can't do better than that around here." Roy's eyes narrowed when he heard the amount again. Ben looked over at Pearl. Her expression shifted according to Roy's mood.

Roy scratched his chest and appeared to be thinking the matter over. He stood suddenly and yelled, "May Dean, you get yourself out here this minute! You done convinced me, Ben Reuben. When's he want her to move in? When's the money start coming in? May Dean! You get out here!"

The young girl came out on the porch, keeping out of Roy's reach.

"Say hello to Mr. Reuben," Roy ordered.

"Hello, Mr. Reuben." Ben nodded at her.

"You're going to work for Mr. Samuel directly," Roy Dean said, waving his arms about for emphasis. "Won't avail you none to try to wiggle out of it neither. Mr. Reuben done worked it out for you to be a maid over to the big place. Time for you to be making your own way and paying us back for all we done for you."

May looked over at Pearl who sat tight-lipped on the porch swing, nursing Nellie. "When am I to go?" she asked.

Roy Dean shrugged.

"Soon's possible," Ben said, standing. "Mr. Samuel has the house finished and needs cleaning help right now."

Pearl shifted Nellie on her lap and pouted. "I need you here, May Dean, and that's a fact, but we need the money worser yet. This here Mr. Samuel will pay wages to us for you." The woman started to cry, wiping her nose on her dress sleeve.

"Go on and pack your things," Roy said gruffly. "Ain't much to take. When you wanting to take her over there, Ben? Can't leave myself. Too much work to do around here."

Ben tried not to laugh. He watched May go back inside the house, both of them knowing full well that Roy had no intention of doing any work around there. "I'll be happy to take May Dean over, and now's as good a time as any." He untied his horse and swung into the saddle.

May returned quickly with a faded carpetbag.

"Climb up behind me," Ben said, giving her a hand. "I'll keep the bag up here. Light as it is, won't be no trouble at all, will it, Penny?" The horse whinnied and shook her mane.

Roy leaned over the porch rail. "I'll come see you every week to get your pay and make sure you ain't doing nothing to make us ashamed. That's when she gets paid, ain't it, Ben?"

"Every week. Yes, sir," Ben answered. "Hold on now, May Dean."

Pearl blew her nose into the open air, turning her head slightly to be polite. "Nothing to keep you from coming around from time to time," she called after the departing horse.

———

MAY COULDN'T BELIEVE her good fortune. She held onto Ben as they rode away, amazed that her life could change so much, so completely, in the space of a few minutes. Here she was galloping down the road to the mysterious big house, the mansion everyone talked about, and she was going to be paid real money for working there, too—more money than she'd ever had or seen before! She remembered that Lillie Reuben said good things come to those who wait. Well, May had waited long enough, and now God was answering her prayers. She wished that Mrs. Reuben was still alive so she could tell her what was happening.

The only time May's folks ever talked about the Lord was to use His name in vain. She hated it when they did that. She never saw her parents pray, and the only Bible they had was kept in a box tied up with string.

Life had to be better at the Samuel place. And maybe she could see Jasper from time to time. There would be no more children to worry about, no siblings to pester her. She certainly wouldn't miss sharing that miserable excuse of a mattress with Molly either. About the only one she would miss was Nellie.

Doubts arose. The farther they rode, the more May Dean wondered what she was doing going to a rich place like Mr. Samuel's house. Why would he want her there, a poor girl with only two dresses to her name and little else? What would be expected of her? Probably there would be glass things that break easily, floors you couldn't even walk on. Would she have to ask for her pay, beg for it?

"He's a Jew, isn't he, this Mr. Samuel?" May asked over Ben's shoulder.

"Far as I know," Ben answered.

"Pa has nothing good to say about Jews," she said. Of course she knew that he had nothing good to say about anyone.

It was a hard ride. May contented herself by watching a passing train off in the distance. It made a push-away, push-away sound. She felt drowsy, hypnotized.

An hour later Ben pulled in the reins, bringing Penny to a halt. "Here we are," he said. May peered over his shoulder and saw the Samuel house rise before her like a picture in a fairy tale, so beautiful, so foreign that she felt almost giddy. She had never been this close before. Oh, she'd seen it from the road when the family went into town in the buckboard. Her pa would spit in the road when they passed by. He would call Mr. Samuel bad names and say he was come to show off and mock poor folks.

Ben rode through the front gate and helped May down. He handed her the carpetbag and smiled as she thanked him for bringing her all the way. She turned toward the porch, feeling shy and awkward, like an intruder. Ben walked up the steps and rang the front bell. She heard a train whistle off in the distance; its familiar cry reassured her. She craned her neck to take in the third-floor windows, the attic above those. What a good view of the trains she would have here, she thought. She could watch the smoke curl up and over the rows of clattering cars, watch its dark trail fade away with the passing caboose.

May waited, wondering if Mr. Samuel liked the sound of train whistles, too. She blushed when a tall, good-looking man opened the big door and smiled at her. He was younger than she had expected, and he shook her hand, just as if she were a grand lady and not a slip of a girl come to be his maid.

———————

The samuel house was arguably the finest in all the unnamed counties from Kansas to Texas. Its three stories of Victorian architecture rose over the prairie like a delicate ship moored in a harbor of green hills. The exterior was carved with all manner of scrolling and delicate curlicues; blue shutters laid flat against the ivory exterior walls. Four pointed towers glistened with light where the sun shone on stained-glass scenes depicting David and Goliath, Moses receiving the Ten Commandments on Mount Sinai, a desert blossoming with roses. The wrought-iron fence had been shipped from France and was set two hundred feet from the house on all four sides, enclosing an immense yard. Its four gates opened onto brick sidewalks, each lined with flower beds where iris and petunias, zinnias and hollyhocks, phlox, and larkspur would bloom. Flagstone paths wound through the backyard. Wooden benches were already placed in the planned rose garden, a canopy of young trees providing shade. Lacy trellises awaited morning glory and emerald-colored ivy to mature and wind over their delicate iron.

The interior was even more grand with inlaid hardwood floors hand-pegged by craftsmen brought all the way from St. Louis and Chicago. The walls were finished with dark paneling, rising fourteen feet to crown-molded ceilings. The marble floor in the foyer spread its creamy surface toward a double parlor on one side and an immense dining hall on the other. In the middle rose the carved stairway winding its mahogany banisters up from the center portico, hinting at the beauty of the studies and bedrooms above. Isaac's library was on the first floor, its walls filled with books and paintings. *Objets d'art* collected on his trips abroad could be seen in every room. Also downstairs were the breakfast room, kitchen, two servants' rooms, and an enclosed back porch.

Isaac Samuel had spared no expense to achieve his esthetic vision. What set his apart from other grand houses of the day was the high wooden porch and mahogany doors on all four sides. It was not affectation that prompted him to build so many entrances. His grandfather Ezra Silver had taught him that a house should be open on all four sides to show hospitality to the poor. Ezra told him that the patriarch Job made four doors to his house—on the north, south, east, and west—so the poor would not be troubled to go all around the house. Isaac's porch with its four points of entry was a tribute to honor the memory of his grandfather.

At the mansion's completion, the town newspaper praised its features under the headline, OPULENT ELEGANCE OPENS ITS DOORS TO THE TERRITORY.

Isaac bought a copy and read the account to his cook and his new housekeeper:

The prairies take new definition as Mr. Isaac Samuel demonstrates what American ingenuity and determination may achieve, given scope and opportunity as he closes the door on construction of his Victorian mansion built right here in the heart of Indian Territory.

Mr. Samuel, an educated man of independent means, hails from St. Louis. He said that he visited our community several years ago and was impressed by the friendliness and dedication of its populace together with the natural beauty of the Territory. His first visit in 1889 prompted his determination to return here to live. Mr. Samuel said he was attracted to our fair clime because of the immense potential of the land itself and its prospects for statehood. Well-wishers from throughout the county have been invited to pay their respects at the Samuel house.

The newspaper story was brief, barely touching on the facts of Isaac Samuel's background because no one knew what they were. Inherited wealth had certainly paved his way in the wilderness. He could have gone anywhere in the world and done well, so people said. That he had chosen to move all the way from St. Louis, a great metropolis, to settle in Oklahoma Territory and build his Victorian fancy farm was a wonder. Most of the residents had never known a Jew personally. The scant few they had met lived in towns and were merchants, lawyers, or businessmen.

"Capitalizing on the pioneers!" some said, not that anyone could find anything to blame. This was America, and it was also Oklahoma Territory, open to Jews and Gentiles alike. Still, it was a mystery why a relatively young man with no wife and children would come to this particular place, starting a farm as if he'd done it all his life.

———— ◦ ————

ISAAC WAS BORN IN ST. LOUIS in 1868, the son of Esther and David Samuel. His parents were a wealthy and pretentious couple whose physical passion was released once and for all in the conception of their only son. The two shared a relentless desire for wealth.

As a child, Isaac experienced both the joy of exclusive attention and the silence of long, rainy afternoons when there was nothing to do but read and sketch. A student of the classics, he was tutored at home by well-paid intellects. Though not a remarkable or original thinker, he nonetheless made it his life's work to acquire knowledge and wisdom. His chief interest, before his grandfather introduced him to the study of Torah, was architecture. This he studied from the ancients to the present, longing to make his mark one day with a significant edifice.

For such singlemindedness, Isaac Samuel had his grandfather Ezra Silver to thank or blame. The old man moved in with the family when Isaac was two years old and proceeded to lead the boy into what Ezra called the treasury of the Torah.

Ezra Silver had achieved his significant edifice in the form of wealth, having amassed an impressive fortune through various enterprises. When Isaac was older, his grandfather hinted at what those enterprises had been, saying it was no longer important. He mentioned gold mines, fur trading, profiteering. He told stories of adventures in the Indian Territory, of ventures with railroads, cattle, kerosene. Ezra had seen the prosperous plantations, the government, the slaves of the Civilized Tribes.

"Such industry and intelligence!" he would say.

Ezra's parents had demonstrated their industry and intelligence by leaving England and settling in Rhode Island, the one British colony tolerant of Jewish worship and traditions. Ezra was born in Providence in 1811. Raised according to the traditions of his faith, he nonetheless disappointed his parents by venturing west where he finally opened a mercantile store in St. Louis at the age of thirty-four. Finding the merits of assimilation conducive to financial success, Ezra gradually abandoned his Jewish roots. He fell in love with a girl named Margaret Hicks, a Gentile who worked for him, and married her. Margaret bore him three children: Esther and the twins—Aaron and Joseph.

Ezra's sons were provided a suitable education to prepare them to carry on his business interests, but the Civil War interrupted their dreams and plans. Both were killed in separate military actions, a tragedy that sent their father reeling. Ezra consoled himself with further travels, leaving his wife for months at a time. During one of his absences, Margaret died of a broken heart. Esther, the surviving daughter, subsequently married David Samuel. Grief brought Ezra to his knees and to a resurgence of faith. When his grandson Isaac was born, the aging man felt hope return. He delighted his daughter and her husband by turning over his enterprises to them. It wasn't long before he moved into their townhouse in St. Louis.

Esther and David were not religious Jews; their beliefs were the result of assimilation and choice. They held that religious fanaticism was imprudent in business and society. They believed themselves part of an enlightened age and adopted a tolerant attitude toward all viewpoints while concentrating on acquiring wealth.

Thus Ezra took Isaac's religious instruction upon himself, selecting the best commentaries for his grandson's enlightenment. They were the prototypes of renewal, their spiritual roots grounded firmly in Zion. Isaac was introduced to the Talmud, to its extensive records of study and debate held by Palestinian and Babylonian Jews for seven hundred years and more. When Isaac heard the Wisdom of the Fathers, his heart quickened, and his soul was knit with the soul of his grandfather.

"We are blessed indeed to learn the fear of God from the rabbinic fathers," Ezra once said. "Here is the basis for all civilized conduct and thought if we will but reach out and take the proffered wisdom."

They kept the Sabbath, sometimes able to persuade Esther and David to join them. On such occasions, Esther would wear a Belgian lace veil and even light the candles and say the blessings. Ezra always spoke gently to his daughter and her husband so that neither took offense. They also did not change. Ezra knew of the deceitfulness of the human heart through the knowledge of his own. For him, the study of Torah was salvation. Life was the temporary framework to hold the teachings of the ineffable God, the God who on Mt. Sinai condescended to give His Law through Moses.

"What more could a man ask of the framework of life than to study the Torah and the commentaries passed down by great rabbis through the ages?" he asked Isaac, causing the young man to ponder his own framework.

In 1880 Ezra was sixty-nine years old and in relatively good health. He rejoiced to see the effect of the Word of God in twelve-year-old Isaac. Isaac told him that he felt the words coming inside him when he read them out loud.

"To study God's Word is to be covered with something that protects you, like plaster poured over rocks," Isaac said during one study session. "Once it gets hard on the rocks, even the rain can't break it. I am the rock, the Torah is the plaster that covers me, and the rain . . ."

Ezra rocked back and forth with his eyes closed in deep contentment.

"Yes, yes, my son. And what is the rain that pours over the stones?"

Isaac thought and answered, "It is trouble. The rain is the picture of the bad things that come down all around you. They cover you completely in the way that real rain gets you wet."

"Ah, yes, and yet what happens to the one who studies and is covered by Torah?"

"He is protected," Isaac said. "The rain cannot hurt him."

"So the Word of God is strong enough to protect you from the rain of bad things, from the rain of evil, is it not so?"

"I see it," Isaac said. "But how are we to rid ourselves of the evil? Moses established the sacrifices for sin, but these have been taken away. Where is our atonement, Grandfather?"

"Good works and study of Torah are atonement. Who

knows?" he asked. "When the third temple is built and the sacrifices return, when Messiah comes, then we will have peace speedily and soon. It's not for nothing that we long for Jerusalem."

Isaac applied the Word of God to his life. He particularly enjoyed studying about the temple of God, its divine mandates and exact measurements, the materials brought from afar to Jerusalem for its construction, the dedication of King Solomon, and the glory of the Lord filling the house. He and Ezra read through the first five books of the Law each year. They studied Jewish mysticism and prophecy and discussed a time when the land of promise would be restored to glory, when Messiah would come.

They spent long afternoons studying in the dining room where the only sound was the ticking of the clock on top of the French provincial china cabinet. Inside were Esther's Waterford crystal and Ezra's silver menorah. So prized was the candlestick that Ezra wouldn't allow the hands of their Gentile maids to touch it. It was the menorah Isaac looked at many an afternoon.

On one such occasion, before his bar mitzvah, Isaac broke the silence: "Here is a Scripture that says we are to remember our Creator in the days of our youth before the evil day comes. I think this means that if I meditate on HaShem and Torah, then His Word becomes a light for my path. Torah shows me which way to go when I'm young and prepares me to face whatever will happen in life when I'm older."

"Well said," Ezra replied. "We must both study and apply Torah. Think of boys your own age who have never even heard of Torah, boys who have to work hard for a living and who live in darkness their whole lives. Think of where the righteous Creator has placed you and be thankful, Isaac. Be thankful."

Isaac *was* thankful. He was thankful that he lived in an elegant townhouse with grand rooms. He was thankful for a beautiful neighborhood with gaslights and manicured parks. Yet he knew that when one is rich, others covet. Every day his father left the house in a handsome coach drawn by fine horses. Every evening Esther, dressed in the latest fashion, welcomed her husband home. They entertained friends and associates with huge dinner parties, croquet matches, and buffets on the lawn.

It wasn't that Esther had deliberately set out to marry a man who would lead her from a faith she had never embraced in the first place. She had simply fallen in love with ideals and goals identical to hers. She had seen all she wanted of death and grief. Death would take care of itself. To Esther there was a portion of life that you could control, and it was this to which she applied herself, depending upon her husband to do the same.

Isaac grew up, his interest in Torah and architecture intact. His parents sent him to school in Chicago, and while he was gone, Ezra prayed that he would remain pure. Isaac told his grandfather not to worry, that the fear of God was too strong in him. Beyond that, he met no one who held his interest long. Isaac trusted God to bring him a wife at the proper time. He continued with his architectural training. He was well liked by friends and associates and entrusted his heart to none. He followed Torah to the best of his ability and kept abreast of the economic and political currents of the age. Summers he spent at home and abroad, the whole family traveling together to the east coast or to Europe.

"Someday we'll go to Jerusalem," Ezra said hopefully. The Zionist movement to regain the Holy Land had begun. Isaac felt inspired. The desire to go out from his father's house awakened in him. He drew sketches for the home he would one day build.

"I've drawn up plans to build my own house," he announced to Ezra and his parents one evening. The year was 1889, the supper a Sabbath meal before Purim, the festival celebrating Queen Esther's triumph over Haman. Isaac was twenty-one. "My studies and travels have only intensified my desire to build," he said as they all gave him their full attention.

"Lofty sentiments demand concrete plans," was his father's response. Esther nodded in agreement while Ezra sipped his coffee thoughtfully.

"True enough, Father, and I have such plans. I want to build a mansion in the Indian Territory. It will cost me $70,000 and take three years, hardly more."

His father held a wine glass in his hand and looked at the candles through its crystal etchings. "Well, at least you didn't say Palestine," he said, aware of his son's Zionist sympathies.

"Not at this time," Isaac answered. "No, the general area I have in mind is close by the train. President Harrison has agreed to open the Unassigned Lands in Indian Territory. From what I've read, the aspect of the country and terrain are suitable for new development."

"Yes," David said slowly. "I'm sure every huckster in the country will be standing by to dupe hapless fools with dreams like my son's. What date has the president set to raise this momentous curtain?"

"This April," Isaac said.

"So soon?" Esther said. "But I thought the Indian Territory belonged, well, to the Indians."

"Two and a half million acres belong to no one," Isaac explained.

"You think this is a good investment then?" his father asked. "Surely you know I've made inquiries of my own."

Isaac smiled. "An article I read says that thousands of people are going there to stake quarter sections of land, not to grow rich."

"Oh, there'll be plenty of money to be made," David said. "Just providing supplies and food for all these dreamers will see fortunes made!"

"What sort of people are they, I wonder?" Esther asked.

"All kinds," Isaac said. "Pioneers, settlers, farmers, bankers, merchants. Some will stake homesites in the towns that will be developed. Some will stake farmland. The only stipulation is that one work the land for five years to own it."

"Five years is a long time to plow dirt, red dirt at that," his father said sarcastically. "Such an undertaking will prove an expensive enterprise, one that most of these poor opportunists can ill afford to risk. Think of the improvements needed, the building of houses and barns, the fencing of properties, the problems associated with cisterns and wells, not to mention incurring the disfavor of the native inhabitants. And then you have to deal with stock and farm implements and deliberate over the proper equipment or technique to produce a particular harvest. There are any number of imponderables in such a venture. If there's any future at all, it would be in the new towns that spring up. It's tempting even to me, but I'm already heavily invested in petroleum, all because of the demand for kerosene. There will be many failures, Isaac." His voice rose slightly. "For every venture that succeeds, a thousand do not."

Esther folded her hands. "We're an established family here. This is our home. Can you really mean to leave everything we've built up for you and go to such a godforsaken place? Surely Missouri has open land just as suitable."

Isaac answered patiently, "I don't know about its forsakenness, Mother, since I've never been there. I'd like to see for myself before passing judgment."

"A potentially expensive view, I don't doubt," his father commented.

Isaac took a deep breath. "I'll not waste my inheritance," he said. "I've waited for the right opportunity to build my house, and I know that this is what I want to do. Beyond that, I'm interested in farming and husbandry."

"What about being a husband yourself?" Esther asked.

"In good time," Isaac said, laughing. "For now going to Oklahoma is enough."

"You already knew you were leaving?" Esther looked over at her husband with alarm.

"I have two round-trip train tickets," Isaac said. "For me and Ezra." Ezra looked up, surprised.

"Of course, there's only one way to find out if this is worth pursuing. Farming can be learned, and there will be many opportunities to expand my investment in other ways. If the country life doesn't suit me, I'll open a mercantile business and continue with architecture. Someone has to build the cities there. There's every likelihood that Oklahoma Territory will become a state one day." Isaac pushed his chair back. "What do you say to all this, Grandfather?"

"Yes, what do you have to say, Father?" Esther asked. "Surely you don't support this scheme."

Ezra folded his napkin and traced patterns on the tablecloth with his fork. "Only the smallest minority of Jews in this country are farmers," he said.

"Who doesn't know this?" David asked and then, after a sharp glance from his wife, held up his hands. "Go ahead, Ezra. Speak. Speak."

"There are things we should all be reminded of with regard to our heritage. Certainly we know that centuries of persecution drove us from the land. May we never forget. We were driven out to form our own communities on the fringe of the Gentile world. We developed new abilities, both intellectual and financial, to contribute to our own welfare and to serve our host countries. We've done well, or not so well, if you consider the Reform thinking and its conflict with orthodoxy. Where is the desire to return to our true homeland, to Jerusalem? But I digress," he said, noticing Esther shifting uncomfortably in her chair. "Jerusalem is not our subject tonight, though I wish it might be. Our subject tonight is Isaac and what he's going to do with his life. So, Isaac, I tell you frankly that my concern is basic, quite simple. Where will the Jews be in Oklahoma? I fear you will truly be a stranger in a strange land, God forbid. I know. I've been such myself. Dangers and temptations on every hand." His voice trembled.

Isaac reached across the table and touched his grandfather's arm. "I've been taught well," he said. "And to answer your concerns, let me tell you that many people will be strangers in a strange land, not only Jews."

Esther coughed politely. "I wish we could quit feeling so exclusive," she said. "But each to his own. Isaac, I know how different you are from David and me. I've consoled myself knowing that yours is a pure intelligence that will find its reward. Neither your father nor I can refuse you your inheritance. You're a grown man, after all, at the age when men marry and settle down. Your grandfather left his home, and good came of it. It's no good arguing, fearing, debating. You want to go. Go. If you're waiting for a blessing or some such token, you have it."

"You can always return," David said.

Ezra shook his head. "He will not return. But as for my going with you, Isaac, I don't know, at my age. It's a long way, a hard way."

"I want you to be with me," Isaac said. "You planted the vision in my mind with all your stories."

"But that was long ago," Ezra said. "Things have changed."

"And will continue to do so," Isaac said.

ISAAC AND EZRA LEFT ST. LOUIS BY TRAIN, dined in Harvey Houses along the way, and changed lines in Arkansas City before arriving at the Pottawatomie Line. It was there that they joined other onlookers to witness the 1889 Run for the Unassigned Lands. When the gun fired, they saw a surge of humanity tearing away on all sides and marveled at the myriad examples of transportation, the ingenuous methods people employed to reach their promised land. Wagons and buggies they would have expected, but who would have thought to see a man riding a bicycle on the plains or a lady dressed in blue velvet riding habit on a white horse?

Isaac followed a deliberate itinerary to provide Ezra adequate opportunities to rest. They spent days visiting the tent cities that sprang up overnight. They tramped through dusty streets formed only days before and elbowed through jostling crowds to ask questions in makeshift land offices and order questionable food in collapsible kitchens. They rode on horseback throughout the Territory, visiting claims and talking to settlers, bankers, merchants, lawyers, shysters of every background and prejudice.

"Not a single rabbi in this great wilderness," Ezra noted sadly. "Nor many trees from which to hang your harp in such a Babylon."

Nonetheless, Ezra took the holy Scriptures and divined God's will for his grandson from them. The revelation of sevens brought them to a passage discussing Adam, whose name meant red earth. This leading from the Tanakh settled Isaac in his determination to move to Oklahoma. What was not settled was when.

At the age of seventy-nine, only one adventure awaited Ezra. A year after the land run, he died in his bedroom at Esther and David's house. He left his body quietly, having made his peace with God.

Isaac sat *shiva* for his grandfather and mourned his death for twelve months. He matured through grief and with a clear head attended to the settlement of his portion of Ezra's estate. It was sizable, more than he'd expected. Isaac pursued architectural contracts, handling several projects over the next seven years. During this time, he made repeated trips to Oklahoma, bought the land to effect his vision, and reworked his house plans. The day came when he made the purchases and arrangements necessary to begin his ambitious enterprise and ordered construction on his mansion to begin. He was twenty-nine.

Three years later, in 1900, Isaac ordered four freight cars and filled them with house furnishings, china and silver, trunks of books and clothing, farm implements, livestock, and a coach. He bid his parents farewell, made them promise to visit him the next year, and set out on what he considered to be the major adventure and purpose of his life.

Oklahoma captivated him, its strange desolation speaking to him of deserts blossoming like the rose and arousing his longing for Zion. He thought of Ezra, of their time together in the new land. Isaac projected his dreams to the arching sky, thanking its Creator for such a singular expanse, such a vantage point that allowed him to see far and wide in every direction from his own land, his own bit of earth. The clear creek that flowed through his farms, fed by unseen springs and winding its way over rocks smoothed by silent processes, was to him the essence of fertile promise, its banks of red rock and overhanging trees the stuff of repose and meditation.

He spent entire days walking over the property, inspecting fences, searching for something, anything that hinted a new truth, a deeper revelation. He found wild places that had never been turned by plow, high grasses brushing his waist and rippling like a grained sea for far distances. He saw adjacent properties as opportunities for expansion. Here before him was a quiescent thing waiting to be brought to its full potential.

Isaac came home each dusk, received the day's report from his foreman, and when the workers were in their tents sleeping or playing cards, he roamed the empty halls and rooms of his mansion. Here, carrying a kerosene lantern in one hand, he satisfied himself that the details of his plans were being realized. The man-made glory of fine craftsmanship, of work well done, pleased him. He inspected the new barn and stables with the same scrutiny, the same intensity, writing his observations for change or adjustment in a notebook. These notes would then be reviewed every morning to insure compliance and excellence.

Isaac slept in one of the upstairs bedrooms of the existing farmhouse, took his meals in the kitchen, made trips into town for various supplies, supervised the care and feeding of his livestock, and made acquaintances often and easily. He awaited the day when he would assume occupancy of his temple, his tabernacle on the prairie.

Having come of age at thirteen, Isaac had early learned responsibility for his actions. The bar mitzvah ceremony marked the time when he was no longer a son of the covenant but a son of the commandment. Ezra's words on the momentous occasion remained with him in the new land: "Let the poor be members of your household. Do not multiply slaves and maidservants to serve you. Instead invite the poor to be members of your household, and let them serve you; then you will receive a reward for hiring them."

Isaac had been taught to be merciful to the poor, that true deeds of righteousness are those not seen of men or praised by them. He held to no preconceived notions of how his servants should act or what kind of backgrounds they would have. Helga Nordstrom, his hardworking young cook, came to him from a bawdy house. "I promise to do my best for you and the house, Mr. Samuel, sir," she had said, and something childlike and pathetic in her look and demeanor touched his heart. Each of his hired hands had a heartrending story to tell—of hard luck, of missed opportunities. He had only had to let one of them go, and that was because the poor man loved to tip the bottle once too often and provoke the others with his drunken behavior. Now another of the world's strange orphans was coming to work for him, a young girl from a local family, poor but, Ben Reuben assured him, eager to learn.

It was only natural for Isaac Samuel to say, "Come in and welcome," when May Dean stepped into the foyer of his grand house for the first time. He really was beginning to feel that his home was turning into a human Noah's ark. Without the flood.

EIGHT

⬥

AUNT HANNAH HAD LIVED with the Reuben family for two months when May Dean moved into the Samuel house. Hannah settled down and into her own regimen, schedule, and expectations of the household, spreading her tented will until the family was covered. She let the children know beyond all doubt that she would not tolerate insubordination or sickness and, further, that she was to be called "Awnt" Hannah in the British style.

"Don't anyone ever 'ant' me," she said, "like I was some common bug you squash with your foot."

She rejected the second upstairs bedroom after a few weeks of panting up and down the stairs. "It's not good for me to be so far away from the children," Aunt Hannah explained. Aunt Addie was summarily given that room while Aunt Hannah established herself in the same room with Grace and Gertrude. No one dared argue the new arrangement with her.

"Whatever Aunt Hannah says," Ben mumbled in response to Addie's report of the day's events. They were sitting alone on the front porch, and he had asked her why the girls had been so sullen at the dinner table.

"Well, she's saying plenty, Ben Reuben, and you'll find your-self having to get used to it like the rest of us. She had me moved into that upstairs room quicker than that this morning!" Aunt Addie clapped her hands together to show how quick that had been. "And me with my back trouble trying to make those stairs every day, maybe even several times a day. I don't know what's to come of all this. I don't, and that's the truth."

Ben sighed as he looked at her. "Addie, I got enough on my hands managing these farms without having to worry about how you get along with Aunt Hannah. Naturally, I want you two to get on, and I've heard you say you believe in what the Bible teaches and that the words give you much comfort. I hope you turn there at this particular time since you're apparently being tested. Isn't that what Lillie would say if she were here?"

"We wouldn't be having this conversation if Lillie were here now, but, yes, you're right. I have to have my faith tested same as everybody else, and this is one test I surely hope I do not fail. But that woman is a pure wonder, Ben Reuben. She surely is. She's got those kids of yours doing things they never did before."

"Won't hurt them to help out more," Ben said. "In some ways Lillie was too soft on them, doing things for them they could have done for themselves. I'm not criticizing the dead, Addie. Don't look at me that way. I'm not. But you know now that it's not going to hurt Grace or Gertrude either to learn how to do more of the cooking—"

"And the washing and the cleaning and the this and the that! La! She has them turned into house slaves almost, and them so young, so like Lillie. They're not strong girls, Ben Reuben. They take after their mother . . ."

Ben felt a dark pain cross over his thoughts and turned to her with a stricken look. "I don't know what else to do," he said. "They're strong enough—got to be. They'll get stronger. Nothing like hard work to do that. Anyway, there's school coming up on us. I will say I'm glad to see the twins at their little chores, and I know Lillie would approve—"

"Boys doing laundry! I never!"

"—would approve," Ben said firmly. "They got to learn that things don't just up and wash themselves. Tell you the truth, Addie, I don't hear the boys fussing about it at all."

"Only cause they're so dead tired come evening," Addie said. "Once they've had their suppers, they're down and gone to sleep."

Ben was wearied of the conversation and looked for a way to bring it to a close. He had heard enough to know that Aunt Hannah was doing her job maybe a little too thoroughly and that maybe he should have a talk with her, but on the other hand, the house was being kept up, and the meals were coming regularly, and there was no serious disruption that he could see. The business with Addie and the stairs was something to consider, all right. Maybe he'd get around to adding on a room downstairs in the fall of the year, which was right close at that. He was brought up short once more at how time moved along on its own course. This time last year Lillie had been with him still. It seemed like the month that changed all that forever happened only yesterday, and yet here it was the end of summer. Could so many nights have passed since he last looked into Lillie's eyes, since he had heard her pitiful cry, "Save me, sweet Jesus"— words stamped on his memory forever?

He put such thoughts aside, like he had to do every day of his life. He could never be unkind to Aunt Addie. She was a comfort somehow, both to him and the children. Her presence was a link with the near past, her faith a support. And she had taken up more work herself. Ben noticed these things, noticed the sacrifices she was making on their behalf.

"Thank you, Addie," he said, standing and leading her to the front door. "Thank you for letting me know what's happening under my own roof. It'll be all right, though. I know it will. Don't go up and down those stairs more than once or twice during the day. There's no need. Send the girls if you need something. And now I just want to be alone. I do thank you for your concern and loyalty. They mean everything to me."

Aunt Addie smiled wanly, said she would pray for him and, indeed, for all of the family, said she would manage her new room and the stairs and not become embittered over what she could not change and finally went inside to see if Hiram and Herman really were asleep and if the girls had washed up the dishes without mishap or intrusion from Aunt Hannah. She passed the girls' door and heard her replacement snoring away with great zigs and zags of sound.

———◦———

AUNT HANNAH WOULD NOT REST until she got the family and the hired hands in the habit of eating together.

"No house of mine is going to serve two breakfasts on the same morning!" she declared. "Simply isn't done—isn't even worth thinking of except to say it stops here and now." And that was the end of the matter.

Still, she begrudged the hired help every extra morsel that they ate. She served them second, but rarely third helpings, with a slap of the spoon that the girls called a plate-cracker. She didn't like complete strangers, as she called them, coming in and making themselves at home and eating up everything in sight. She was vocal about her joy if any departed Ben's service and just as loud with her criticisms of the new men who took their places.

The last time it happened, Ben challenged her, "How'd you manage your farm then? Did no one suit you, Aunt Hannah?"

Aunt Hannah made a harrumphing sound. "Never had more than one hired hand in any season!" she declared. "My sons managed fine on their own!"

"Well, now, bully for them! I don't have grown boys yet, and I need these here men. So please try to serve them without making them feel like intruders. You should have seen how much they ate when Lillie did the cooking! There was third and fourth servings, I can tell you!"

Aunt Hannah rolled her eyes and from then on bit her tongue when asked to serve up other helpings.

A hired hand might stay as long as two months but seldom longer. There were usually two or three on the place at any given time—solemn, mysterious men with callused hands and creased features. Their presence meant work for the family. Not only did the girls have stacks of dishes to wash after every meal, they had to sweep and mop the floor incessantly. The men were not careful what they tracked in, not after the perfunctory wiping on the mat at the back door. Food was always in some stage of preparation throughout the day. These were the chores that fell to the girls, helping Aunt Hannah with the real work of the kitchen.

Ben officiated at the head of the table. As far as he was concerned, he said, mealtimes were for eating and not talking. Everyone, even Aunt Hannah, took the hint. He insisted on an ample spread with two kinds of meat, vegetables, gravy, biscuits, cakes, cookies, jellies, jams, and always pots and pots of coffee. They raised their own pork and beef, and after seasonal slaughterings, they stored the meat in lard inside sealed containers. Chicken was served fresh on Sundays, either fried or with dumplings.

The silent guests were private men who kept their stories about themselves to themselves. Last names were little more than formalities; first names blended with all the faces that came and went, all except one, a former slave named Primus.

Primus came through that August, the same year Lillie died. He stood off the back porch a ways, his hat in his hands. He said he was looking for work, any work, to tide him over, nothing permanent, and as soon as he could, he would move on. He told Ben he didn't want any trouble on account of his being a Negro, said he wanted to go on west from there, to California.

"You're just in time to settle in and pick cotton with us," Ben said. Though Primus tried to appear enthusiastic, one look at the man's smooth hands told Ben this was not an outdoor worker. It was still light out; the supper table was being cleared, and the hired hands were going back to their own house. Aunt Addie came out the back door with a heaping plate of hot food and handed it to the grateful supplicant.

"I'll find something for you to do," Ben said. "I always need help with my horses, and in the meantime something else may come up."

"I've asked everywhere," Primus said, eating hungrily.

"Been to the Samuel place," Ben asked, "up to the mansion? It's a good ride from here."

"Haven't seen no mansion in these parts," Primus answered.

"Well, we got one big as all outdoors," Ben said proudly. He led Primus out to the barn, to a stall-like room where he put new-born calves and colts. "This stall is private enough," Ben said, "and it's empty and clean. You got a bedroll on your back, and you can put it on this new straw. Anyway, it's dry here, and no one will bother you. I promise you that." Ben was thinking of the way the other men had eyed Primus earlier, how one of them brushed against him roughly when he passed by, how Primus had stepped back, bowing repeatedly and saying, "Excuse me, sir," several times.

"Was Primus really a slave?" Grace asked her father a week later when the family was sitting quietly in the parlor after supper.

Ben looked up from his book, Matthew Henry's commentary on the book of Revelation.

"Says he was, Grace, though it's no business of ours one way or the other."

Aunt Hannah rolled her eyes and cleared her throat. "I say if someone eats under your roof, especially a Negro former slave, you most certainly can make whatever they do your business, and so I asked him myself about his life before the great Emancipation Proclamation." She folded her huge arms for emphasis.

Ben excused himself and went upstairs with his book.

"Tell us, tell us," Gertie pleaded. "I've never known a real, live slave before, and Primus is nice. He sings pretty songs, too, and smiles at us."

"A slave to a couple from Virginia," Aunt Hannah began. "Primus was born to slaves of their family and took their last name, though he wouldn't tell me what it was. It's a mystery to us, children. And that's the only time I've thought less of him for something he said or did. Goodness knows, he works like there's no tomorrow—and polite as all get out! You boys could learn more than a few good things from Primus, and that's the truth!"

The three-year-olds blinked at her.

"During the war, almost toward the end of that sorrowful time, the couple that owned Primus and quite a few other Negroes fell on very hard times. Indeed, who didn't, especially later after the war when the thieves and bullies took advantage of decent folk, some of them our own dearly beloved, too. Where was I?"

"Fell on very hard times," Grace prompted, trying to disguise her interest.

"Yes, so they did. Primus says it was because the old master looked over his left shoulder at a full moon one too many times.

Whether that's so or not, they had to move from the South, which was in its way probably a blessing, though they couldn't have known it or appreciated it at the time. Now would you believe that a long time before all this, a rich man in their vicinity had offered them one thousand dollars for Primus? Yes, he did! One thousand dollars! Wouldn't I be sorely tempted to take it, too, if it had been my decision to make? Well, Primus says his old master said, 'No, thank you. We plan on keeping our Primus here.' He was just a little thing at the time, but I guess he was something special even so for someone to offer that much money."

"I never saw a thousand dollars in my life!" Aunt Addie declared, biting the thread she was working and putting a new color in her needle.

The girls shook their heads in agreement, and Herman started dozing off to sleep. Hiram kept repeating Primus's name with a low chanting monotone.

Aunt Hannah smoothed her skirt and continued. "So Primus and the other darkies moved with them, and Primus's own mother stayed on to care for the old couple after the war. She stayed with them even after they were all set free, and then she still stayed with them, took care of them both right up until they died. Even when they did not own her anymore, she cared that much about them! Primus, for his part, said that he took his opportunity when it knocked at the door and went off and married some mulatto who had a baby girl already, and then they had twin boys, and she left him after six years, and he tried to keep the twin boys, but she came and kidnapped them."

Aunt Addie raised her eyebrows. "You can't hardly kidnap your own children," she said. "Really, Hannah, do you think this is fitting for the children to hear?"

Aunt Hannah snorted. "I think it serves a good purpose of instruction in the ways of right and wrong. We learn by imitation and observation, Addie. You, me, and the children, too. So let them learn by observation of how one Negro's life is turning out, for we are part of that life now in a little way, and we can make of this knowledge what we will.

"So listen, Gertrude and Grace, for the boys are too young to appreciate this now. Good truths go over a baby's head, and that's a metaphor. There goes Herman off to sleep, out like Lottie's eye. Breaks your heart, don't it, to see him so? Hiram, stop that fidgeting and 'Primus, Primus-ing'! You'll give your old great aunt a headache if you don't stop it this minute!"

Gertie and Grace were giggling so hard they almost got hysterical.

"Kidnapped! Kidnapped!" Gertie started exclaiming, clapping her hands.

"Yes," Aunt Hannah said. "You may well sound shocked, missy. That mulatto wife of Primus up and kidnapped their little twin boys. Never heard their names, but they must have been something like."

"What's mulatto?" Grace asked.

"It's a good thing you girls got school coming up so soon; else how will you learn your vocabulary? What's mulatto, indeed? What do they teach at these schools today? Mulatto is when you're not all white nor yet all colored, but part of each."

Grace and Gertie rolled their eyes at each other.

"So should you be amazed!" Aunt Hannah said solemnly. "Yes, it means that one parent was all Negro, and one parent was all Caucasian, and the result is a mulatto. Poor things! Don't neither side want nothing to do with them. It's a wonder that Primus admits to marrying one, but he said she was a beauty."

Aunt Hannah let this sink in for a moment before going on. "As I was saying, she ran off, that mulatto wife, and kidnapped her and Primus's twin boys and took them and the other little girl she already had (who would be even more mulatto than her mother, wouldn't she, Addie?) and took a paid cooking job aboard a Mississippi boat bound for New Orleans. No one has ever seen hide nor hair of them since!"

"Poor Primus!" Grace said.

Gertrude didn't want to commit her feelings one way or the other. "I'll go and put Herman to bed," she said, thus excusing herself from the obligatory kiss—Aunt Hannah's good-night routine.

"Yes, yes, put little Herman to bed," Aunt Hannah said, reaching out her capacious arms and grabbing Hiram in his wild flight across the floor.

"Here, Gertie, see if you can get this little heathen to go to bed, too! You kids have me all wore out!" she said and reached to unbutton the top two buttons of her starched blouse.

Aunt Addie waited for the children to leave the room before she spoke. She laid her needlework on her lap and gazed at where the kerosene lamp sent a faint trail of smoke up its glass chimney.

"Hannah, do you think you should tell the girls stories like this? What good can come of it?"

Hannah went to the other lamps in the room and turned their flames off.

"I don't think it's harmful, if that's what you mean. If it offends you, Addie, that's something else again. What harm can come of hearing real stories about real folks, folks that show up at our doorstep and live with us, eat with us—"

"Primus does not take his meals with us, Hannah."

"That's correct. He does not, though I've said before I don't know why not. He's got better manners than most of the hired help who sit right at our table. I never saw such men in my life. Pigs is what they are, pure and simple. Such snorting and smacking and carrying on with food. I never! I think it's a shame that

Primus has to take his dish out on the back porch, and him too shy to ask for seconds, just like a dog."

"We set up a decent place for him out there," Addie said. "He's got a table and a chair and doesn't eat on the floor. I've a mind to join him sometimes. Anyway, that simply isn't done around here. You don't eat with coloreds."

"Well, you are all more Southern than I ever hope to think about becoming," she said. "One thing I do not want to see while I'm here is for these children to grow up with prejudices. That's what the war was fought for, to put an end to such foolishness."

"And what about your prejudices, Hannah? Are you so free of what you criticize in others?"

"I have not got a single, solitary thing against any human being that I know of, and if I do, I'd like you to just tell me what you think it is!"

"I've never heard you say a kind word about the Indians here or anywhere else for that matter." Addie saw the stricken look on Hannah's face.

"It's different with Indians," Hannah said. "Well, I don't mean anything by it, is what I should say," she said quickly. "I've seen bad things that Indians did. We had some family killed by Indians. And, too, they moved here with all the opportunity any white man would want and lost it by going off and supporting the Confederacy."

"Not all of them fought with the rebels," Addie corrected.

"But you can't deny a goodly number owned rich amounts of land and that more than a few owned slaves, as many as five hundred at a time! Don't ask me to feel sorry for the Indians. They wouldn't change fast enough for these times, and they're suffering for it."

"I can't argue with you," Addie said. "And I'm not making excuses for anyone with regard to owning slaves. Though I may not think it's right and wouldn't have done it myself, the Scriptures clearly teach that if one is a slave, he should make the best of it and be as good a slave as possible. And the Lord tells masters to be good to their slaves, too. No one gets off without a strong admonition on how to live a life that's pleasing to God. We're every one of us learning how to do that if we're really seeking His will for our lives."

"But what has this to do with Primus? It wouldn't bother me to let him eat with us and maybe even break this dread silence at mealtime. We can learn from one another at no better time or place than sitting down to eat. It's where we learn manners and exchange pleasantries and understand others' ways of doing."

"And you'd sit down to table with an Indian, too, I suppose?"

Hannah looked irritated. "Yes! Please, God. I would just to prove to you I could!"

Addie smiled. "Don't worry—it probably won't come up in the first place. I just don't know if it's good for Grace and Gertie to think about whites and blacks getting together and having mulatto babies. There's lots of folks around here that won't stand for even the thought of it. Negroes has got to be careful how they act. As for the dread silence, as you call it, it's what Ben wants. When Lillie was here, we used to talk and laugh and carry on, like tonight here in the parlor. I am glad for that, Hannah, to hear the girls laugh again. I think it's too much for Ben to allow. Maybe when more time has passed."

"More time," Hannah said. "Well, if you ask me, I think Ben Reuben needs to bury his grief before it eats up these kids of his. He needs to get out and away from here, meet a fine woman, get married. Don't look so surprised, Addie! You know it's true. He's not too old, and the children need a mother."

"But it hasn't even been that long!" Addie whispered.

"I know how long it's been," Hannah said, "and a sorrier

time I can't recall except when my own sweet Chris was killed right on our front porch, and I became a widow!"

"The cowards!" Addie said. "To come and shoot him down right there on your own property!"

"'Twas them dirty Sooners that did it, all right! 'Course folks said no one knew who it was, with them wearing those sheets and hoods, but God knows. Those scoundrels wanted our land and was willing to kill for it, too. Only I didn't leave. They couldn't run me off. Ah, they will never be caught till Judgment Day," Hannah said, wiping her eyes. "Surely my Chris is with the Lord, though. He was a believer."

"Death comes to us all," Addie said softly.

"Yes, it does," Hannah replied. "And we got to make the most of what life we have left. That's what I say about Ben Reuben and his grief. You may as well know, Addie, I can't stay here forever and never had any intentions of doing so in the first place."

Addie rocked quietly.

"It's hard, yes, it is, to take on another woman's household and her children and do all the things that young women are by nature and inclination prepared for. I'm not that young anymore, Addie. I knew it when Ben asked me to come, but I felt I somehow should. And, too, I loved Lillie dearly."

"I do hope you don't go off for a long time yet," replied Addie, "or at least until Ben Reuben does marry again, if he does, I mean. You do know, don't you, how special a woman she'd have to be to marry a man with four children?"

"She'd have to be a saint is all," Hannah said. "And I don't know anyone who fits that description at the moment."

"Nor do I. But even if I did know, I can't do anything tonight because I'm just too tired to say another word."

"Go on to bed, Addie. There's days and days for us to study on these things."

"And pray for God's will to be done," Addie said as she went up the stairs to her room.

"Yes, God's will."

Hannah waited before going to her own bed in the room she shared with Gertrude and Grace. She was still thinking about Primus having to eat alone and sleep out in the barn. The barn was nice enough, but it was still a barn, a place for animals. She was sorry for the former slave who through no fault of his own apparently had lost what little he'd ever had and didn't even have his children as a consolation.

His plight reminded her of her own loss so many years ago. She hadn't done anything to deserve it. She knew there would never be another man like Chris to love her for herself, the good and the bad. Chris had seen the good in her and made it better while he was alive. So she never had another man after him, or before, for that matter. She was too fat, too plain, too outspoken. But maybe she could do something still, some meaningful thing or other. Like taking care of Ben Reuben's family till the handsome widower found a new wife, as he most surely would. Taking it all in all, Hannah knew Ben Reuben would be a good catch even with four children tagged on to his suspenders. He was as good as any and better looking than most and well-to-do besides. She was surprised that Rose hadn't pursued him. But Rose was married now, content and hoping for a baby. Not that contentment was everything, not that it could protect you from tragic happenings.

She hoped and prayed that tragic things like what happened to her Chris were well over now, that men in this community didn't ride around in sheets trying to take what didn't belong to them, trying to scare folks. Prejudice was a right ugly thing when you came down to it. Hannah didn't like to reflect on such matters for long. The immediate needs of the present time were enough for her to face and handle.

"Well, I loved and was loved and thank the good Lord for it, too!" Hannah said to herself as she settled into bed. She determined to speak to Ben about Primus, to resolve where he was to eat and sleep after this. She would find a time, but it would have to be after the breakfast and the ironing. All that laundry, a full day's work!

One thing about Hannah was that when her massive head nestled into a pillow, she slept the sleep of the blessed till it was time to get up.

NINE

———————◆———————

MAY DEAN FELT AS IF SHE were enrolled in a new kind of school when she started working at the Samuel house. The first days consisted of one lesson after another. Helga showed her how to polish silver, how to dust and sweep properly, how to do laundry with store-bought soap and then wring the clean wash through a gadget that threatened to pinch her fingers if she wasn't careful. Her work started at six in the morning and went until six at night. She was busier than she had ever been, and happier. Not only was Mr. Samuel polite, he was also generous, giving her Sundays off and an extra dollar a week. He told her the money was for her own needs, that she did not have to give it to her pa. Mr. Samuel was also pleasant, never moody or unpredictable. To be in the same room with him was to be noticed and thanked for whatever task she had completed or was working on.

The only fear she had was that she might break some precious thing and incur the censure of the house. The house! Never had she imagined that so much space could be contained inside and in such pretty ways, too. At night all that space surrounded her, wrapped her up in dark quiet. When the wind had hit the

Dean shack, May feared the roof itself would fly away. The wind against the Samuel house found its match as it whistled about the corners and glass, never finding entry.

All the stairways scared her at first, winding up to other floors with their long halls and empty rooms, rooms that Helga made sure were cleaned on a regular schedule. May couldn't understand how all the furniture came up those stairs, especially the furniture in her own room. Maybe the walls had simply been built around the double-poster bed, the large wardrobe and dresser, the chairs. It was pure luxury just to sit and look out the bay window toward the north, across the fields and trees, to see, as she had hoped she could, the trailing smoke of locomotives. There were new curtains, too—real curtains made from yards and yards of muslin.

"It can't be my room!" May exclaimed the first time she saw it. She was embarrassed to set her pitiful little carpetbag down in such a luxurious place.

"And whose room should it be if not yours?" Helga asked, her Norwegian accent slightly contemptuous of the newcomer. The two girls had been introduced shortly after Isaac Samuel's initial greeting, and they took a guarded liking to one another.

May listened to everything Helga said, envying her starched dress and apron, her white cap pinned to lively blonde curls. Helga showed her through the whole house and all the work attendant upon keeping it through the next few days. She would take time from her work and huff and puff about the place, stopping on the stair landings to catch her breath. The plump cook seemed to enjoy enumerating all the housework that had to be done on a daily basis, emphasizing that May Dean was expected to discharge such tasks in a manner befitting her station. She pointed out the house's fine points, emphasizing her own pride in being employed there and stressing that it was she, the cook, who was in charge. May listened intently, fearful of smiling foolishly or appearing inattentive.

"Und another ting," Helga kept repeating with each new tour, "don't be calling the entry way the front door neither. It's the foyer. Say it. Foyer." May complied each time, trying to memorize the unfamiliar word and grateful to be given the opportunity to learn new ways and not sound ignorant.

As they grew more accustomed to each other, Helga spoke more freely. "You look at me all a-wonder and thinking where I got my talking," she said. "I know I sound peculiar to your ears. Vell, I come from Norway, the land of fjords and mountains, of reindeer and snow. My people vas killed by Indians some time ago far and away north of here. Only I survived that terrible slaughter," she said, shuddering. "So here I am and that's all you need to know on me." They were sitting in May's room. Helga regarded herself in the dresser mirror and tucked a strand of loose hair back under her cap.

May wanted to assure her hostess that she hadn't meant to ask any questions at all, but Helga continued before she could get a word in. "It could have been my room," she said, walking to the windows where she adjusted a curtain fold. "I had my choice, for vasn't I the first one hired? Ja. And didn't I live over to the other place, too, the small one, before the mansion was finished?"

May blushed at Helga's reference to "the small one." How would this Norwegian beauty describe the Dean house?

"But it's the stairs that don't agree with me," Helga continued. "I'm rather to being on the first floor of any building, thank you, house or shop, church or school. Ach! I get dizzy, and there goes the legs. How we made it tonight with all the upping and downing is the wonder to me. I been meaning to ask you, where is your other tings? You only brought one bag, and it's been the long while now. Should a trunk be coming?"

May Dean was embarrassed. "The bag is all I brought," she said. "It's all I have."

Helga looked a little more kindly at her charge and clucked her tongue. "Poor ting," she said, shaking her head. "Vell and all, you picked a good place to try your hand at housekeeping, and there's the truth. No man is kinder than our Mr. Samuel, and I should know, for I been here these three months myself, me still grieving for all my woes. He treat you proper, May Dean, and you vill surely have more going out than you brought coming in if you're smart and learn some thinks."

May would have preferred to be alone at end of the day, but putting up with a curious Helga was nothing compared to how she used to have to take care of all her brothers and sisters. She was still too shy not to be agreeable. The clock on the dresser said six o'clock; it was still light outside, and she hoped to see Jasper later.

She was wearing the nicer of the two dresses she owned, a simple blue cotton with a white pinafore that tied in back. Her shoes and stockings had belonged to Mrs. Reuben before she died. Mr. Reuben told May Dean that they had never been worn. Though she was hesitant to put them on, she had never seen anything so lovely as the little buttoned shoes. Beyond these items of clothing, May Dean had one long nightgown, one slip, some cotton underwear, a hairbrush, a cracked mirror with a tortoise-shell handle, and an oval locket her mother gave her long ago.

She felt Helga's eyes watching her every move, saw the pale eyebrows shifting slightly now and then. "You got a fella?" Helga asked suddenly.

"No one special," May Dean answered.

"You know boys from men then?"

May Dean looked at her interrogator. "I know about boys and men," she said, offering nothing further.

"Ya. I be tinking so. Girls what knows such tings has this way about them."

May didn't want to be the object of conversation. "Do you have a beau?" she asked, hoping Helga would take the hint.

"Ach, no more. But did I have? Yes!" Her eyes glazed with memory. "It was when I was doing all the cooking and wash for a bawdy house over to Guthrie. I had a fella fine. He vas a real cowboy, dot one, with the horse and the hat and the chaps and the spurs. He took me riding many times. Gallop so hard it make me all to bounce and hurt. Ach!"

"What happened to him?"

"He vas all the time looking away from me at other girls, whatever girls vas there. And, too, he liked to dance. He finds a pretty face with skin and bones to match, and off they go, dancing away from me. Ach! He vas no good, that one, and so I cried my bitter tears. There vas someting in the paper about a Mr. Samuel needing a cook, and, tank the Lord, here I am. No mens no more. Just cook and save my wages."

May wondered how much Helga got for cooking but thought it wouldn't be polite to ask. She went over to the dresser to brush her hair. "Oh, look! A pin!" she cried, picking it up and showing it to the startled Helga.

"Ya, so vat means a pin you find on any dresser top?" Helga asked.

"It's good luck if you pick it up," May said. "Like the verse says. 'See a pin and let it lay—bad luck you'll have all through the day. See a pin and pick it up—all through the day you'll have good luck!'"

Helga laughed. "So you vill be having the good luck here, and there's the pin to prove it so. Ya."

"Yes," May Dean said, turning the pin in her fingers before weaving it through her pinafore. "Shall we go to the kitchen? I feel like something to eat again."

"You vants your privacy, I know," Helga said. "And vhat an appetite! But come—another piece of pie can't hurt us, eh?"

Later Helga washed the dishes while May dried them. They peeled some potatoes for Mr. Samuel's evening meal; he always ate late. "Yours isn't to serve the master, though," Helga said. "Only set the table. I do the rest."

When all her work was finished, May went outside and walked around the yard. There were sounds here, but not the crazy sounds of an unruly household. What she heard were the indistinct voices of men finishing up a day's work, the occasional neighing of horses, and the movement of cattle. Mr. Samuel's fine carriage was parked outside the barn; Jasper had been cleaning and polishing it through the dusk. It was a beautiful thing, black and sleek; it looked as if it would fly over the ground. Brass sconces held small lanterns on either side of the driver's seat. It would hold at least six passengers, she was sure, and all enclosed with little side doors and folding steps for climbing in and out.

Jasper looked up, smiling at her approach, and set his cleaning rag aside. He told her he had been through for a long time, that he just enjoyed the act of polishing. She knew he had been waiting for her, though. He showed her the gatehouse at the entry to the property. It was a tiny, two-story cottage built of brick, completely furnished. "Though it gots no gate as you can plainly see," he said, glancing about before opening the front door. "Mr. Samuel, he ordered one, though, all the way from Paris, France. A big gate, too. I saw a picture of it."

"Who lives here?" May asked, scarcely daring to breathe.

"No one. Me and the other men live in the farmhouse, but no one stays here."

Her heart raced when he took her hand and drew her inside.

"Don't worry, May Dean," he said. "Ain't nobody looking this way."

"It's right pretty in here," she said.

"HOW'S MAY DEAN GETTING ALONG?" Ben asked Isaac a couple of weeks later. The two men were drinking coffee in the kitchen at the Samuel house.

"She's a good worker and seems very conscientious," Isaac said. "Helga is teaching her how to use a kerosene iron, and she's already baking challah bread. You're eating some of it now, as a matter of fact."

"Hollow bread?"

"Challah," Isaac corrected him. "You have to say it with a guttural sound. Sabbath bread."

"Pretty tasty," Ben said between bites. "I'll bet Aunt Hannah would like the recipe."

"Simple enough. I'll ask May to write it down for you. Helga hasn't learned to write English yet."

"So May likes it here?"

"As far as I know. Helga did say that May doesn't spend much time visiting with her father when he comes for her wages—that she acts glad when he leaves."

"That doesn't surprise me," Ben said. "Roy Dean's not the sort anyone wants to be around for long."

"Well, she doesn't have to worry about her family while she lives here," Isaac said.

"You needing any more help?"

"May and Helga are getting along fine."

"I know. I know. But what about you having a butler?"

Isaac laughed. "Don't tell me. You just happen to have one on hand—isn't that right?"

"A man that was born to it," Ben said, nodding his head. "Used to be a slave, in fact."

"Where'd you meet him?"

"Came to my door one evening looking for work. I could tell right off he was no outdoor help, but he fairly begged me for a place. I put him up in the barn because the other men wouldn't have him sleep in the same room with them. His first and only name is Primus, far as I know. He's seen a bunch in his time, and that's the truth. Man like that would be a good addition to your mansion. Only place he's like to fit in, for that matter. Will you see him, talk to him?"

Helga came up from the basement and poured them more coffee.

"I'll talk to him," Isaac said. "Only don't make him any promises."

"Wouldn't think of it. Glad to have you handle the whole thing, one way or the other. How's your well water? Your men dug up the other five yet?"

"I'll show you." Isaac led Ben out the back door and down the porch steps. The ground had been prepared for grass seed since Ben had been there last. Finished walkways crossed the yard. Isaac went to the beautifully bricked well and drew up a bucket full of water.

"As good as any," Ben said, relishing the taste. "Cool and fresh."

"I told my men to start digging the other wells next week. I'm obliged, too, that you suggested we make the cistern bigger than the original plans," Isaac said.

"Never hurts," Ben said.

Isaac shook his head. "I've been puzzling over how you were able to find water here."

Ben laughed. "Well, no mystery to it. You saw the whole thing. It's mostly guesswork and mostly prayer. I guess that's what faith boils down to. You ask the Lord for guidance and then go on believing He's answered. 'Course there are more things in heaven and earth, Horatio . . ."

"I took you for an educated man," Isaac said, "and so you are, too."

"I've read a few books," Ben said modestly. "Used to teach school, too, long time ago. That's how I met my wife, God bless her memory."

Isaac looked away. "I knew you were a widower. Thought you'd mention it when and if you wanted to. It must be difficult to raise children alone."

"Hope you never have to know how hard it is," Ben said. "But you have to get on with your life. That's all there is to do. Lillie and I used to talk about it some. She had great faith in God, a hope of heaven. Ever lost anyone yourself?"

Isaac nodded. "My grandfather. It's been several years, and I still miss him. That part never goes away. Sometimes I get a feeling about him and look up almost expecting to see him there."

"It's the same with me and Lillie," Ben said. "You never married then? Or is that too personal? Seems I'm prone to butting in when I shouldn't."

"It's all right," Isaac said. "No, I've never married. Not that I wouldn't. It's just that other things have been first in my life."

"Not many eligible women around these parts," Ben said. "But you never know. We're expecting a new schoolteacher, a young woman from Arkansas, any day now."

"I'm not looking for a wife, Ben. God will provide me one in His own time."

"Not many women of other faiths around here either," Ben said.

"You mean not many Jewish women, don't you?" Isaac asked, smiling.

"Well, yes, that is what I mean."

"I'm not concerned about that," Isaac said. "I want to fit into the community, do what I can to help others, make good on my farming."

Ben looked at the sky. "'Pears it's going to rain," he said. "I expect I'd better be heading for home, Isaac. Thank you for the coffee and the talk. I get too much of one and not enough of the other, it seems."

"Send Primus over tomorrow," Isaac said, walking Ben to the front gate, "if the roads don't get backed up with mud, that is." He held out an open palm as the first drops of rain began to fall.

"Will do it," Ben said, turning up his shirt collar. "Knew I should have brought that duster with me. Happens every time it rains, and you'd think I'd have learned by now." He leaned over his saddle. "It's a good thing you got such a big place, Isaac, so you can fit in all the strays around here."

"There is certainly room," Isaac said.

"Lillie always said May Dean was a jewel, a girl with rare potential."

"Seems she was right," Isaac said.

"Lillie was generally right about most things," Ben said. "She'd be after me today for not wearing a coat, and that's for sure. Better be off then. See you, Isaac," he said, digging his heels into the sides of his horse.

"And you," Isaac called after the departing rider. By the time he reached the top of the covered porch, the rain was falling in solid lines. It would be good for the grass, he thought, going on into the house.

TEN

———◆———

I T'S NOT ONE SINGLE THING, but how all of prophecy fits
together," Ben said. He and Isaac sat in the Samuel library,
warming their feet at the fireplace. Primus had just been
introduced and his services engaged. The new butler was settling
in as the two men talked.

Ben was telling Isaac about a book he was writing, something he hoped to publish at his own expense. "It's called, and I
hope you don't think this is too high for the likes of me, 'What
the Seven Thunders Uttered.' From the book of the Revelation."

"I'm familiar with the book but not that reference," Isaac
said. "You sending it back east?"

Ben shook his head. "Nah. We can publish books like I'm
talking about right here! No hard cover like these in this here
room. Mine will be the kind you can bend, like a sort of pamphlet. There's a place does it over to Guthrie. Bindery and everything. You ought to ride over that way sometime and have a look.
It's quite a place, quite a little city, bound to be the capital."

"If Oklahoma becomes a state," Isaac said.

"*When* it does," Ben said, emphasizing his words. "Bound
to happen."

"Are you prophesying now?"

"Not exactly," Ben said. "But, like I said, it all fits together. It's a series of things I'm trying to write. You've got the settlement of America close at hand, but that's only one event in the greater scheme of things. People coming here for religious freedom and then denying it to others. It's always been that way. Long ago you had the pope running things and forcing people to believe what he said, and that office was and is still thought to be infallible. Did you know, Isaac, that on his crown is written in Latin clear as day, 'Vicarius Filayee Dayee'—Vicar of the Son of God? And if you take that and figure it out in Roman numerals, which I tried myself and it works, those letters come up to the number 6 6 6, which you find in Revelation chapter thirteen as being the number of the beast himself."

"I'm not well versed in the New Testament," Isaac said, "though I remember many discussions with friends when I went to school in Chicago. Some of them thought the end of the world was coming. But we've turned the century, and it hasn't happened yet. My grandfather and I studied the prophets of Israel. Those writings I know. What I'm not settled on is how these words relate to our times. As a Jew, I bear no love for the papacy, but I'm not so sure the office should be equated with what you call a beast or, for that matter, why the number 6 6 6 has anything to do with history at all."

"Read it yourself," Ben said. "It's all there in the King James Version, which was translated direct from the Greek. This beast is supposed to come up out of the earth and make people wear a number on either their forehead or their right hand, and that number is 6 6 6. Leo Tolstoy wrote about it in *War and Peace*."

"I've read that, too, and now that you mention it, I'm reminded again."

"Good. Then you remember the character Pierre thought the

beast was Napoleon and wanted to assassinate him. He was wrong, of course. It's the pope."

"In your opinion."

"Naturally."

"And this convinces you that these are the last days?" Isaac asked.

"That and other things. There's interests and then there's interests, if you take my meaning. There's men who can get control of a single industry, and no one knows how they do it or why the government lets them get away with it and run other folks right out of business. Look at that Rockefeller! And there are others who do it, too. My point is this, if one of these men can get that kind of power in such a short period of time, what's to prevent the man of sin doing it? The Bible calls him that over in First or Second Thessalonians, the Antichrist. He's going to be something like we can't believe. Says so. That's why I work like I do so my kids'll have enough that they don't have to take anybody's mark but get by on their own. I see Oklahoma as a haven from the forces being loosed, one of the last havens there is probably."

Isaac sat in stunned silence. He found himself thinking of his grandfather, of Ezra.

"This interests you immensely, I can see that," Isaac said. "But how is one to resist this beast of yours—"

"Not mine, not ever mine!" Ben said, interrupting abruptly.

"No, of course not. I didn't mean it the way it sounded. There's a reference in the book of Daniel to the abomination of desolation—"

"It's in Daniel and in the Gospel according to Matthew, too."

"I didn't know that," Isaac said.

"Jesus had the most to say about the latter days. You should read it."

"Yes," Isaac said thoughtfully. "Jews have taken the reference in Daniel to mean the days of affliction under Antiochus Epiphanes . . ."

" . . . who sacrificed a pig on the temple altar," Ben said. "He was bad, all right, but he doesn't hold a patch to the man of sin who's coming later, in the last days."

"We celebrate a feast each year to commemorate the Jews who resisted the tyranny of Antiochus. They refused to worship him or his idols. In a way, they refused to take the mark. The feast is called Hanukkah, the Festival of Lights."

"Well, I never," Ben said.

"Yes, it's true. And now could I ask you something?"

"Ask away."

"Please don't misunderstand what I'm about to say, Ben, but I'm beginning to feel like you're trying to convert me."

Ben stared dismayed. "Is that what you think I'm doing? I'm no preacher, Isaac Samuel, and no saint either. I'm only telling you what interests me. Take it for that and that alone. No offense intended. I'm just telling you what my little book is going to be about."

Isaac shook Ben's proffered hand. "No offense taken. I'm sorry I said anything."

"It's all right," Ben said, standing. "We got to keep honest inquiry going between us, Isaac. I'll be listening to you and your ways, and I'd expect you to do the same with me. Well, I see this morning has plans to wear on with or without me, and about the only thing I've accomplished is getting Primus over here and you butlered."

"It's coming up on the Sabbath," Isaac said.

Ben nodded. "I been keeping the seventh day for some time now. Seems like that's the way I read my Testament. What I need to do is go see about that schoolhouse before the new teacher starts. It's going to need some repair—patching here and there. As head of the school board, it's my responsibility."

"You take a lot on yourself," Isaac said. "Finding work for young girls and slaves, digging wells, managing a subscription school. And yet you still find time to ponder the end of the world."

Ben laughed. "It all goes together, Isaac. It surely does."

PRIMUS WAS GIVEN THE ROOM behind Helga's kitchen, adjacent to the pantry. He told his employer it was too much and more than he deserved, but anyone could see that Primus was really pleased. Isaac drove him into town the following Monday and ordered him two suits along with shoes, shirts, ties, undergarments, gloves, and handkerchiefs. Primus beamed when he wore his butler suit for the first time.

"Never saw such quality, not since the old days before that most unfortunate war," he said to May and Helga as he rubbed the suit fabric between his fingers appreciatively.

"You are so elegant, so grand," Helga said. "And I slap the first one what laughs at you, Primus. See if I don't!"

Isaac had talking tubes installed to facilitate Primus's supervision of the cleaning and cooking. Primus proved his efficiency and earned the young women's respect right away. He was polite and helpful to all. Under his direction, the activities in the big house ran more smoothly than ever.

Primus served his employer with a deference and grace that had been missing before. Isaac was glad, too, to have another man living in the house. Though accustomed to being around servants, the ones he had dealt with in St. Louis in his parents' house were professionals, a unique society unto themselves. May and Helga would never be in that class. They were more like poor country cousins one was obliged and happy to assist. The girls were also more independent, like they had other lives, other dreams that they would fulfill in their own good time. It could be distracting.

Primus was the first one up in the morning and the last one to bed at night. He made sure the kerosene lamps were filled and trimmed the wicks; he polished the silver every week, whether it needed it or not, and prepared a hot bath for his master at the same time every night. He kept his own room as clean as he expected May Dean to keep the rest of the house. He was a gentlemen to the young women and gave the hired hands a wide berth. The only special thing he asked was that his employer allow him to borrow books from his library to read in his room at night.

"When all my tasks is done, suh," Primus said.

Isaac was surprised at the books Primus chose. He seemed almost to devour one after another, from the plays of Sophocles and Euripides to the tragedies of William Shakespeare. He said that while he enjoyed William Blake's *Song of Innocence*, he preferred the lofty grandeur of Milton's *Paradise Lost*. His insights proved astonishing in their depth.

"It's like I done died and woke up in heaven coming to work for you, Mr. Samuel," he said. "Lord knows I do love to read, suh."

ELEVEN

B EN WAS RIGHT. The country schoolhouse was in a sad
state of disrepair. It hadn't helped matters that the last
schoolteacher had left in the middle of the year. As he rode
into the schoolyard, he blamed himself for not tending to matters sooner. The storm that all but took the roof dated back to
the week Lillie died. He'd had other things to tend to before and
after that awful time, other thoughts to occupy his heart and
mind. The building was small, though, some thirty by forty feet,
with a dry cellar in good shape. Ben had insisted that the cellar
be built.

"You don't miss a cellar till you need one!" he said. "Just
wait till one of those cyclones comes through, and it'll be 'Katy,
bar the door!'"

Each landowner contributed money for expenses beyond
what the government provided. Such funds were used to pay for
the blackboard, erasers, and chalk, for maps and books and the
globe, for the upright piano. Parents also paid subscription fees
for their children to attend. Everyone contributed a certain
amount of firewood through the winter.

A large, potbellied stove occupied the center of the schoolroom. The back door opened onto a fairly large yard with swings and a merry-go-round. The privies, one for the boys and one for the girls, stood a good bit away from the schoolhouse and away from each other, too.

One thing all the settlers wanted was a proper school bell, one that could be rung from inside. What they had was a large iron triangle that sent out its own unmistakable sound when struck. During the school year, this occurred every morning at eight o'clock, at recess, and at noon.

The land the schoolhouse occupied was parceled out for this particular purpose on two acres of ground adjacent to the county road that led to town. Ben had of course been the one to dig the well, a shallow one that was done by hand. It was a blessing that it was close to the school, too, little more than a brisk walk in cold weather. It was necessary to keep a bucket of water indoors on bad days. When snowdrifts made it impossible to walk the road, there was no school.

Schoolteachers came and went, easily discouraged by the long hours and meager pay of twenty-five dollars a month. Few had received more than eight grades of schooling themselves; fewer still had attended normal school. Teaching forty or more children of all ages was a daunting challenge, even for the most stouthearted. Ben appreciated this as he prepared to meet the sixth teacher in the school's brief history. He hoped to at least have the building ready before her arrival, especially with school starting less than two weeks away. Farmers needed every hand available till then, even their children.

It was the first week of September and still hot. The morning promised a day that would be miserable with heat, the kind that forms a pocket and won't let anything out or in. Ben had to remove his hat and wipe his forehead several times before he reached the school. When he got there, he drove the wagon around back to water the horse, sizing up the abandoned yard while washing his own face and hands. Even the water felt hot. The ground was beaten down with hard use and weather; what grass there was came up in little yellow spikes. The trees cast a brown shade on the ground. There was no breeze; the wooden swings sat stone-still.

Ben went to the back door and tried it. The knob turned in his hand easily, but the door had warped and stuck. Inside was a swelter of heat. He opened all the windows, three on each side, but it did little good. The dust and cobwebs were thick.

He took out a pad and pencil stub and wrote down the supplies he would need to clean the place. The floors would require a good sweeping and mopping. Every surface would be dusted, the wood polished with linseed oil. The desks were a uniform size, consisting of plain tops with a shelf under each to hold books and papers. He wouldn't have to worry about firewood for a couple of months. Septembers in Oklahoma were as hot as August, Ben had found, and it stayed that way far into October most years. Some lessons would have to be held outside for relief from the heat. He worried about all the sickness that was sure to come.

Ben looked the windows over to see what repairs were needed before bad weather set in. He was glad he'd insisted on having wooden shutters installed to protect against wind. He was testing the floor boards on the front porch when a horse and buggy drove into the schoolyard. He looked up in surprise as the driver, a young woman, drew in the reins.

"Whoa, there. Whoa, now." The horse, an elegant little gelding, stopped. The driver stepped out of the buggy and secured the reins to a post.

"Hello," she said to Ben, extending her hand. "My name is Rainie Truden. I'm the new schoolteacher."

She was tall for a woman, with a trim figure and attractive features. Her hair was thick and reddish brown. Ben could see some of the older boys winding up with broken hearts that year.

"Ben Reuben," he said, shaking her hand politely. "I'm the chairman for our subscription school here. You could have missed me, though. I was paying an unscheduled visit to see what repairs are needed. Tell you the truth, you weren't expected until sometime next week."

He became aware that he wanted to speak not only politely but with his best grammar.

"I came earlier than I'd planned," Miss Truden said. "I hope this doesn't inconvenience anyone." Her voice bore the slightest trace of a Southern accent.

"Not in the least. Glad to have you here, early or late. I had it in my mind one way, and you're here sooner than I thought, that's all. Where you staying, Miss Truden? In town, I don't wonder."

"Temporarily," she said. "Oh, my. It's hard to tell which way I just came. Seems like it was south, though."

"That's the spot," Ben said, pointing. "Where are you staying temporarily?"

"With the Long family. Are you acquainted with them? They have three girls. Mr. Long is in banking."

"Yes, I know them," Ben said. "The Longs were my wife's kin. Maureen Long is, I mean, was her sister. My wife died last spring in April."

"I didn't know," Miss Truden said. "Your sister-in-law hasn't said anything about you or your wife. I am sorry to hear of her death, Mr. Reuben. I was orphaned myself."

"It's a private grief," Ben said, looking away. "As the Good Book says, 'Oh that my grief were thoroughly weighed, and my calamity laid in the balances together!' I think your horse could do with a drink of water, Miss Truden. We'll have to go round back for that."

"I can't think of a Scripture for thirst right offhand, but I know we can both use a drink," she said. Ben took the reins and led the buggy around to the watering trough.

"Your letter of intent said that you've taught school before," Ben said.

Miss Truden shaded her eyes with a gloved hand and walked toward the back door.

"I've had a little experience," she said. "I know already from the way you're looking at me that you think I'm too young. Oh, it's all right. You don't have to apologize. I'm pretty well used to people saying something about my age."

Ben smiled. "It isn't that so much, Miss Truden, that I'm worried about. We have some rough boys around here, and I just hope you can handle them is all."

"You think I'm too delicate to whip someone? I've found that respect is something you have to demand from the very first day, Mr. Reuben. You let everyone know exactly what you expect, set the rules, and then don't budge one inch. Otherwise, they'll get the upper hand soon enough, and then there are scoldings and whippings and what have you. I've been teaching two years now, and I know."

Ben's eyes widened.

"A fine and honorable profession it is, too," he said. "Used to do it myself. It's hard to find qualified folks that want to teach. I posted our opening in the Arkansas papers 'cause I already know who's qualified from here, and that's no one—no one who wants it, I mean. We have only two applicants for the job, Miss Truden, you and a widow woman who lives over to Guthrie. Your recommendations determined our decision to ask you to come."

"I liked Fayetteville well enough. That's where I started out.

We had a two-room schoolhouse there. I taught girls mostly, up to the age of fourteen. I wanted to see what Oklahoma was like. Anyway, I'm twenty-two years old, and I think I can do a credible job here."

Ben held the back door open for her. "After you," he said.

Miss Truden walked resolutely to the teacher's podium, a raised platform with a large desk and chair. She went over to the stove and, after removing her gloves, examined it inside and out. She ran her hands over each desktop, studied the rolled up geography maps briefly, and blew dust off the globe. Ben saw her eyes fall on the paddle hanging on a nail by the door.

"From what you said, you know how to use this," he said.

"I prefer not to, but there are those occasions when the application of discipline cannot be avoided, and then you can trust me to do my duty," she said. "It's very warm, isn't it? No breeze at all. It was better riding over here in the buggy." She took a handkerchief from a small handbag and dabbed at the moist circles under her eyes.

"Might be a bit more comfortable back outside," Ben said, holding the door again. There was no discernible difference in the outside temperature, however. Where the indoors had felt unbearably close and suffocating, outside was a bright heat. They walked to the water trough and washed their hands and faces.

"I see there's a cellar," Miss Truden said, wringing her hankie. "A day like this makes it hard to imagine we'd ever need a cellar. I know it rains, though. Folks say it does."

Ben looked up at the sky. "Summertime can be deceptive," he said, "and every other season, for that matter. Days like this make you think it must never rain or snow, much less storm. But the wind can turn when you least expect. We've had several wind storms, regular twisters, since I settled our place, and that's been over ten years ago."

"I've never been in a cyclone. I've heard about them, read accounts in newspapers, but I've never seen one."

"Well, I hope you never do, but it's pretty much inevitable around here. You'll be glad for the cellar if one ever does dip down our way."

"I expect that's so."

"You'll hear it first, like a thousand trains going at full blast. The sky gets dark as sackcloth, and the clouds churn every which way. They come from the southwest most generally, and you know it when they do. No mistake about that."

"I've heard they do strange, queer things."

"You heard right. Why, I saw a pitchfork driven all the way to its hilt into the side of a barn. That was just last year. Couple years before that, I saw a house that had been lifted up off its foundation and turned ever so slightly and set back down again. I reckon that was strange enough. Another time there was this wagon standing up on end with its tongue driven straight into the ground. There it stood, like some giant had just picked it up and jammed it into the dirt."

"Horrible! And think of the people who get picked up and carried away or hit by something!"

"Not if you're in that cellar," he said reassuringly. "That's why we built it."

"Well, I'm glad to hear it. Weather is about the only thing that does scare me," she said. "It's so unpredictable and all."

"That kind of storm usually happens in the spring of the year," he added. "Anyway, the cellar is safe and clean."

"It appears there's quite a bit of other cleaning to get ready for the first day," she said. "Are there enough books and supplies, do you think?"

"You'll want to go over the records from last year's class," Ben said. "Should be in the top drawer of the desk. You can take them with you when you leave. That'll give you a better idea on what supplies to buy in town. Of course, the subscription pays for everything."

"How much are the subscription fees here?" she asked.

"We started out with two dollars for each child, and we've had to take it on up to two dollars and fifty cents. 'Course there's lots of families can't afford even that, so we pass the hat and make up the difference where we can. Subscription pays for supplies and your salary, too, of course."

"Yes," she said.

"My girls and I are coming over next Monday to start in on this cleaning. I doubt it'll be much cooler even so, but a breeze might come up. You just never know."

"You sound very competent and experienced about school," she said.

"Well, like I said, I used to teach."

"Where was that, Mr. Reuben?"

"In a little town in Kansas that I doubt you've ever heard of. Don't care if I ever hear of it again myself, to tell you the truth. This is home right here. And I wonder what you think about our prospects for becoming a state?"

"Oh, I think it's likely," Miss Truden answered. She sounded so sure of herself that Ben had to smile. "I think it was all determined when Congress passed the Organic Act on May 2, 1890. Establishing seven counties between Texas and Kansas west of the 102nd meridian could only mean only thing. And though there are some who want a separate Indian state, I feel quite certain that will never happen. The Oklahoma Territory's first legislative assembly let everyone know that a real foundation for statehood is being laid. We've seen civil and criminal laws enacted, provision for public schools, a new college and university established, and even a normal school for teacher training. I'm most interested in that."

"Whew! You sure know your history!" Ben said appreciatively. "What you said is true, and all this means one thing to me. We're definitely headed for statehood within the next decade."

Miss Truden nodded her head.

"There are too many financial interests and political pressures for it not to happen," she said. "Our population is amazing, and more people are moving in all the time. I read that there are over sixty thousand living in the Territory alone, and as more come in, we'll see more towns and business and schools. Oh, I think we'll be a proper state, all right. I'm interested in seeing this come about and being part of it, Mr. Reuben. These are historic times, as all times are in one sense, but what I mean is that we have a chance to see it happen and be here to help when we're needed."

"I'm gratified to hear you say it. Gratified to know you'll be teaching my girls."

"And how old are they?"

"Grace is twelve, and Gertrude is eight."

"Grace will be a big help, I'm sure. And I look forward to having Gertrude in class, too. Do you have other children, Mr. Reuben?"

"Yep. Two boys, twins. That's Hiram and Herman. But they're not even four. They won't be to school for some time yet."

"I shouldn't think they would be a bother at all. I wonder that your sister-in-law didn't mention . . ." She broke off in embarrassment. "It's none of my business, I'm sure."

"You'll know sooner or later," Ben said. "She doesn't have much to say to my face, so I'm obliged she doesn't talk behind my back. It's a long story, this silence of hers, a difference of opinion, you might say, and it goes back a ways."

"I'm sorry, I'm sure," Miss Truden said, sounding confused and ill at ease. "Of course, I won't be staying with them long.

They've let me understand that it's only until I can find a place out this way so I can be closer to the school. Do you know anyone who would put me up? I'm a dependable boarder."

"Doubtless," Ben said. "I'm sure someone will come to mind. Wait here, and I'll get those records for you."

"Here you go," he said, returning shortly with a paper notebook. "I don't mind telling you about my family, seeing as how you live with some of them."

"If you really want to," she said curiously.

"When this land was opened up for settlement, folks could stake a farm or a town site, depending on which way the wind took them. From the very first, I wanted a farm, and Lillie's family wanted in town. Her sister wanted us to live close by to keep our families together. Also, my brother-in-law wanted me to invest what money I had in his bank and open a dry goods store. He called farming a futile thing, like pouring money down a rat hole. Well, I stuck to my guns and they to theirs, and what was just a difference of opinion turned into something that divides and conquers at last."

"It's a shame," Miss Truden said. "Surely it doesn't matter where you chose to live, or them either. You didn't have to tell me, Mr. Reuben. I rather wish you hadn't."

"You're bound to hear talk, and you should know the real story. I am not, nor never was one of those Sooners who came in illegally, but that's what Maureen Long has always called me. I have finally concluded that she wishes they had a farm now, and the whole thing is sour grapes, pure and simple. 'Course I bear no grudges."

"I shall have to find another place to live," she said.

"Not on this account, I hope."

"No, but they said they didn't have room for a long-term

boarder. I wonder that they even took me in seeing as their own girls go to school in town."

"I'll study on finding you another place," Ben said. "Something will turn up, Miss Truden. It always does. How long are you planning on teaching, if you don't mind my asking?"

She stepped into the buggy. "Mr. Reuben, I've been trained to be a teacher, and that's what I plan to do from here on out. I mentioned before that I was orphaned at an early age and raised in places you couldn't imagine. I've got no family to be concerned for me or with which to concern myself. I answer to no one but myself and my employers, and of course, to Almighty God. I say all this because some folks do not take me seriously, and yet I am a serious person and will find a way to earn respect in this community. I expect to stay here a good, long spell."

Miss Truden took the reins in her hand and adjusted her gloves and hat as she spoke, demonstrating that she was not one to waste time or effort and that she could handle two things at once. The lesson was not lost on Ben Reuben.

"I'm sure you will do just that, Miss Truden. Do rest assured that we have every confidence in you."

He patted the horse and from force of habit ran his hands around its mouth to examine its teeth. "Is this your rig?" he asked.

"Yes, it is," Miss Truden said proudly. "It turns out I had an aunt who died last spring. She thought enough of me to leave me a small inheritance with which I purchased this horse and buggy. I thought it was a justified expense, given my travel needs as a country teacher."

"I appreciate a good horse," he said, patting the animal's neck. "You got a good one here—young, strong, a little sassy."

"I know something about horses," she said. "Prince is a fine gelding. He takes the harness well. I'll have to have room for him and my buggy wherever I live."

Ben thought he saw the least bit of color in her cheeks.

"You might want to come out to the place and see my horses," he said. "I do some trading and have built up quite a herd—got some good stock."

"Certainly it's something to consider," Miss Truden said. "It would be fine to meet your family, too."

"Well, then, how about today?"

"I wouldn't want to inconvenience you."

"It's no trouble. You can follow me over and stay for dinner. How's that sound?"

"I wouldn't want to be out after dark, and I promised the Longs to go to church with them tomorrow."

"You'll get back in plenty of light. No need to worry about that. And you can keep your promise to the Longs, too. I know that's what Maureen, my erstwhile sister-in-law, would want. Can't neglect that church business. Now my family and I, we don't often get to town on Sundays. We have services at home. I'll go get my horse, and we'll head out."

Miss Truden hesitated and then spoke slowly and deliberately, obviously trying to make an important point. "Mr. Reuben," she said, "I do appreciate your kind invitation, but I really would prefer meeting your family at another time. I'm afraid what with this heat and the long ride to and from town, well, I believe it would be best for me to limit my activities today to our chance meeting here. I'll tell you what I will do, though. I'll study this notebook and prepare a thorough list of supplies we'll be needing and get it to you Monday. You said you and your girls would be here then to do some cleaning. Thank you for your kindness, and now do please excuse me."

"Of course," Ben said. "There's time for dinners and introductions." He bowed slightly, never taking his eyes off the small buggy as the horse pulled it effortlessly into the road and up the hill out of sight.

Ben couldn't help thinking how cool Rainie Truden looked even in the heat, how unruffled with her observations and plans. He regretted that he had not bought prettier dresses for Lillie, dresses like the one Miss Truden was wearing, white with little pink roses all over it. The new teacher was certainly self-possessed for her age, and what a direct way she had of looking you straight in the eyes, never flinching, never hurrying to gaze elsewhere. Even the color of her hair, brown with auburn highlights, reminded him of his wife. And to think that she knew as much about the Indian Territory as he did! It was something he could not help thinking about all the long ride home, something he would dwell on later.

TWELVE

INDIAN SUMMER SPREAD ITS INDEFINITE season over the countryside until the atmosphere seemed ready to burst with the expectancy of wanting something new, some cooler wind to blow away even the memory of heat, of the unrelenting sun. The hint of crisper air held back, high and out of reach behind the curtained sky, waiting for the stamp-stamping of its anxious audience before making its scheduled fall. Now it dropped front and center, right smack over the land, spreading a patchwork blanket of red sumac and yellow leaves. The breezes brought a flirting respite before the latter rains. The clouds were kinder, too, muting the sun's receding light and holding out the promise of milder days. October was off to a sluggish start, though, weighted still by the backward tug of summer's heat. Then came the steadier rains—hard, wet ropes that lashed the thirsty ground.

The cotton crop was respectable that year, but it hadn't always been so. Ben's girls were expected to pick at least eighty pounds on the days they could work with him and the men. They worked half-days through the week and all day Saturdays till all the cotton was in. It was grueling labor; cuts and bruises from handling the sticky pods opened new wounds and reopened old ones. Ben Reuben planted at the right time, and he followed his own advice never to put all his eggs in one basket. It was the one-cropper farmers that never fared well. People like the Deans concentrated on one crop in a season, and if there wasn't enough rain or too much, it could make all the difference between having a little and having nothing. The fact was, Roy Dean planted later than he should have, so there was nothing to show in his fields when the others were bringing in thick bolls to sell at market.

"It's the story of the ant and the grasshopper all over again," Aunt Addie said when she heard Ben relate the Deans' latest run of bad luck.

"It isn't that Roy Dean is lazy," Ben said. "He just doesn't know how to do, that's all."

"Well, he could learn, same as everyone else," Aunt Hannah said. "Speaking of which, learning, I mean, it seems our new schoolteacher has the harvest program well underway. Look at this here invitation Grace and Gertie brought home today." She held up a piece of brown paper cut in the shape of a turkey inviting them to attend the Mount Vernon School Harvest Home Program that Friday at 7:00 P.M.

The girls smiled and would not tell what the program was about no matter how often they were asked.

"It's a secret," Gertie said.

"You'll see soon enough," Grace added. Ben thought her attitude much improved since school started. "Everyone has to bring something to eat."

"That's right," Gertie said. "Something different. Miss Truden said she didn't want twenty cherry pies showing up."

The night of the harvest program fell in mid-November. Buggies and wagons started pulling up at the country school-house around six o'clock. Many children hadn't bothered to go home first, choosing to stay and help their teacher prepare for the performance.

"Thank goodness the weather is clear, so we can have our play outside as planned," Miss Truden said. "We'll have more room that way."

Inside, the desks were pushed against the walls and covered with quilts to serve as tablecloths. Desserts were placed on these, along with plates and silverware, cups for punch and coffee. Colored paper streamers draped from the corners to join in the center of the room. Here a four-sided pumpkin that Gertie had made hung with swinging abandon. It was a big pumpkin, bright orange with a greenish-brown stem. Outside, rows of chairs and benches were set up. The piano was placed to one side of a makeshift stage where candles set inside tin cans served as lights.

The Thanksgiving program was written by the class and directed by Miss Truden. Ben thought she looked charming in her Pilgrim costume. Different scenes were featured, including life aboard the *Mayflower* with real buckets of water thrown to create the illusion of a storm and waves. Then followed scenes of the first step on Plymouth Rock, the first meeting with the Indians, the first harvest, and the first Thanksgiving. Every child had a part to play. What their costumes lacked in detail, the actors made up for with a glad exuberance.

At the finale, Miss Truden played the piano while everyone joined in a tearful rendition of "We Gather Together."

Refreshments and punch were plentiful as families lingered to praise the celebration, to visit and gossip, to listen to piano music, and even to dance. The men smoked pipes, sharing tobacco and matches; the women herded their children and babies while mourning their fleeting youth; the children, young and old, ran and played, yelled and jumped and stuffed themselves with sweets. It was a great and noisy time. "Miss Truden's triumph!" everyone agreed.

"I'll stay and lock up," Ben told Aunt Hannah when the party came to an end. "Go on home and put the children to bed."

Ben asked two older boys to help him move all the furniture back inside before they left. He saw to it that the schoolroom was ready for the next Monday and then started to take down the colored streamers and pumpkin.

"I wish you'd leave them," Miss Truden said. She had finished shaking out the mop at the back door and untied the kerchief from around her hair. "The children can enjoy them for a while yet."

"All right then," Ben said. "We'll all enjoy what happened here for a long time to come. It was a fine program, Miss Truden. Excellent." He paused, observing her. "You look about worn out."

"I am for a fact, but so is everyone else. I'm gratified that you were pleased. The children worked so hard on it."

"I can't remember when we've seen anything as good, not in this schoolhouse anyway. You and the kids put your hearts into it, all right. Didn't you see how the ladies cried?"

"Yes, I did see it. Thanksgiving does that to us, though, doesn't it?"

"And now it's over for another year."

"Now it's over."

"And you've got to ride all the way back to town."

"Looks like. I'm still hoping to find a place to live out this way. I believe I've about worn out my welcome at the Longs'."

"Didn't see them here," Ben said. "'Course I didn't expect to. We need to get you settled, Miss Truden, especially before the weather really does change for the worse. Roads get to be long, miserable journeys when it's cold."

"I wish I could move, really I do, Mr. Reuben."

"Don't I know! Maureen Long can't take much pushing, and that's for sure. She gets it in her head that something has to happen a certain way, and if it doesn't, or not in the time she wants, well then, that's a problem for all concerned. I'm surprised she hasn't found you another place herself."

"She's tried."

"Well, I've tried harder and been successful," Ben said. "I should have told you sooner, but the person whose concern it is wanted to come tonight to meet you. He's left already, gone to make sure your room is ready."

Miss Truden stared in disbelief. "You didn't tell me! You didn't let on at all!"

"Like I said, your new landlord wanted to see you first. You can appreciate that. You met him, Miss Truden. It's Isaac Samuel who will open his place to you."

"I remember him," she said, "the tall man with dark, curly hair. He's the one with the mansion, isn't he? Oh, but I could never afford to pay for a room there! What did he say?"

"Isaac Samuel doesn't have to charge much, an arrangement I think you'll find most satisfactory. It'll be between you two, of course. It's no one else's business. There are other folks there, too, Miss Truden. I know you're thinking about him being a bachelor and all. Anyway, that house is so big you'll be in it a week and never run into anybody."

She laughed. "I doubt that, but I'm sure it's wonderful!"

"Come on. Isaac will be expecting us. Get into that buggy of yours and follow me."

"Isaac Samuel is one person the Longs do talk about," Miss Truden said as they rode along. "They say he's a rich Jew from St. Louis and that he put big double doors on every side of his house! Mr. Long seemed to find that a great extravagance. I've noticed that your brother-in-law is cautious with any criticism, however, especially since Mr. Samuel has increased the assets of his bank considerably."

"Have you ever seen Isaac's house?" Ben asked.

"Only from the road," she said. "My goodness! It's a beautiful thing, what with that grand fence. I never saw anything like it except when I lived in Fayetteville, and even then the houses were older, not nearly so fine. Mr. Samuel must have a lot of servants to keep it up."

"Three is all. There's a cook, a housekeeper, and a butler. They all have their own rooms. You'll have two to yourself up on the third floor. Plenty of privacy."

"An upper floor! Oh, that'll mean a view. That's one thing I've missed since moving here from Arkansas, Mr. Reuben. We had hills there and lots of trees. I've longed to be someplace high where I could see what's around me. Oh, this is wonderful!"

"We could get you moved in by Sunday night if you want to."

"Yes, I suppose we could."

"There'll be papers to sign, a mere formality. Of course, you're expected to spend the night. It's too late to be going back to town now."

"But what about Mr. and Mrs. Long? They'll worry. I know they will."

"I already sent someone in to tell them. Won't Maureen be surprised?"

"It would appear that you've thought of everything, Mr. Reuben, but I can't be cross. It's simply too good to be true. And there's room for Prince and the buggy?"

Ben laughed. "Just wait till you see that warehouse Isaac Samuel calls a barn. There's room for twenty horses and buggies!"

MAY DEAN WALKED DEJECTEDLY toward the stairway that led to her room. She hadn't said a word on the way back from the Harvest Home Program.

"What is it, May?" Helga asked, putting a hand on her friend's shoulder. "You not been yourself all this night, and what a good time it was, too. All that program and all that food. Lots of foods and nice talking. What is the matter then? You just as vell tell me 'cause I find out one vay or the other."

May looked at Helga and burst into tears.

"It's my pa!" she cried. "He was there tonight, Helga, and he didn't come to see the program either. He came to see me and to ask why I haven't been home to visit."

"Ach, so that ghost of man vas your pa, was it? Meaning no disrespect. I say no more, or I say too much. So I see you, too, with the tall one, that Jasper Knight what works right here on the place, and you never saying a vord about him to me. Ya. I notice lots of tings, Miss May. So vat you tell your pa? Why don't you go to see them, your own family? I told you to go, but you don't do it, and now see the grief."

"They got no grief over me. As for Jasper, well, he's good to me. He's a decent sort. We went to school together last year. But my family aren't good, Helga. You saw them. They can't even be civil to strangers. I don't want to go home. I don't ever want to leave here!"

"No place is so nice as this, and of that I'm sure and certain, but them's your people all the same and so deserving of you sometime. Not all the time, just the visit here, the visit there. No one asking you for all your time, May Dean."

"Pa threatened to make me come back, though. He said they needed me at home, said they'd made a mistake." She leaned against the wall and sobbed.

"Here now and here now. Up you get, and let's go to your

room and talk it out. No good for Master to see you like this, all these tears. Ach. Come, May Dean. Take my arm and upsadaisy—here we going."

May Dean fell across her bed.

"Put this blanket around you," Helga said. "You shiver so. Now then, tell me why it is he vant you to move back? Is the money you make no good to him no more?"

"It isn't that," May said. "It's other reasons, he said. My ma's not well, he says. She needs me back, he says. And all the time he's saying how she needs me back, he's touching my hair and getting close to my face so that I can smell his breath. It's like he used to be, like I had almost forgotten since I've been here. He drinks whiskey, Helga, and when he does, he gets mean. He does and says things . . ."

Helga put her hand over May's mouth.

"Stop and say it no more, May Dean. I know what sort he is, and a bad one it is for sure. Like my old Uncle Otto. Ach! And didn't he come to evil in the end, and just you vait and see if it doesn't happen to your pa, too. You stay right here and think no more vat he say. Threats is all that is!"

"He said he can force me to come home 'cause I'm just sixteen. He said he can get the law after me and drag me home. It was awful, Helga. Awful!" She buried her face in her hands.

"Mr. Samuel vill protect you."

"Pa said he'd kill him. 'I'll kill that stinking Jew!' is what he said. He said other bad things, too, about me living in a house with a black man under the same roof. That made him madder than anything. I was so scared and so afraid that someone would hear, but no one did, I guess. And then Had Coonrod came up and whispered something to him, and Had smelled bad, too. They both laughed in a mean way, and Pa said for him to shush—that they knew how to take care of Negroes and Jews. It made me scared for Primus and Mr. Samuel. Then Pa shook his finger in my face and said he'd tend to me later. What am I going to do, Helga? What am I going to do?"

"Nothing tonight can be done," Helga said. "But I worry, too, about what they said. Threats comes to no good, men taking matters in their own hands and hurting others who's different. Tell Mr. Samuel in the morning. Ya. That's vat we do. You sleep now, May Dean. Everyting be all right."

Helga patted May's head and tucked in the blankets around her. "Sleep," she said from the stairs, and she closed the door behind her.

THAT ISAAC SAMUEL WAS FOND of May Dean he would never think to either admit or deny because his feelings had not yet reached a conscious stage. When he first met her and saw that hopeful expression on her face there on his front porch, when he later observed that she was so obviously longing to please him and indeed everyone, he told himself he would do everything he could to improve her life. He had not expected to see such an arresting gaze, such fresh beauty. At the same time, May Dean seemed small, vulnerable. He wanted to protect her, to alter her destiny for the better.

But not like Pygmalion, he told himself. Isaac wasn't interested in creating a perfect statue and seeing it come to life. And May Dean was nothing like the designing women Ezra had warned him about. Scarcely more than a child, years from being a woman. A woman! If "the child is father of the man," what glorious maturity would she become, this flower, this jewel?

He was pleased with her attitude toward her work and how she did the work itself. She seemed eager to perform not only the services requested but also to anticipate the needs of others. He watched her listen to Helga and then follow her instructions on housekeeping and cooking.

"It's plain as the day that she never did learn the proper ways of doing tings," Helga told him. "But she's got a good heart, dot one. She learns quick and makes my work the easier. She turns the corners of sheets just so and has no bulges under the cover tops. She does good washing, too, and ironing that I hate. Then see what shine she makes to polish with the furniture and walls!"

Primus also praised her. "She wants to improve herself," he said. "She's not too proud to ask for help, and now she wants to learn to cook. Helga is mighty pleased to have her for an audience. Mighty pleased. And to help her in the kitchen, too. Don't know what I'll do, sir, if she wants to learn butlering."

Ben Reuben invited all of them—Isaac, Primus, Helga, and May Dean—to Miss Truden's Harvest Home Program. Only Primus declined. "I'll stay here and keep the lights on till you folks come home," he said. "And get the rooms ready for our new lady, for Miss Truden."

Isaac told Ben he wanted Miss Truden to tutor May and Helga in exchange for her room and board. "I wouldn't know what to charge her," he said. "Lessons for Helga and May seem a fair exchange."

"Indeed," Ben said, "and more than fair to the girls. You've taken quite an interest in helping them."

When they arrived at the school, Ben introduced Isaac to Rainie Truden. The two men winked at each other as their agreed upon sign that Isaac approved of her. He was glad Primus had stayed behind now to prepare a place for the new schoolteacher.

This was Isaac's first excursion to a community event, and he thoroughly enjoyed himself. He visited and ate, listened as Ben pointed out repairs that needed to be done, promised sums of money to cover the expense. Isaac found himself looking for May Dean. She appeared to be enjoying herself around the other boys and girls, children who had been her classmates only the year before. He saw her spend several minutes talking and laughing with one of his hired hands, Jasper Knight. When they saw Isaac looking their way, they moved out of sight. Later Isaac saw her again with her parents. She was obviously distressed by something they were saying to her. He went over and spoke to them. Roy Dean did not acknowledge Isaac's outstretched hand.

"Your daughter should make you feel very proud," Isaac said, addressing his remarks to Pearl. "I think we ought to consider a raise in pay for all her hard work. Would you folks be agreeable to that?"

Roy Dean leaned forward, his breath reeking of whiskey. "She sure is worth a lot to us," he said thickly. "I think a raise would be a right nice thing. How much you talking about?"

"What would you say to an extra dollar a week?" Isaac asked. He added, "Starting this week, of course. I'll be happy to pay you now and save you a ride over tomorrow."

Roy stared at him blankly but grabbed the envelope Isaac handed him. He was weaving back and forth. Pearl Dean offered a weak smile, acknowledging that she missed her daughter. Encouraged by the way Mr. Samuel listened to her, she went on to complain that May Dean had not been to see her once since she moved away, that she was more than likely ashamed of them, her with her fancy airs and now riding about in a carriage, of all things.

"Shut your mouth, Pearl!" Roy ordered, and the poor woman flinched as if she'd been struck.

Isaac found the conversation awkward and unpleasant. He extricated himself from the pair and told Helga and May Dean it was time to go. On the ride home, May Dean sat in a corner hugging her legs to her chest and staring out over the dark fields. Later she climbed the porch steps and went straight to the kitchen without a word.

Ben and Miss Truden arrived shortly thereafter, and the matter of Miss Truden's residence was settled. She agreed to tutor May and Helga in payment for her room. She insisted, however, on paying for whatever she might eat there.

Isaac didn't argue the point, stressing how much work it would be to help the girls with their grammar. "They will require considerable attention," he said. "I'd also be obliged if you took them into town next week. They both need dresses and winter coats. I'll give you enough money to cover the expense."

Ben said good night, lingering a bit hoping for an opportunity to take Miss Truden's hand. She thanked him again and followed Primus up the stairway to her new rooms on the third floor.

———————◆———————

LATER AFTER BEN HAD GONE HOME, Isaac finally retired, but he found he could not sleep. The meeting with May Dean's parents had been fraught somehow with a chilling undercurrent. He put on his robe and slippers and went downstairs to the library. It occurred to him that all three floors were now occupied by someone, that only the attic and basement had no residents. He planned on keeping it that way. Yet even with a houseful of people, Isaac felt alone. He had neglected his Torah reading for some weeks and no longer kept Sabbath in the old way. It seemed that Ezra's fears had come to pass; solitude's many faces were making themselves known.

The actual physical work of farming proved more demanding than he'd imagined. Isaac discovered something else in conjunction with this. He liked the work itself, liked the feel of leather across his palms, the blisters and calluses that came from days of working the soil under the merciless sun. He enjoyed the sweat and pull of oxen and plow, his muscles learning new ways to extend and become what they were meant to be all along. What peasant ancestor was responsible for this awakening of his blood?

He didn't know. He did not see the changes in himself—they were so gradual. The scholar was still there, but the hands were no longer the hands of a reader or an architect. The mind was still there, active and alive as never before; only now it stood on the edge of untried frontiers.

The evening played itself over and over in his mind, his visit with Ben and Miss Truden, the unsettling encounter with Roy and Pearl Dean. Isaac felt that some restless thing had been unleashed. It drifted on the edge of his awareness, pulling him on. He went into the library and stared at the titles of hundreds of books. Nothing interested him. Words seemed hollow in the lateness of the hour. He sat in the darkness for an undetermined time. It wasn't a book he wanted nor the sublime interpretations of tired, old men whose blood had long since gone cold.

He thought of May Dean and how pretty she had looked. She was so happy on the way over to the school program and then so somber on the way home. And what did Jasper Knight have to do with all this?

There was no isolated moment when he remembered seeing her in a new light. It wasn't a particular thing that she did or said. He couldn't say, "Here was what I liked about her," or "That was when I saw this new facet of who she is." It wasn't that he had noticed in any conscious sense how she went from room to room, how lovely all her movements were. It was the accumulation of all that was she, the impulse itself that was May Dean, the revelation of her soul and life.

That she was unaware of her effect on him he knew. Here was no trace of affectation. Oh, he was well acquainted with the fairer sex. He had generally found them to be rather silly creatures. He had seen the predatory nature of the female shamelessly revealed, and he was not amused. He had certainly not pursued.

Ezra had impressed upon him God's assessment of such women through the writings of Isaiah the prophet. "Because the daughters of Zion are haughty, and walk with stretched forth necks and wanton eyes, walking and mincing as they go, and making a tinkling with their feet: Therefore the Lord will smite with a scab the crown of the head of the daughters of Zion."

How well the words described the women of the society he had known. Their end, according to Isaiah, was to be "burning instead of beauty."

This was not May Dean. The contrast between her innocent charm and the Liliths he had met could not have been greater. He could no more disregard her than stop breathing. Some part of her, her essence of being, her spirit, had penetrated his defenses and taken what remained of his childhood captive. This was a siege that transcended space and time, a pitting of personality against personality. Hers was the stronger, more alive and vibrant, not because she was younger, but because she was so completely herself. Her presence in his life had forged its own foundation, one he came to rest upon.

Isaac had so subdued his conception of evil impulse that he was blinded to its real power. For all these years, his conception remained nothing more than an untried theory. It was one thing to deny what you didn't desire in the first place—another to resist the living temptation. Hadn't Ezra said that once a man pursues unchastity, all his limbs obey him? And conversely, when a man tries to do good, these same limbs impede him. So the evil impulse was strong indeed. Yet Isaac believed he had broken its power. Like others of his faith, he did not believe in original sin. He believed people were sinners because they sinned, not that they sinned because they were sinners. As long as the evil impulse was controlled by the flame of Torah, it could be commanded by him who holds it to the fire. He believed this.

Isaac paced the room, remembering Ezra, wishing he could talk to him again. "Remember, my son," his grandfather had said, and it seemed that he spoke even now from the corners of the room, from the books on the shelves, "whoever yields to his appetite when the evil impulse drives him on will die early."

Isaac was thirsty. He looked at the kerosene level in the amber lamp on his writing desk and turned it off. The house was quiet, the grounds still. From every quarter there was only silence, save for the moaning wind. The wind crept along the sides of the house and rustled through the trees. More leaves would be falling outside, falling under a crescent moon. He was acutely aware of the wind. It seemed that its force was able to see inside the house and mark his movements there.

He went to the kitchen to get a glass of water, noted the door that led up to May Dean's room. He decided to have a talk with her in the morning. He would find out what was wrong. This resolution was followed by the soft sound of water pushing into water. Isaac knew it wasn't raining.

The door to the stairway that led to May's room also opened to the basement. He opened it slowly and heard the liquid rush again, this time more distinctly, closer. The basement was twelve steps below, a wide and spacious place designed to hold the furnace that heated the entire house. A large bin stood beside the furnace with a chute for shoveling and storing coal. The furnace was still on a low heat now; the weather had not yet turned cold. Isaac had designed the basement to be both functional and attractive, not like a cellar. No expense had been spared to make this space as beautiful as the rest of the house. There were finished rooms for laundry, for sewing, for canning and storing. Large brass tubs hung gleaming on the plastered and painted walls. There was a stove for heating irons and a large metal sink with its own water pump. It was here in this warm and protected place that the servants came to bathe.

Isaac walked down the steps slowly, clearing his throat. He did this in a quiet way but distinctly enough so that he could be heard by whoever was down there. The only response was the sound of the wind and the water.

"Primus?" he asked softly, though his blood had already informed him. There was no man there.

Every sense quickened as he stepped down and into the space. Isaac was instantly aware of two things at once—the soft flame of candles on the basement ledge and the glow they cast over May Dean's shoulders as she sat in a burnished tub. Though her back was turned to him, he distinctly saw where each drop of water shone on her glistening flesh. A smell of scented oil hung over the room. The diffused glow was what a painter would try to coax from his brushes, to express on canvas the elusive textures of sense and skin, the blush beyond sight and knowing.

That she heard his voice and knew him to be standing there he saw. She held herself still, never turning, scarcely breathing. His heart was wild with longing, though far afield from thought or lust. She had become, in one translucent moment, the stillness of the place itself, the glow of candles, a living poem. May turned her head, so slowly that the water scarcely stirred. The blackness of her hair melded with the shadows, draped in its own night. This is what Isaac saw—all in a moment. As far as his eyes were concerned, the rest of her awaited conception.

When their eyes met, Isaac thought he detected movement at the basement window. *It must be the wind,* he thought.

The event lasted but seconds.

"Excuse me," he said softly, turning to go back up the stairs. "I heard something, didn't know . . ." Something irretrievable had taken place. Shaken, he left her alone and returned to his room.

It occurred to him that if flesh is not resisted, it perforce becomes one's lord, and thus, in turn, the tie that binds, awakened to birth and mastery through the intercourse of sight.

"YOU'VE BECOME A REGULAR NOAH'S ARK for humankind," Ben said to him some days later. Isaac had sent a man for him, asking him to come have a look at one of his horses. Ben ran expert fingers over the horse's leg and stepped back when the animal reared and stamped. The horse had sustained a bad fall, but Ben saw it was not too serious. It seemed to him that Isaac was distracted.

"If you keep sending people to live here, I'll have to build another house," Isaac said.

The weather had finally turned a corner into winter. The cattle stood outside, huddled along the fence, steamy wreaths shooting from their nostrils. The barn, though snug, was not warm by any means; a chill air dominated. All the horses wore blankets on their backs.

"Poor thing," Ben said, stroking the horse's neck. "This leg looks bad, but I've seen worse. Keep him off it for a few days, though. I have a harness sling out in the wagon. It raises an injured horse and keeps the weight off its legs while it's healing."

"I couldn't use yours," Isaac said. "I'll pay you to make me one."

"Take me at least a day to do that," Ben said. "In the meantime, this horse has to be elevated. You can go ahead and use mine. I'll send Si over in a day or so with a new one. You got any more problems here I can take care of? Don't want to be getting out any more than I have to on days like this, even for you, Isaac Samuel."

He went to the wagon and removed the harness and sling.

"Everything else is going well," Isaac said. "Let's go inside and have some breakfast. I want to talk to you."

"It'll take three men to finish up here and get this horse hoisted," Ben said.

When the job was done, the horse secure, Ben patted its neck. "That'll do her. 'Course you'll want to get food and water on a level she can reach."

They walked briskly to the house and stamped their boots on the doormat. Primus, officious in summer and fall, now proved his worth in winter. He opened the door before his employer had time to ring the bell. "Best you gentlemen get in this here house," Primus said, "and let me take your coats, if you please. Helga will bring your breakfast to the library directly."

"That'll be fine, Primus, fine," Isaac said. "Is May helping her? I haven't seen her today."

Primus looked thoughtful, like he was trying to remember May Dean's schedule. "Well, now, this being Tuesday and being morning, Miss Dean, she be doing ironing I expect down in the old furnace room. Nice and warm there. Oh, yes. Very warm indeed. 'Course, could be that she's doing the churning. Now that's a possibility."

"Thank you, Primus. Tell Helga we're waiting."

"Yes, sir. That I'll do."

Ben looked around the room, appreciating the high ceiling with its arched windows, the dark paneled walls, the shelves of books. "I don't wonder this is a grand place for study," he said. "Has Miss Truden frequented it as yet?"

Isaac motioned to the chairs by the fireplace. Primus had managed to get a good fire going, and with that and the heat from the furnace, they were soon comfortable.

"Miss Truden keeps a good deal to herself," Isaac said. "She comes in from school and works in her room until supper. She takes her meals with us in the kitchen, at which time she engages Helga in light conversation to improve her English. She tutors both girls, reads for an hour—no longer—in the parlor, and afterwards retires. I know as much about her personal life today as I did the day I met her. She's very private, Ben. Helga says that Miss Truden writes at night when everyone is asleep."

"Helga must be snooping a bit to discover such a thing. But this isn't what you're worried about."

Isaac shook his head. "No, not at all. Rainie Truden is the perfect boarder—thoughtful, quiet. The trouble is this, Ben. Roy Dean wants his daughter to move back home."

Ben leaned forward. "You told me she was getting on so well here."

"Yes," Isaac said. "She is."

"Then what . . ."

"I don't know. All I know is that he acted very strange toward me the night of the school program. I don't recall if you spoke to him or noticed. I greeted him and his wife, told them how well May Dean was getting along, and said I wanted to give her a dollar a week raise. I gave Roy her weekly pay with that extra amount. He refused to look me in the eye, though he took the money fast enough."

"And Pearl?"

"What a pathetic and dreary woman she is! It's hard to believe that she could ever have a daughter like May. Pearl whined about missing her, about May taking on airs and not visiting them."

"Come to think of it, I did see Roy drinking with Had Coonrod. It occurred to me at the time that the two were trouble getting ready to happen. But no fights broke out, so I forgot about it."

"There are bad feelings inside that Roy Dean, Ben. I could feel them, feel the contempt and hatred."

"Toward who? Not you! He's always been this way."

"That anger was directed at me, Ben, as much as at his circumstances or his poverty. I've seen that kind of look before when I lived in St. Louis and later in Chicago. It's the look some Gentiles turn toward Jews."

"But he didn't tell you he wanted her to come home, did he?"

Isaac shook his head. "No, but he told May. She came home all in a state and afterwards cried about it. Helga told me. Helga said Roy Dean had harsh words with his daughter, said he was mad about her living in the same house as Primus, of all things. She said May was terrified of going back home."

Ben nodded his head slowly. "I can see why and so can you. She comes here with her pitiful little bag, and in no time at all she's smiling and happy and wearing new dresses with hardly a thought for what she left behind her. You've never been to the Dean house, so you don't know what I'm talking about. Still, I've always felt real sorry for Roy and for Pearl, too. Don't know what's going to happen to them. He spends any money they have on liquor—bad stuff, too."

"I don't want to send her back to that, Ben."

"I know. I know. You feel responsible, and God bless you for it, Isaac. 'Course there's this to consider, too. She's not yet old enough to go against her folks' wishes. If she was eighteen, it'd be different."

"Can you talk to Roy and get him to change his mind?"

Ben shook his head. "I don't know, Isaac. I don't know what's driving this here thing. It may be Pearl is missing May, pure and simple. It may be they don't want her living in a house near a black man. It may be other things we don't want to think about."

"What things? What could scare May Dean so?"

"I told you once, Isaac. Poor folks have poor ways. Roy may be hankering after her."

Isaac's eyes widened. "I don't believe it! Are you suggesting he would do something indecent to her? But that's immoral! It's against the law!"

"Only if you can prove it, and who's going to tell, and how're you going to know anything like that for sure in the first place? I've seen it in these parts, Isaac. Folks get to thinking there's only them and their own in all the world, and what they do is between and amongst themselves. It's bad. And woe to the man or woman, however well-intentioned they may be, who tries to interfere or question their morality. Yep, it's bad, all right, but it's nothing you can prove."

Isaac opened and closed his fists. "I'll give him more money," he said.

Ben looked up. "How much more?" he asked, watching Isaac intently. "It'd go against what folks think is decent if you gave him too much, you know. What would people think?"

"I could care less what people think of me! I'll offer him ten dollars a week for her to stay on. They need the money. You said they did. Especially with the winter coming on like it is. You said it was going to be a bad one, and that's confirmed in the almanacs I've been reading, Ben. Ten dollars a week should settle him down."

Ben whistled. "Ten dollars a week! That's something, that is. Why, that's more than the schoolteacher gets paid, more than many white men. You don't want to go telling this around, Isaac. It's got to stay right here in this library room between you and me. 'Course Roy will know, and we don't know who he'll tell or brag about it to. It's a lot of money to pay for someone to clean house. You surely realize that, don't you? It's too much, Isaac."

"It's little enough to ensure that girl's peace of mind till she's older and can tell them to leave her alone. I'd pay twice the amount, Ben."

Helga peered through the glass doors from the hall. She held a large tray with covered plates. Isaac got up and opened the doors for her. "If that be all, I vill leave you to it," she said after setting the side table for them.

Ben waited until she had left. "So that's how it is." He buttered a biscuit and started to eat. "May Dean has gone and got you to fall in love with her."

Isaac looked up, stunned. "No, Ben! I swear it! It isn't like that." He stared, helpless to defend his feelings.

"Then how is it, I wonder? I know you for a gentleman, Isaac Samuel, one that's found out he isn't too grand to get his head turned around when he least expects it. I can be pretty slow sometimes, and this sure is one of those times," Ben said.

"I didn't set out . . ."

"'Course you didn't. Now you just listen to me, Isaac Samuel. I never once had any thought that something like this would happen if she came here. Why, to me she's just a little girl, not much older than my Grace. 'Course I've seen how she's changed. I see it now anyway. Tell you the truth, I wasn't thinking as much of May Dean as of the whole Dean family when I asked you to take her on here. At least I think I was. Who's to say now? Things like this have so many ways of being looked at when you stop and think about everything. Like what it is that moves us to do the things we do."

Isaac stared at the fire. "What should I do?"

"Do what you think best," Ben said. "You're a grown man, after all—a man of means and influence. You're doing well enough that you've earned everyone's respect for miles around. I've heard them say so. Like the way you took on Primus and Helga and Miss Truden, not just May Dean. And you've done your part many a time when funds were needed for school repairs, fixing bridges, and such. And there's other things besides. I know you're a good man, Isaac Samuel. You can do as you please in this and every other thing. As for May Dean, well, she's growing up, and it doesn't matter if it's right here under your own roof that she's doing it. You can bide your time and see how she feels—about you, I mean."

"You mean marriage?"

"Happens all the time," Ben said. "Older men, young women. I was ten years older than my Lillie." Ben felt the familiar ache at the thought of his wife. He was startled to find how close it still was, front and center to his life, a sad presence that wouldn't be comforted.

"You could be thirty or fifty or twenty," Ben said. "Life's short when you get right down to it. Take what happiness you can, Isaac. I don't mean rush into anything or go off and do something foolhardy or wrong, something that could only hurt you both, but don't rule out marrying May Dean. If that's what you really want."

"I don't know," Isaac said. "I never thought . . ."

"You don't have to say any more. I'd wait on that Roy Dean thing. It'll all blow over. He was drunk and doing what he does when he's drunk. Young girls can exaggerate things, you know. But if you do give him more money for May Dean being here, don't jump all the way to ten dollars all at once. Start out slowly."

"That's wise counsel," Isaac said. "I don't know what I was thinking."

"I do know, though," Ben said. "I know too well. You were afraid you were going to lose someone who means something to you, more than you thought."

"We understand ourselves so little," Isaac said. "How about you, Ben? Are all your feelings clear to you?"

"Too clear, I'm afraid," Ben said. "I loved my wife, Isaac. If you could have known her, you'd see what I mean when I say that. Lillie was everything to me, or at least I thought she was. I see now how alone I was even with her as my wife, even with her love. In one moment, it can all be gone. It can all be over just like that. God knows how I miss her. Yes, I do. But I'm still alive. I'd like to marry again someday. I don't like being alone, even in the face of uncertain mortality."

"Not many eligible women around here is what you told me when we first met."

"I know one, I think, if she doesn't find a younger man more to her sort, if she doesn't move away."

"I don't think Rainie Truden is going anywhere real soon," Isaac said. Ben looked at him quickly. "She told Helga she never wants to leave, that this is the perfect place for her to accomplish her life's work, her writing."

"Well, I'm not surprised," Ben said. "She said as much to me, not about the writing part but just wanting to stay. My girls tell me she writes a fair bit of poetry, too. Don't misunderstand me, Isaac. I find many qualities to commend Miss Truden. Only I'm in no hurry, and I think she's content to remain single a while."

"You'll have an opportunity to be with her next week when you all come for *Shabbat* dinner," Isaac said.

"Looking forward to it, too," Ben said. "If Helga's suppers are as good as her breakfasts, I may have to move in myself. But what if the weather turns bad?"

"There are enough beds for you and your family to spend the night if that happens."

"Mighty kind of you. Only don't go spoiling my children, Isaac."

"It isn't spoiling to share what God has been gracious enough to give to me. In fact, it's an obligation."

RAINIE TRUDEN WAS PUTTING the last touches on her Christmas poem. She had been working on it since September when she first started teaching at Mount Vernon. Every day she wrote a little more or went back and struck something that didn't have the perfect cadence or rhyme she was striving for. And then she had to rewrite the entire poem, now grown to six pages of white paper, all over again. She was proud of her penmanship and couldn't bear smudges beside the fine cursive. It was the one talent she had developed in the orphanage, one for which she was praised. But it required a great deal of time. The even flow of her writing demanded complete concentration.

The poem, titled "Angel Wing," was to be her offering as part of the evening's entertainment when the Reuben family came to celebrate Hanukkah. What the children would do to entertain the adults, she wasn't sure. Grace had said she just wanted to sit in the lap of luxury, but Gertie said she would bring pictures she had drawn for Mr. Samuel and for Primus, too. Mr. Samuel made it clear that everyone in the house was to be included at the table, even Primus and Helga and May Dean.

Rainie was delighted when Mr. Reuben and the school board

agreed to let the school close midweek. This gave her two extra days to work on her poem. She didn't want to be selfish with her time, however, and offered to help Helga with preparations for the meal.

The busy cook's reply had been firm, final. "No such a ting, Miss Truden, begging your pardon," she'd said. "There's so much to do, I be having to tell you ever little ting, and that takes too much time. No, ach. I can do it myself with May Dean baking the breads."

Rainie then asked Isaac if she could help him prepare for the Friday night festivities. It was Thursday; they had just finished their supper. Isaac told her he would be delighted.

"Tomorrow's supper is a Sabbath meal," he said, "a time set apart to honor this day, the queen of the week. As such, she deserves the best. I have china, silver, and crystal reserved for Sabbath alone and have always enjoyed the preparations. Of course, it's been a long time."

He opened the sliding doors into the large dining room and turned on the kerosene lights. The wood surfaces shone where May Dean had dusted and polished every piece of furniture.

"I've never taken a meal in this room before," Rainie said. "It's so grand and rich. You said the Friday night meal was Sabbath. I thought Sabbath came on Saturday."

"Sabbath extends into the seventh day," Isaac said, "but it actually begins on Friday night when the first three stars of the evening are visible. We'll have the Reuben children watch the sky and tell us when they see them. That's when we light the candles."

"Two candles for the Sabbath," Rainie said. "And nine for the menorah, for Hanukkah. But I haven't seen you lighting them at night."

"I'm going to light them all tomorrow," Isaac said. "This

menorah belonged to my Grandfather Ezra. We lit the candles together from the time I was a child. Of course, we lit the Sabbath candles, too, one for creation and one for redemption."

Rainie felt a thrill of sensation as she touched the menorah. "It's beautiful," she said. "Do you observe all the Jewish customs?"

Isaac shook his head. "Sadly, no. Though I understand their profound significance, and I do try to apply myself to Torah, to the teachings. It's harder to observe when you have no family."

"Yes, I expect so," she answered quietly. "Yet one may always study alone. Haven't you found that to be best?"

Isaac opened a drawer and removed two beautifully tapered white candles. He set them in silver candlesticks and placed them at the head of the table. Beside them he placed a gold matchbox.

"Individual study is better than none," he said. "Yet it's best to discuss what is read with another or with several at a time to hear other viewpoints. I miss that."

Rainie listened intently. "Some say that the Torah consists of the first five books of Moses," she said.

"You're a good student, Miss Truden. Torah may refer to these, the Pentateuch, or to the writings and teachings entire. They are also known as the Tanakh."

"I didn't know that," she said. "We had daily Bible study at the orphanage where I was raised. We studied both Testaments and had to memorize the order of the books in the Bible, as well as Psalms 1, 23, 91, and 100 by heart."

"Were you rewarded for such efforts?"

Rainie shook her head. "Unfortunately, the church that ran the orphanage was not one to reward you for good works. However, punishments were inflicted for failure. We were expected to learn what we were told to learn and to suffer the consequences if we did not. For my part, I'm thankful that the

Scriptures became alive to me so that I wanted to learn them. There were some children there who did not."

"Why would any rational person try to force a love of God's Word on another?" Isaac asked.

"I don't know. I do know that it all worked for good in my life. I learned the truth even in the midst of other people's wrong interpretations. My belief is here in my heart, the bedrock of my whole existence. I couldn't any more deny it than to try to stop breathing."

"So you were able to forgive. I should have found that impossible."

"Ah, but perhaps you never had to face such a test," Rainie said. "Yes, I forgave. Yet it is more accurate to say that Christ in me forgave others. I don't know how else to explain it. I realized that anyone who hurt me was to be pitied, that my Lord had suffered and died for them as well, and if I could hope that God would forgive me, knowing myself as I did and my many sins, then how could I not forgive others? It is also a commandment that we do this."

"It's a paradox," Isaac said, "this forgiveness. Yet it is true of Torah also. When we forgive our enemies, Torah says that we heap coals of fire upon their heads."

"That sounds rather vengeful on the surface, doesn't it?" Rainie asked. "Perhaps the meaning goes deeper to illustrate the altar of sacrifice. My goal shouldn't be to punish the one I forgive but to seek God's forgiveness for him as well. And this comes at the altar where we find the coals of fire."

Feeling suddenly self-conscious, Rainie stopped. "My, how I go on. Please excuse me."

Isaac smiled at her reassuringly. "No offense taken, I assure you. I would know at once if you were trying to convert me, Miss Truden. I would be instantly aware of any such attempt and deal with it accordingly. For my part, I know that we both profess to believe in one God. The difference between us is that your Messiah is not the one I'm seeking."

"At the risk of pushing my point, I feel compelled to add one thing," Rainie said.

"And what is that?"

"Perhaps this Messiah is seeking you."

Isaac looked into Rainie's eyes and again felt no offense at what she said. Long habits of resisting this Gentile Savior rose up, only to be silenced by the calm spirit before him. Within her eyes were peace and a deep joy. He found himself strangely warmed and moved, and anxious at the same time.

"Shall we continue?" he asked.

Rainie nodded enthusiastically.

The dining room was designed to seat fifteen comfortably on each side of a long mahogany table. It was not crowded even with the addition of a large buffet, sideboard, and china cabinet. The room's size was a mirror of the double parlor on the other side of the foyer. Crystal light sconces spaced at five-foot intervals were styled after the Waterford chandelier that hung from the vaulted ceiling. The armed chairs were upholstered with tapestries of pastoral scenes.

Isaac opened the accordion doors of a tall walnut cabinet and removed several items stored there. The first was the largest single tablecloth Rainie had ever seen, a marvel of Belgian lace. Isaac placed table pads on the table, and then they spread the lace cloth on top of these.

"These also belonged to my Grandfather Ezra," he said, removing a silver goblet, a silver bowl, a large linen napkin and towel and setting them on the table. Isaac then lifted a cylindrically shaped object wrapped in red and purple cloths. He removed the coverings slowly. "And this was Grandfather's Torah."

Rainie stared in awe. The outer casing of the large scroll was inlaid with silver and inscribed with letters from the Hebrew alphabet. "I've only seen pictures of scrolls like this," she said. "It's so beautiful."

Isaac's eyes shone. "This Torah came from a synagogue in Germany. My grandfather and I were careful not to handle it often. I think Ben and his family would appreciate seeing it, though, even as you do. We'll leave it by the menorah."

"I had no idea there would be so many things needed for a Sabbath supper," Rainie said.

"We still have to set out the red wine that has been blessed by a rabbi. That will be poured into this silver goblet at the appropriate time tomorrow. The silver bowl is filled with water and passed for a ritual washing. Besides these, there will be two loaves of Sabbath bread. May Dean will bake those tomorrow. And then of course there's the dinner itself. Helga has a lot of experience feeding a number of people at a time."

"It will be so lovely," Rainie said. "I've never eaten at such a table before, much less a Sabbath meal."

"Primus will do the rest tomorrow afternoon, setting each place. I've already promised him that he could. He sets great store by the china and silver and takes his butlering most seriously. He's had May Dean wash all the napkins and iron them this week, and they weren't even soiled. In fact, I don't think they've even been used since I moved here."

"Will there be a centerpiece?"

Isaac nodded. "Helga has arranged some dried foliage and holly. I'm afraid we'll have to settle for whatever our woods have provided."

"Mistletoe would work, too!" Rainie said. "You see it everywhere. But tell me the significance of the Sabbath candles."

"It's the Jewish belief that the Lord God, Creator of the universe, commanded us to observe the Sabbath day," Isaac began. "Six days of labor are to be followed by a day of rest. In the early days of the Israelites, a shofar, or ram's horn, was blown to signal everyone to stop their work and start observing the Sabbath. Lamps were lit just before the sun set. It has been so for centuries. The custom is for a woman to light the two Sabbath candles because it was Eve who disobeyed God and ate the forbidden fruit from the tree of the knowledge of good and evil. Her disobedience put out the light of eternal life."

"What a wonderful tradition!" Rainie said. "I've never heard the fall of man explained in such a way before. And to think that this has continued down through the ages."

"We still take a different interpretation on what you call the fall of man. The two candles represent creation and redemption," Isaac said. "We remember and observe both. Some families, I understand, light many candles, one for each member. But our home was different. Usually only my grandfather and I kept the Sabbath."

"But your parents . . ."

"By pure coincidence, they both had Gentile mothers who bore no fondness for religious observances. It was my grandfather who taught me Jewish ways. His parents were devout and theirs before them for as long as anyone can remember."

"Do you know what tribe you came from?" she asked.

"Let me read it to you in Hebrew." He took the Torah and unrolled it to a familiar place. When he spoke, Rainie thought the words sounded like rushing waters. "It's in Genesis 49:3-4. 'Reuben, you are my firstborn, my might, and the beginning of my strength, the excellency of dignity, and the excellency of power: unstable as water, you will not excel; because you went up to your father's bed; then you defiled it; he went up to my couch.'"

"The tribe of Reuben! But his birthright as the eldest son was given to the sons of Joseph, and Jesus' genealogy is not to be reckoned after the birthright."

Isaac stared at her in wonder. "Where did you learn . . ."

"The history of Israel has long been my passion, Mr. Samuel. I cannot tell you why, for indeed I don't know myself. I only know what has been placed in my heart. Jesus came from the tribe of Judah through the line of King David. But Reuben received no blessing from Jacob. I wonder that you can trace your history to him. It's a miracle!"

"The existence of Jews is a miracle," Isaac said. "Yet here we are, the product of long tradition. We know where we came from. That's what makes us different from all other peoples. There is a continuity that holds us together and will do so forever."

"I believe that, too," Rainie said. "Tell me about the wine."

"The silver goblet is set next to the candlesticks on the table beside the bread. The father recites the *Kiddush*, or sanctification prayer, over the cup of wine, which in turn symbolizes fullness and life and joy. Tradition dictates that the one who holds the goblet must do so at the base so his fingers point toward heaven."

"Like we're reaching up to God."

"Even so."

"To think that Jesus did this, too," Rainie said, her voice nearly a whisper.

"If He kept the Sabbath," Isaac said.

"He kept the whole law in all its perfection."

"Well, that's a difficult task. I'd say it is impossible," Isaac replied. Then he added, "It would be good, of course, if one could do it. One holy man, when asked if he was keeping all the law, always answered with two simple words: 'Not yet.'"

"Does everyone drink from the same cup?"

"Yes. Of course, we each have our own glasses, too."

"Then there's the silver basin," she said, pointing to the elegant bowl.

"That we use for what you might imagine—to wash our hands. This shows our gratitude to God for setting us apart. We wash our hands and lift them towards heaven."

"And you say you haven't observed the Sabbath for some time?"

"Not in a formal sense, not for a long time now. I didn't realize how much I've missed it."

"No one's stopping you from keeping the Sabbath again. I know that I would participate if you let me."

"Your sincerity is touching, Miss Truden. And I will definitely consider it. We'll see how tomorrow evening goes with the Reubens."

"Do you think it's possible that the Reubens have Jewish ancestry?"

"I've wondered, but I haven't asked him. Ben Reuben is a great student, you know, of the prophets. Anyway, there's been so much cultural assimilation that it's difficult to trace a genealogy unless you're Jewish. We take it very seriously."

"So do I. Being orphaned at the age of two and sent to a home for unwanted children, I have some experience of the difficulty."

"I'm sorry," Isaac said. "And your name? How did you come by your name?"

"That, I fear, is the product of an active imagination. Someone at the orphanage named me."

"Well, Miss Truden, I think it's a lovely name, and I hope you'll do us the honor of lighting the Sabbath candles tomorrow night."

"I'd love to, but is it quite proper? It would seem that the proper person to do it should be a mother."

"You're a spiritual mother; look at all the children you teach every day. I think it's perfectly proper. All you need to complete your role as the candle-lighter is this." He turned to the chest and removed an exquisitely designed lace veil. "Please wear this tomorrow evening. My mother gave it to me."

"Oh, really, I couldn't."

"Please," Isaac insisted, handing the veil to her. "I wouldn't ask you if I thought it wasn't absolutely appropriate."

Rainie held the lace carefully. "Thank you, Mr. Samuel. I'd be honored."

"You wear it loosely draped over your head and let it fall over your shoulders."

"Mr. Samuel, there is one final thing I wanted to ask you."

"Yes?"

"After we have the Sabbath ceremony and dinner, would it be all right if I read something I've written?"

"But of course. I'm sure we'd all be delighted. You may read it after supper when we go into the parlor."

THIRTEEN

————◆————

AUNT HANNAH OBJECTED to taking the twins out at night, but when Ben told her more about Isaac Samuel's house and the wonderful food that would be served there, when he reminded her that the boys would get to see Primus again, she relented.

"If the weather turns bad, Isaac said we could sleep over, so there's nothing to worry about," Ben said.

"Still and all, it's just the time of year for the whooping cough, croup, or what have you. We'll have to bundle them up good," she said.

When Ben asked the boys how they felt about bundling up and going over to Mr. Samuel's house, both Hiram and Herman jumped up and down, shouting with excitement.

"Mamshun! We see the big mamshun!" Herman cried.

"It's mansion, silly," Grace said. "And anyway what's so special about that?"

"You know you're dying to see what it looks like inside," Gertie said, "even if you won't admit it."

"Am not!"

"Are, too!"

"That's enough!" Ben said. "Whether you want to go or not, we're going, and you'll all be glad you did. After all your hard work shelling corn every night, this dinner at Mr. Samuel's will be a special treat."

Friday afternoon found Ben converting the buckboard into a covered wagon for the family to ride in. He was concerned about a bank of gray clouds moving in from the northwest. "This canvas will keep us dry should it rain," he told Aunt Hannah.

She was standing on the porch eyeing his work and the sky all at the same time. Her hands were planted firmly on each hip, a sign Ben had learned to interpret as silent disapproval. "Best get some fresh hay on that floorboard," Aunt Hannah said. "Grace! Gertie! Where's them blankets and pillows I told you to bring out here? La! You'd think we had all day to set out on this ill-advised venture."

The girls banged open the front door, their arms full of bedclothes. "Brrr! It's cold!" Gertie said, shivering.

"You get back inside that house this instant and put your coat on, missy!" Aunt Hannah cried, shaking her head. "Wonder we all don't catch our death of cold tonight."

Ben laughed. "Letting on that you're not the least bit curious about seeing Isaac Samuel's house won't work with me, Aunt Hannah. Who's been cooking up surprises in the kitchen all morning?" he teased.

"I could have seen Mr. Samuel's house when the whole blessed Territory saw it opened 'fore fall," she said, snorting her disdain. "I thought then, and I think now that our own house is quite good enough. You go traipsing off to see other folks' wealth, and coveting is sure to follow. Ostentation has never been my way, and I hope to the Lord I've done kept coveting to a minimum, too."

"There's a difference between coveting and admiring," Ben said. "Anyway, I know you're going to have a good time tonight. After all, Aunt Addie's taking her famous shortbread."

"Humph! Guess I've got some food fixed up, too." She turned and went back inside.

Grace spent a solid hour getting herself ready for the evening out. Gertie, for her part, was satisfied to put on a clean pinafore and run a brush through her hair but only because Aunt Addie pressed her.

Ben looked at his watch at 5:30 and told his family it was time to go. The horses appeared restless as the children piled in, fussing and pushing until everyone was settled in for the long ride. Aunt Addie rode in back with them; Aunt Hannah said she preferred to ride up front. "So's I can see what's coming at us," she said.

"Everyone cover up good now," Ben said. "It's looking a bit doubtful we'll get by without rain. I do know she's going to be one cold night."

"How long till we're there?" Grace asked.

"About an hour, give or take," Ben answered. He released the wagon brake and urged the horses on.

Aunt Addie engaged the children in rowdy caroling the first half hour or so. When they passed houses along the way, they waved and hooted their presence out the back of the wagon. Voices grew tired presently. It was too cold to do much more than huddle. Winter sounds of dogs barking and horses neighing filtered through the frosty twilight.

Ben broke the silence. "Listen up now, children. You sing this to the tune of 'Old Beulah Land.'"

"Not the 'Homesteader's Malady' again!" Gertie groaned.

"It's 'Homesteader's Melody!'" Grace corrected her. "You

know Dad loves it, and at least he can carry a tune, which is more than you can do!"

Ben's voice rang out lustily, "'I've reached the land of corn and wheat / And pumpkin pies and potatoes sweet / I got my land from Uncle Sam / And now I am happy as a clam / Oh, Cheyenne land! Sweet Indian land! / As on my cabin roof I stand / I look away across the plains / And watch the lines of wagon trains / And as I turn to view my corn / I vow I'll never sell my farm.'"

Herman and Hiram clapped their hands and bounced up and down while their sisters groaned through the next two verses. Aunt Hannah managed to get tickled in spite of herself. She laughed outright and so hard that everyone got infected. When the Reubens pulled up in front of the iron gates on the south side of Isaac Samuel's grand house, they were a noisy crew indeed.

Isaac came outside and greeted them warmly, taking each visitor's hand in turn, from the oldest to the youngest. Aunt Hannah and Aunt Addie presented him with a basket tied up in gingham and filled with shortbread, jams, and honey.

"Thank you, kind ladies, and welcome; welcome to the tribe of Reuben," Isaac said. "Your happiness and joy are most contagious and so welcome in my home. Come in and get out of this night air. Look, Miss Truden, do you see any stars yet?"

Rainie stood on the porch in a dress of rose velvet, its pink lace collar highlighting her eyes and flushed cheeks. A black shawl was draped about her shoulders. "There!" she exclaimed. "I see one, no, two! Oh, there are more than I thought! Are we too late to light the Sabbath candles?"

"Not if we hurry," Isaac said.

"Not too late for supper, I hope!" Ben said, laughing.

Rainie smiled at him and said, "Just you wait," as Primus led them from the foyer to the dining room.

The family's joviality turned to a high pitch of excitement the moment they stepped into the magnificent house. "Ohhhh . . . ," each one exclaimed and then looked quickly at the others. Quiet elegance enfolded them. Hiram and Herman were so intimidated by the dining room that they clung to Aunt Addie's skirts. They warmed up when Primus swung them up in the air and seated them on bolsters in the huge, grown-up chairs.

"Did you ever . . . ," Aunt Hannah whispered to Aunt Addie.

"No, I never did. It's a house for dressing up in if I ever saw one. And would you look at May Dean! Isn't she a pretty little thing, though? What's that Mr. Samuel is wearing on his head, I wonder?"

"She doesn't have any idea how fortunate she is to be here," Aunt Hannah said, keeping her voice very low. "Let's hope she has the good sense to make the most of her life now. I expect that's to do with Mr. Samuel's religion—that cap. Maybe he'll tell us."

"Look, Grace!" Gertie pointed to the domed ceiling overhead. "It's a painting of angels and clouds!"

When they were all seated, Isaac stood and motioned to Primus to turn down the lights. "Tonight is a special night for many reasons," Isaac said. "The Sabbath is here with its blessings of rest awaiting us. As I say the Hebrew prayers, Miss Truden will light the Sabbath candles, one for creation and one for redemption."

Rainie stood, a lace veil draped over her dark hair, and lit the candles as Isaac brought in the Sabbath.

"'*Baruch attah adonai elohenu melech ha-olam*,'" Isaac began. "'Blessed art Thou, O Lord our God, King of the universe.'"

The Reuben family sat with rapt attention as he said the

Kiddush over the wine. "'Blessed art Thou, O Lord our God, King of the universe, who brings forth the fruit of the vine.'"

The silver cup was passed around the table for all to take a sip. Isaac then blessed the washing of hands as Primus took the silver basin and linen towel to each guest in turn. "'Blessed art Thou, O Lord our God, King of the universe, who has sanctified us through Thy commandments and instructed us concerning the washing of hands.'"

When all had washed and dried their hands, Isaac held up the two loaves of challah bread. "'Blessed art Thou, O Lord our God, King of the universe, for bringing forth bread from the earth.'" He broke the bread and passed the pieces down the table.

"Since I have no wife, I will recite Proverbs 31 for all women present," Isaac said. "If you know any part of this Scripture, please speak it out loud with me." Aunt Addie was the only one to join in, her voice finally breaking when they said the last verse together: "'Many daughters have done nobly, but you excel them all. A woman who fears the Lord, she shall be praised!'"

A moment of silence descended upon all. The Sabbath candles cast their light over the linen and china, over the silver and crystal, their flickering radiance enhancing each face so that all were beautiful in this time and place.

"And now to bless the guests at this table," Isaac said. "I'm deeply honored to have you all here at my table. Please return my joy and begin your meal."

Aunt Hannah raised her hand self-consciously. "Shouldn't we say grace first?" she asked timidly.

Everyone laughed.

"We've done had grace in abundance," Ben answered.

Isaac held up his hand. "No, no. Aunt Hannah is right. We will say yet another grace, thanking God for blessing the food,

but we do that after we eat, not before. It must seem a little backward to you. It's all right," he assured her, smiling warmly.

"Long as we do it right," Aunt Hannah said, placing a white
linen napkin in her lap and watching Primus hand Isaac one platter after another.

"What amazes me," Aunt Addie said, "is that Jewish folks
just like you are doing this same thing all over the world."

"Yes, it's true," Isaac said. "The tradition is thousands of
years old."

"What's that?" Herman asked, pointing to a long, curved
object on the buffet table just behind the steaming food.

"Would you like to hear?" Isaac asked. "Hand me the shofar, please, Primus."

Isaac put the ram's horn to his lips and blew. Its piercing
sound resonated in the room with a ponderous summons to
silence. "The ram's horn calls us to worship," Isaac said, handing the curious object back to Primus.

"Like the last trumpet on the day of the Lord!" Ben said. "I
always wondered what that horn would look like, and now I
know."

"Remember what I said to you and Helga and May," Isaac
whispered to Primus and indicated the three waiting places. "I
expect you all to join us when the food is served."

"Yes, sir, Mr. Samuel," Primus said, bowing. "If you insist,
sir, and we know that you do. I'll tell the two young ladies, and
we'll be right in."

Ben and his family greeted May and Helga warmly when
they took their places at the table. Both young women were
dressed in similar white dresses with lace on the bodice and little pearl buttons from the hem all the way up to the neck. Helga
wore her hair in a tight bun on top of her head. Tiny blonde
strands escaped to form a frantic halo around her round face, set-

ting off her fair complexion. May had pinned her own much darker hair with tortoise-shell combs and let it fall down her back in a black cascade. They each wore an identical cameo brooch.

Aunt Hannah and Aunt Addie tried to engage Primus, who was sitting opposite them. He was polite but seemed distracted, with little appetite for conversation or food. Hardly fifteen minutes had passed when Primus abruptly excused himself, saying he needed to bring the dessert.

"Why, he scarcely took a bite," Aunt Hannah said to Aunt Addie. "And such good food, too. I've never had turkey and fish at the same meal."

The others took their time enjoying the fine supper and listening intently as Isaac told them about Hanukkah, the Festival of Lights.

"This festival," he said, "is celebrated in the month called *Kislev*, the same month as December. It lasts for eight days to commemorate the Jewish victory over oppressors who tried to defile the temple in Jerusalem and kill all the Jews. An elderly priest named Mattathias started a revolt that was carried on by his son Judas Maccabaeus."

"Excuse me," Grace said, raising her hand. "That's not the same person as Judas Iscariot, is it—the one who betrayed Jesus?"

"No, it isn't the same man," Isaac answered. "Judas is a fairly common name, though. According to the Gregorian calendar, which Gentiles observe, Judas Maccabaeus would have lived around 160 years before the birth of Jesus." He paused. "On the twenty-fifth day of the month *Kislev* in 164 B.C., this Judas Maccabaeus, the son of the high priest, led a small army of Jewish soldiers into Jerusalem to cleanse and rededicate the temple after the heathens had defiled it."

"What's *defiled* mean?" Gertie asked.

"To make it dirty," Grace answered.

"Yes, but there's more to the definition than that," Miss Truden said. "The temple was supposed to be a holy place where only the designated sacrifices were to be offered, sacrifices for sin and cleansing. The only animals allowed to be killed for the sacrifice had to be clean, and even those could have no blemish whatsoever on any part of their body."

Isaac nodded his head approvingly and went on. "Clean animals included sheep and goats and bulls and even pigeons. But the Greeks went into the most holy place and offered unclean sacrifices by putting slaughtered pigs on the altar itself. It was a horrible thing!"

"We slaughter pigs!" Gertie said. "And I hate it. I always have."

"But you never say no to a piece of bacon or ham, do you?" Ben asked, and everyone laughed.

"Liking it is one thing, killing another," Gertie said between mouthfuls.

"Please go on, Mr. Samuel," Aunt Hannah said. "I find this fascinating."

Isaac's voice took on a solemn tone. "Our tradition says that while the temple was being cleansed, one of the priests found a container with unpolluted oil inside. The candlestick that sits in the holy place was replenished with this oil. It was a small amount which should have lasted only one or two days, but it lighted the candles for eight full days!"

"How could that happen?" Gertie asked. "Was it magic?"

Isaac shook his head. "No, it was a miracle, and that's why we celebrate the Festival of Lights every year for eight days."

Grace was counting on her fingers and saying something to herself. "But you said that the month you do this is called *Kislev* and that it's the same as December, and we're in December right now!" she exclaimed.

"That's why I invited you tonight," Isaac said. "Christmas is celebrated on the twenty-fifth of December and Hanukkah is celebrated on the twenty-fifth of *Kislev*, except that Hanukkah lasts for eight days."

"Do Jewish children get presents all eight days?" Gertie asked.

Herman and Hiram looked up at the mention of presents. They looked forward to receiving one small toy and maybe an orange each year.

"Some do," Isaac said, "if they can afford it."

"Now don't you kids go getting any ideas that we might extend Christmas," Ben said. "Two days a year is enough for anybody to get presents."

"What's the other one then?" Gertie asked. "Have I missed something?"

"Your birthday, of course," Grace answered. "Pass the rolls, please."

Primus brought in a chocolate torte with cherries and fudge flowers worked into the icing. "There's other desserts coming," he said. "Got to have Miss Hannah's pie and Miss Addie's shortbread."

After everyone had eaten their fill, Isaac stood and offered the last blessing. He then led his guests into the double parlor. When they were still in the hallway, Aunt Addie drew May Dean aside and asked her to direct her outside to the privy.

"You don't want to go outside," May Dean said. "It's way too cold for that."

"Well, I'd rather not, and that's a fact," Addie said. "But the twins here have got the fidgets, and I know what that means. If they don't relieve themselves quick, we'll have an accident for sure and right here on Mr. Samuel's fine carpet, too. These boys can't hold it for long. I can't either, to tell you the truth."

"Follow me," May said, leading them down a side hall past the library.

"Any old chamber pot will do," Addie said, scurrying along behind her. Hiram and Herman each held onto their great aunt with one hand and their pants with the other.

"You won't need a chamber pot, Miss Addie. Mr. Samuel's house has a water closet right indoors!" May stepped aside so the astonished older woman could see for herself.

"Well, I never!" Addie exclaimed. "A privy right inside the house and what pretty wood, too! Would you just look at that little sink with the pretty flowers painted on the porcelain. La! I think I've died and gone to heaven!"

"It was a mighty big surprise to me, too, when I first saw it," May said. "I was afraid to even come in here."

Hiram kept pulling the chain and flushing the toilet.

"Stop that this minute!" Aunt Addie cried. "Unless you want me to put you to bed. 'Course we'd have to go up those big stairs first and past that painting of the lion you said you didn't like! I bet May Dean has a room upstairs where she locks up bad, little boys."

"Don't want to!" Hiram cried.

"Then you be good and you, too, Herman, or I promise you a paddling you won't forget! Wash your hands now, both of you. La! How'd you get that chocolate in your ear, Herman. Well, we'll just have to clean it out."

Herman pleaded not to be locked away. Aunt Addie hugged him and said she shouldn't have threatened such a thing in the first place.

When everyone was finally settled in the double parlor, Primus pulled the sliding doors shut and busied himself clearing the dining room. Aunt Hannah and Aunt Addie occupied the largest sofa and sat the twins on the carpet in front of them, each with a pillow, and told them to be still. Isaac handed the twins two stereoscopes and stacks of viewer cards. "There are lots of pictures of trains and ships in there," he said.

Ben sat in one of the large chairs by the fireplace. Grace and Gertie wanted to be as close to the fire as possible, and so they chose to sit on the floor where the thick carpet met the marble hearth. May Dean and Helga shared a sofa while Rainie sat on a third.

Isaac took the chair opposite Ben. "Helga, please hand Grace and Gertie each a pillow from the divan," he said. "They may decide to stretch out before the evening is over. Miss Truden has prepared something special for us. She's going to read a poem out loud, one that she wrote herself. If we're all agreed and comfortable where we are, I'll ask her to begin."

"I think I would prefer to stay seated if you don't mind," Rainie said. "My poem is entitled 'Angel Wing,' and it's about a little girl who finds an angel's wing in the snow."

Isaac rose suddenly to his feet.

"Miss Truden, please excuse me for interrupting, but would you mind waiting a few more minutes before reading your poem? I almost forgot something. Everyone stay here, and I'll be right back." He left the room and returned moments later with a large box full of wrapped presents.

"Ohhhhh, look!" Grace and Gertie cried together. Herman and Hiram were all attention in a moment.

"Isaac, you shouldn't have done this!" Ben exclaimed.

"Done what? You don't even know what I've done yet!" Isaac set the box down in front of his chair. "Here," he said, "you young ladies help me pass these out, please. That's it, Grace. That one is for Miss Hannah, so please take it to her. And this one says, ah, yes, Miss Addie. Gertie, if you will do the honors. Let's see if there's something with Grace's name on it. Sure enough! Here you are, Grace. You can open it in a minute. And now the boys. Hiram, try this out. Don't worry, Ben. It doesn't make any noise. And, Herman, you get one just like it, only a different color. Ben, you weren't forgotten, and now who does that leave?" Isaac rolled his eyes. "Something for Miss Truden, and that leaves one last package still in the box."

Gertie flushed with excitement.

"How could I possibly forget?" Isaac asked, laughing. "Of course! This present says 'To Gertie Reuben,' so it must be for you," and he handed it to her anxious, little hands.

"But what about Helga and May?" Gertie asked. Then seeing the look on her father's face, she wished she hadn't.

"Oh, but we got ours already," Helga said. "Ya, we did, too. See vat you been looking at all night, missy. This beautiful brooch is vhat the Master gave Helga and one also to May. Und Primus, he got gold cuff links. Been flashing them all evening, too."

"Now open. Open the gifts," Isaac said, "and you will have received, I think, your first Hanukkah presents ever. I hope you enjoy them quite as much as I enjoyed picking them out. May Dean did a wonderful job of wrapping the gifts for me. Please," he said, "open them."

They took turns opening the gifts so that everyone would see what the others had, beginning with Herman and finishing with Aunt Hannah. The twins received toy fire engines made of iron, each drawn by a single horse. They were fine, sturdy toys with wheels that really turned. Grace was thrilled to open her present and find a little silver hand mirror and a beautiful tortoise hairpin. Aunt Hannah and Aunt Addie each received a box of lace handkerchiefs in pastel shades with their initials embroidered on them. Ben took out a small leather-bound Psalter, translated from the Hebrew. Rainie expressed her delight over an elegant box containing a new fountain pen and a crystal inkwell. Gertie was perhaps the most pleased, however, when she unwrapped a leather valise containing a sketch pad and a box of charcoal pencils.

They all thanked Isaac for their gifts, and Isaac had the twins gather up the wrappings and put them in the fireplace where they made a bright burst of light.

"Now I think we're ready to listen to Miss Truden's poem," Isaac said. He asked Primus to dim all the lights but the one on the table next to Rainie.

Gertie opened her valise and removed one sheet of paper and a charcoal pencil. "Just in case I think of something to draw," she said.

Rainie began: "'Angel Wing.'" Her voice sounded low and sad and far away.

> "When Sarah Jane was ten years old,
>   a child of grace, ethereal,
> death found a home and lived in her
>   to make her youth eternal.
> She and her mother lived alone
>   on a little farm with house and land,
> and they would take short walks alone,
>   but never far and not for long.
> There was so much to ponder on
>   at ten going on eternal."

Aunt Addie sighed deeply, watching the little boys near her legs and gently nudging them every now and then with her feet. The twins rolled their fire engines on the floor, making every effort to be good and quiet. Rainie's voice rose and fell with a peaceful lilt.

> *"She studied long her mother's fear,*
> *a widow made so by the war,*
> *but Sarah Jane was not afraid.*
> *She early sensed the death of life*
> *and all its interchangingness.*
> *She thought of death as one long sleep,*
> *and one more road for her to walk,*
> *and one more woods for her to roam."*

Ben's thoughts drifted to a quiet place on a hill far from the Samuel house. *One long sleep,* he thought to himself. *Yes, death is a very long sleep indeed.* He wondered what scene held Hiram's attention as the little boy stared into the stereoscope. The words continued like a spoken song.

> *"She loved the woods, the trees, the words*
> *that poets wrote about the woods,*
> *and her voice was sweet and strong.*
> *She searched the woods for hallowed things,*
> *for hidden beneath the surface things,*
> *the lonely and forgotten things;*
> *sharply defined and tangible,*
> *these talismans of nature's craft*
> *were treasures she could find and store.*
> *She kept the trove beside her bed*
> *in a wooden chest from long ago.*
> *Stones of every shape and hue,*
> *and leaves with veins of red and brown,*
> *cocoons of metamorphosed life,*
> *and flowers! roses, daffodils,*
> *with tiny nests and strips of moss:*
> *each written in her careful hand*
> *with penmanship both fine and firm,*

for Sarah Jane would take her time;
she knew there is so little time.
Each stone, each leaf bore secret names
on lines within her ledger book,
all written in her graceful hand,
the sleeping and the laid to rest.
'The keeper of the lost I am,'
and this was what she called herself."

May Dean stared at the fire and thought of secret things and secret places. She thought of these in connection with Jasper and all the times she had spent with him, especially since moving to the Samuel house. She thought of her mother and how she hadn't been home for so long. She couldn't recall ever making her mother smile. She thought of her pa, too, and secretly wished he had been killed in a war, like the little girl's pa in the poem. As soon as she thought it, she was sorry. She hoped the poem wouldn't be too sad because she didn't want to cry in front of all these people. May Dean wondered how in the world a person could write so many words in the first place. She found herself trusting Rainie in an unexpected way. She loved the sound of the young teacher's voice and thought her the perfect lady.

"The year was coming to its end
with time adventing on its way,
and it was nearly Christmas now,
with Christmas Eve on Saturday.
The morning opened full and wide
with kitchen smells and snow outside.
'I'd like to take a walk,' she said,
and feared her mother would say no.
She watched her mother pound the dough,
shaping it for Sunday's bread.
'I'll wear my scarf and everything,'
at which her mother stopped and sighed,

> *for Sarah was beyond her grasp,*
> *and how could she deny her life*
> *when life was rare and time was fast?"*

Helga felt the rumble of digesting food cross her stomach like it was a new frontier. She smiled to herself, thinking of the triumph of her chocolate torte. It was hard for her to understand all the words that Rainie said, but the rhythm was pleasant enough, she thought.

> *"'It's bound to snow more later on,*
> *so promise me you won't be long,'*
> *and Sarah pulled her black boots on,*
> *but there were tears upon the bread.*
> *Her boots made tracks into the snow,*
> *deep and wide, midst stabs of pain,*
> *but she would press on, just a while,*
> *trying to ignore the strain.*
> *Snow had covered house and land,*
> *and all was whiteness everywhere.*
> *The beauty of that afternoon,*
> *that late, raw-lazy afternoon;*
> *the spilling of the cool, gray sky*
> *was all that Sarah yearned to know.*
> *The future vanished as a dream.*
> *This was the true awakening."*

Aunt Addie picked Herman up and laid him on the sofa. He grunted softly and slept with his head in her lap. She felt a rush of tenderness for the child and found herself caught in the spell of the poem.

> *"A rabbit bounded from the woods.*
> *She cried to him a wildish cry*
> *which stopped his stride and made him turn.*
> *She quivered at his whiskerings,*

so private and so wild and free.
    Their breath rushed out in blasts of air
with finest agitation there.
    But he did break the spell at last,
racing through the land and air.
    'A treasure fast, a treasure rare,
the springing little country hare,'
    she cried, as flight became a blur.
She searched the ground for many signs,
    for tiny pinpricks in the snow
to trace the path of bird or deer,
    the pie-crust etchings of the crow.
The glisten on the sheets of land,
    the diamond light on every hand,
were all the signs that she could see,
    and wind was racing through the trees."

Grace hugged the sofa pillow to her chest and bent over, staring at her face in her new mirror. *It's a pretty face I've got,* she thought. *Mother used to say so.* This memory and the poem made her think of death. She sighed as her beloved teacher read on.

"She pushed her hands into her coat
    and turned to see how far she'd come.
The distance to the farm below
    was far more than she cared to know.
'All my fields are covered now,
    lost beneath the sleeping snow.
Patient, rest beneath their flow,
    and I will find you with the thaw.'
But she was tired and ceased to sing.
    She felt her sadness crystallize
as silence filled the woods and trees.
    Till there against a speckled line
of aspen trees bent down with snow,
    a thicket was revealed to her
where pulsed a soft, diffusing glow.

> *A different whiteness held her sight,*
> *a brighter tint of white than snow.*
> *Almost a silver sheen was there,*
> *almost another subtle thing:*
> *lines of hand-drawn, beaten gold*
> *with fainter lines of tracing.*
> *She could not think for certain how*
> *that here there ran a silver gleam,*
> *or there inlaid, that gold could tip*
> *the edges of the fallen wing,*
> *But she knew it was a wing."*

Gertie drew in a deep breath of pure joy. She could see it all—the thicket, the wing, the shades of light and shining. She leaned forward ever so quietly and started to draw. Her charcoal pencil flew over the paper with strokes now broad, now fine, always controlled.

> *"She knelt before the royal thing*
> *and laid her aching body down*
> *where flowed the first great bursting joy*
> *of grace attending heavenly sight.*
> *It made her warm and made her glad*
> *and bade her look and look again.*
> *She could not leave it in the woods,*
> *however still its snowy bed.*
> *Her mind raced quickly to the farm*
> *where she must bear it forth at once*
> *to place within her wooden chest*
> *and thus become its foremost prize:*
> *this, her pride of treasures all,*
> *a glorious pearl of heaven's craft,*
> *this, her rarest angel wing!"*

May Dean leaned her head back on the sofa and sighed at the lovely words and scenes evoked. She found her eyes straying from time to time to where Isaac Samuel sat. His calm repose stirred her somehow. It confused her when this man looked at her. She remembered how he'd come down the stairs that night when she was bathing, after she had been with Jasper. She remembered how Mr. Samuel had seen her from the back. *Funny,* she thought, *how I'm not afraid around him, and I should be embarrassed, but I'm not.* She thought of Jasper Knight and how he said he loved her. She saw Aunt Hannah observing her as the poem ran on.

> *"She gently raised the heavenly rift,*
> *   five feet spanned across her hands,*
> *and saw that it was feathered, yes,*
> *   but not with down of country fowl,*
> *and struck on edge with meshlike steel!*
> *   She found she had the voice to sing,*
> *'Angels, we have heard on high!'*
> *   but there was thunder all around*
> *which called down snow with ice and hail,*
> *   and she was but a mortal child!"*

"Oh, mercy!" Aunt Addie said softly. Rainie looked up briefly and continued.

> *"She ran with hard solemnity,*
> *   tearing the ground with fearful tread,*
> *and it was far to the farm below*
> *   with Christmas Eve upon her head.*
> *At last the porch steps reached to her,*
> *   at last, the open kitchen door,*
> *and there she saw long rows of bread,*
> *   heard, 'Sarah, Sarah, oh my child,'*
> *and felt the floor and then the bed.*
> *   But she held to the angel wing*
> *though she herself was nearly dead.*
> *   She felt cool sheets against her skin,*
> *she felt the chill within her grow,*

>   and dimly saw her mother there,
>   till midnight sleep came fast and fair."

Ben took a kerchief from his back pocket and wiped his eyes. He hadn't expected to be touched like this by anything again, much less a poem written by a young schoolteacher. He hadn't expected or even looked for it, but here it was, wringing his heart, exposing his soul's deepest need.

Rainie, he thought, and then he thought of Lillie.

>   "The house was still when she arose
>   with no sound but the wind and snow.
>   And there it lay upon the quilt
>   nearly stripped of all its glow.
>   She made herself sit down somehow
>   on the little rug beside her bed
>   and take her ledger and her pen
>   and empty lines to fill which read:
>   'Born: This day on Christmas Eve
>   To Sarah Jane of Salter farm,
>   Immanuel, the Angel Wing,
>   Arrayed in white and kept from harm.'
>   This she wrote with shaking hand,
>   a noble entry shining there,
>   emblazoned now by shafts of light,
>   the light that fell that Christmas morn,
>   far brighter than the sun and moon
>   and all within her little room.
>   When Sarah dared at last to look,
>   no longer mortal, strangely still,
>   she hoped to look and never cease
>   or turn her sight at once away
>   and never see or dream again,
>   so great was her out-rushing joy,
>   the vastness of the voice of peace,
>   with words of endless origin.

'Fear not, for none will harm you here.'
  She knelt before the moving light.
'Rise up, my child, and do not kneel,
  for we are servants, you and I,
of Him before whom all must bow,
  and HE IT IS WHO sends me now!'"

"Oh, glory!" Aunt Addie cried. "Glory, glory!"

Rainie looked up and smiled at her audience. She was more than gratified. Her voice quivered with emotion.

"But if he stood or if he sat,
  she never said in later years.
His presence rather filled the room
  with no consent to solid form.
Yet he was altogether real,
  and more than flesh,
and more than more."

The charcoal pencil lingered over Gertie's sketchbook for a long time and then moved again. She sat with one side of her face turned toward the fire, the other toward the center of the room. The light from the flames cast her shadow against the far wall; it leapt higher or lower depending upon how fast she moved her pencil. Ben stared at her and the shadow, his eyes dancing from one to the other. He felt hypnotized by the moving outline of his child on the rich tapestry that hung there, mesmerized by the lovely voice.

"'I ask you for my sleeping wing
  which fell from me in fields of snow.'
And as she looked, she gazed upon
  a singlet nestled in his robe.
She handed him the dying mate
  and saw them leap to life again!

Rekindled by the Living Word,
  the wings were firm and whole again,
ablaze with meshlike threads of light
  and golden nets of liquid steel!
All in the twinkling of an eye,
  they rose to life, the child and wings!
She looked into his deep-set eyes
  where danced great wheels of fire and light;
and when she heard his voice again,
  was richly thrilled by Jordan's song.
'You saved it where it lay, Sarah,
  upon the earth, and art thrice blessed,
for you have seen a heavenly thing,
  a vision of forever's plan!'
Her heart, her eyes, her mind aflame,
  she wept. She yearned to know it all.
He held her close with every thought
  and pierced into her very soul.
'When a child is called from life,
  her angel drops his wings in prayer,
and though he grieves in charity,
  a hope lies in the mystery,
for at the blessed rising day,
  the Christ of Resurrection comes
and brings the souls of all with Him
  and then bestows on us new wings,
the wings of our salvation there,
  and these can never after die.
Thus we share the grace of death,
  the promise of eternal life!'
As she looked into his eyes
  she saw her name encircled there.
This knowledge joined with wonderment
  as he rose up into the air!
'You are His child, oh favored one,
  and He is your Immanuel!'"

Isaac listened in stunned amazement. Where had these images come from? How had this young woman, this relatively untried schoolteacher, come to such depths of feeling and expression? *Immanuel!* he thought. *God with us. God help me not to think about May Dean in any ignoble way. She keeps looking at me. Such beauty!*

> *"Lost in worlds unspeakable,*
> *she fell before the seraphim*
> *now summoned forth in time's great flight.*
> *Midst molten cadences of light,*
> *the angel's glory shone and flew.*
> *She stood, transfixed, a secret time,*
> *and dreamed of Resurrection dreams.*
> *She lay, transfixed, in fields of prayer*
> *and fell at last in rushing sleep*
> *and dreamed of distant things come near.*
> *With morning came fresh tears again,*
> *her mother weeping close at hand,*
> *but Sarah, wrapped in roads and worlds,*
> *stretched forth her hand upon the bed*
> *where fresh and whole and laced with steel*
> *and flecks of gold and silver, too,*
> *a single feather lay.*
> *'Immanuel!' she cried,*
> *and rose to life on Christmas Day!"*

A reverent silence filled the parlor; the only sounds were Gertie's charcoal pencil and the crackling fire. No one spoke or wanted to. Long moments after Rainie Truden laid her manuscript quietly on her lap, after her small audience dried their eyes and cleared their throats, Isaac Samuel rose to his feet and walked over to her. He took both her hands in his.

"Please let me express our profound gratitude to you, Miss

Truden. I know I speak for everyone here. You've given us a truly remarkable vision—one I'll never forget."

Ben leaned forward and looked over Gertie's shoulder. "Looks like we have another vision, too," he said. "Gertie, show them your picture."

Gertie turned and held up her drawing shyly. Now it was Rainie's turn to weep as she saw her poem come to life. Gertie had drawn two studies on the same page. One showed a little girl asleep in bed, her mother kneeling in prayer beside her. In the doorway, just out of sight, stood an angelic figure in a long robe with only one wing. The second study was smaller, showing the same little girl kneeling in the snow and picking up a delicate angel wing.

"How quickly you did it all!" Rainie said in amazement.

"It seemed to sweep over me," was all Gertie could say.

"Put it away for now, Gertie," Ben said, stroking his daughter's hair. "It's late and we need to be getting home. Try not to wake Hiram and Herman while I go get the horses and wagon."

Ben didn't know what to say to Rainie. He waited his turn as May and Helga and both the aunts and Grace went up to her and thanked her and hugged her. Finally, he drew up his courage and shook her hand. "It's a wonderful poem, Miss Truden," he said. "It's more than that, but I don't know how to express it. I'm proud that I could be among those to hear it read for the first time."

"Thank you, Mr. Reuben," Rainie said. "I appreciate all your kind words. I really do."

Later on the way home, Ben heard the steady gait of the horses, the snuffling sounds of sleeping children in the back of the wagon, and the older sighs of contentment and fatigue from the two women who took care of his family. All blended into the cool, clear promise of the twice holy season. He gazed past the sleeping fields and thought long on the beauty of the poem and of the one who had read it. It seemed that the wife of his youth was watching, too, that in the stars above he could see the reflected light of her distant and approving eyes.

———◦∙◦———

"MAY DEAN? WILL YOU STAY A MOMENT?" Isaac waited to ask her until the others had gone to their rooms. She was tidying up after the guests left. "You can finish straightening things up tomorrow."

May picked up the sofa pillows that Grace and Gertie had left on the floor. "There's not so much to do really," she said. "Primus washed every one of the dishes and dried them, too." She turned questioning eyes to him. "Mr. Samuel, I was so excited about my brooch that I didn't even thank you. I'm so sorry. It's the most beautiful thing I've ever had. And the poem Miss Truden wrote is the loveliest thing I've ever heard. I think this was about the best night of my whole life."

"I'm glad," Isaac said. "Your smile is thanks enough."

"All our work fixing the food and serving and then eating the Sabbath meal and hearing the blessings makes me feel good, like this is the way things are supposed to be and can be all the time if we let them."

Isaac stirred the embers in the fireplace with a brass poker.

"You contribute to a peaceful household here, May. I think we were all reminded of our possibilities in life and that God is ordering our steps even if we can't see the whole plan. Life can be good, like you said. It's not just my heritage. It's yours, too."

May sat in a chair by the fire. The newly escaping flames illuminated her face so that her large eyes shone. Noticing this effect, Isaac looked thoughtfully at her and said, "Your hair blends into the darkness behind you so that I can scarcely see where one begins and the other ends."

"Must make me look pretty strange then," May said.

Isaac shook his head. "Not strange," he said softly, "but like the other night . . ."

Their eyes met. "Oh," May Dean said, remembering, "you mean when I was bathing in the washroom. I wondered if you were ever going to talk about that."

"How could I?" Isaac asked, staring resolutely at the flames. "I was hesitant, yet neither one of us planned for it to happen."

"'Course not," she said. "It just happened—no harm done."

Isaac cleared his throat and kept his eyes on the fire. "I hope not. Seeing you the way I did, though, made an impression on me. I hope you don't feel that I violated your privacy."

"I was just taking a bath," she said. "I was so upset about my pa telling me he wanted me to come back home, and I wanted to be alone and to think about what he'd said and how happy I am here and how I don't want to go back. I never meant for anyone to come down the stairs and see me. Primus never leaves his room once his bedroom door is shut of a night. Helga sleeps like a log, and you never come into that part of the house anyway."

"For good reason," Isaac said, leaning his head against the back of the chair. "May . . . ," he started and turned to look at her. "Oh, May, have you any idea how beautiful you are?"

She felt her breath catch and quicken at his words. "I . . . I don't know what to say, Mr. Samuel."

He went on, his eyes closed tightly. "I've tried to put that night out of my mind. I try not to think about it at all, and just when I think I've succeeded in dismissing the image that haunted me so, then I see you, and it comes to me again. You enter a room, and everything comes back to me. You walk across the yard or pause over something as simple as washing the dishes, and it's like a white light surrounds you. I look at other people who may be around to see if they see it, too. It's there now, in your eyes, your hair. I feel like a smitten schoolboy who doesn't know what to do!"

May leaned forward. Isaac hoped beyond hope that she would not stand up and move toward him. When she did, her right side facing the fire, he moaned deeply and embraced her at once. She placed a tentative hand on his dark hair and stroked it gently.

"You don't have to do anything," she said softly. "Only I thought you were in love with Miss Truden."

Isaac looked at her, flushed with revelation and peace. "Why? Because I let her light the Sabbath candles?"

"Well, that, and because she's so smart and can write poetry and reads with such a pretty voice. She knows how to talk to folks. She acts like she belongs here."

Isaac stood and led her back to her chair. "I'm not in love with Miss Truden," he said. "Miss Truden is a lady, May Dean, and so is comfortable in any setting."

She relaxed into the chair and smiled sleepily. "I don't know about being a lady, but I like Miss Truden very much and want to be like her. I'm almost seventeen. My mother had me when she was younger than that. I want to stay here and be like Miss Truden and never have to go back to my folks again. I want you to talk to my pa because you're good, and maybe he'll listen to you. Any white man that would invite a colored man to eat at his own table has got to be good. Pa would never do that. He would never . . ." She paused, looking frightened. "Don't ever tell him that Primus ate at the table with us. Pa would never let me stay here if he knew that. No telling what he'd do!"

Isaac breathed a sigh of relief, feeling in control once more. Here was an anxious young girl he was expected to protect, not make love to. "I intended to talk to your father if the need arose," Isaac said. "He's already getting more money for you to work here."

"You gave him more? But three dollars a week is so much already! He just spends it on himself. Not a dime goes to my ma."

"I don't see any other way to make him leave you alone," Isaac said. "I know he's getting the benefit of your hard work, but I'm willing to pay you some money that he doesn't have to know about."

May looked startled. "How much more?"

"We could start out with two dollars a week more. You have no expenses anyway, so you could put it in the bank. Then at the end of the year, you'll have something to show for your work, and the bank would give you interest, too."

"What's interest?"

"It's money the bank gives you for keeping your money for you. They use it, along with all the other savings from other people around here, and make investments to increase their capital."

The confused look on May's face silenced him. "You don't need to think about that," he said. "I'll give you the money, and you do whatever you want with it."

Her eyes widened. "Thank you, Mr. Samuel. I don't know how to thank you for everything you've done."

"Just let me take care of you, May."

"Do you want to marry me?" she asked suddenly.

Looking at her, Isaac realized how very young she was, how naive. He blushed. "I know you'll make someone a wonderful wife someday, but we shouldn't be talking about that now."

May Dean thought of the ways Jasper Knight had declared his love for her. She had held back her essential self from him, and she would hold it back from any man. She held back now even though it was good how Isaac Samuel was talking to her and offering to give her more money. If only he would hold her again and tell her that he loved her. Still, she thought it was decent that he didn't try to kiss her.

"Mr. Samuel . . ."

"Yes, May?"

"Mr. Samuel, I'm not good with saying things. I don't think about getting married because I'm sixteen, and I don't know what it is I do want, not yet. But that's not important now. You can still love me. I don't care about that or about how old you are. It's all the same to me."

Isaac's blood raced. "I see," he said. "You don't care if I love you, but you don't want to think about getting married. Is that correct?"

May nodded.

"Don't you know, May, that it's wrong to have carnal knowledge of another person outside of marriage?"

She stared at him. "You make loving someone sound bad," she said. "I know folks say it's wrong to do it, but I don't feel inside my own self that it is. It's like when you came to the basement when I was bathing, and you saw me there in the water, and we looked at each other. You weren't ashamed, and I wasn't. It just happened. Sometimes loving just happens."

"All manner of grief follows when you break the commandments of God," Isaac said.

"But we're not breaking any," May said. "We like each other, that's all. That's the way it is between a man and a woman."

"If you think that, then you've been treated shamefully," Isaac said. "But it doesn't have to be that way anymore, May—not here, not in my household."

"Well, Mr. Samuel, I know how men feel about women and how it won't leave them alone, and so they can't control what they think or do. I don't know if it's wrong or not. It just is. It seems to be natural to feel what you feel and not be ashamed since it won't go away anyhow. I know something else, too. I can be here with you like this, and no one has to know. Not my pa, not Helga, not anybody in the world."

For a moment, Isaac felt younger and more vulnerable than the self-possessed girl before him. The wrong step could plunge him into the sort of oblivion he'd always feared, of giving himself unconditionally to another. He summoned control. "It isn't a mistress I want," he said. "I wish I could make you understand that what I feel for you is better than that."

She moved from her chair and sat at his feet, placing her head against his leg. "I know you don't want no mistress," she said, taking his hand and kissing it. "What you want, Mr. Isaac Samuel, is me. Isn't that so?" she asked, lifting her face.

Isaac moved his leg away from her. "I can't deny it," he said, "but that's as far as it's going to go. It would be best for you to go to your room now and not think about this anymore. Also, I don't think we should be alone together, not for a long time anyway."

May never took her eyes off his while he said these words. She rose in the full splendor of her youth so that Isaac was sorely tempted. After she left the room, he was glad for the darkness that came and the embers that barely glowed through the next hours, the hours of wanting and not taking what she offered him so freely.

FOURTEEN

WELL, IF YOU ASK ME, that May Dean sure has set her sights high!" Aunt Hannah said to Aunt Addie. "Going off to work in a rich man's house, and next thing we know there she is sitting in the parlor like the Queen of Sheba herself." The older woman was scrubbing out a stubborn stain so forcefully that she scraped her knuckle on the metal board and cried out. "That's what I get for getting all worked up about that girl, but, la! Did you see the way she was carrying on, Addie? Did you see her sitting there all la de da?"

Laundry filled the kitchen on a rainy Monday morning. Ben had driven the girls to school in the buggy on his way to town to do bank business. Herman and Hiram had played themselves into an early nap so that the house was otherwise still. The smell of simmering stew filled the air; every once in a while Aunt Addie got up to stir the pot so it wouldn't burn.

Aunt Addie came back and started scrubbing a large pile of aprons in her tub. Her head bobbed up and down not in agreement, but in response to the physical demands of the task at hand. "What I saw," she said between scrubs, "was a pretty, young girl growing up and having the first chance in her life to enjoy decent company. Think where May Dean has come from, Hannah dear, and try to be more charitable. And pray that it doesn't get any colder so this rain turns to snow."

Aunt Hannah craned her neck and peered out the kitchen window. "Charitable, haritable!" she cried, relishing the silly rhyme. "I'm telling you, Addie, that I saw the looks that passed between her and Mr. Samuel, and those looks tell the tale plain as day. No, I will not ignore what's sure to be a scandal. Brazen is what she is! A brazen, little hussy going after a rich man and thinking she can do it, too, just because folks make over her good looks all the time. Though, for the life of me, I can't see what there is in that little bag of bones that you could call one bit attractive. Say what you will, Addie, you can't make a silk purse out of a sow's ear, and she's a sow's ear if ever I saw one. Never, never! Well, I declare! There went a button off. Help me find it, Addie, won't you? I can't see a thing in this water."

Aunt Addie left her scrub board and plunged her hands into the murky water as Hannah leaned back to make way for her. "You could wait till we throw the water out," she said, "but it'd likely get lost that way. Here, let me feel around." She fished in the water, finding the bottom ridges on the tub and working her way between the metal grooves. "Here it is. Ohhh!" As she held up the soapy button, her finger was bleeding profusely.

Aunt Hannah laid the button on the table and made a clucking noise. "How'd you go and do that?" she asked. "It's bleeding like a stuck pig. Here, here. It'll stain your dress if you're not careful." The large woman stood up and went to the medicine cabinet on the back porch. She brought in some ointment and bandages and set to work with Addie's wound. "It's a deep cut," she said. "Must have caught on that rough place at the bottom of the tub. I've been meaning to ask Ben to pound it out and keep forgetting. Should have gone and done it myself."

Aunt Addie fervently wished that Hannah had done so. The sight of blood didn't bother her as a rule, but her finger felt like it was sliced to the bone. The soft flesh kept feathering back like a peeled onion, and she knew it would take a long time to close. "It's just the worst sort of luck," she said. "Grace and Gertie will have to do all the washing till this thing heals, and I reckon it'll be a while, too."

"Yes," Hannah said, grimly setting her teeth and wrapping a dry bandage around the finger. "You know, Addie, we probably should get Doc Pierson to sew it up. Ben could go get him when he gets back home."

Addie frowned and shook her head. "Not in this weather."

"You want me to do it instead?" Hannah asked doubtfully.

"Nobody's going to sew nothing," Addie said forcefully. "I'll watch it and keep the bandage changed regular. It'll do, Hannah. And I don't want you upsetting Ben about it either."

Hannah held up her hands in surrender. "Not a word, upon my life! It's all this talk about May Dean done it. Lord have mercy, but I've got to learn to keep this mouth shut and not get all riled up about things that has nothing to do with me. Addie, dear, I am sorry. Will you forgive me?"

Addie's finger throbbed steadily, each pulse sending out a fresh ripple of blood to soak through the wrapping. She tried to smile. "Nothing to forgive, Hannah. These things happen, and if it teaches you not to fret and carry on about things other folks do or don't do, then it was worth a sliced finger, I reckon." She drew herself up and took a deep breath. "'Course it does look like the rest of the wash has fallen to you."

Hannah, her hands set firmly on her hips, was sizing up the situation for herself. She nodded. "Sure does look that way. Well, talking isn't doing. You just sit back down on that stool there and visit while I finish up. I won't rant and rave no more, Addie. But just tell me if you did or did not see something between May Dean and Isaac Samuel, and if you say you did not see a thing, then I will shut up and change the subject altogether."

Addie eased herself into a kitchen chair and pinched her finger at the base to staunch the flow of blood. "You may as well change the subject now, Hannah," she said, "'cause I didn't notice anything like what you seem to be thinking, and I wouldn't care to discuss it if I did."

But Hannah had trouble keeping her promise. She had to be reminded more than once to change the subject before Ben and the girls came home and all the wash was hung to dry on small ropes tied across the back porch.

———◦———

SCHOOL WAS LET OUT EARLY the day Aunt Addie cut her finger. Miss Truden considered dismissing the children after the first clouds blew in. Less than an hour later, she settled on it. "Go straight home," she told the boys and girls, "and don't try to come tomorrow if the roads are snowed in. I don't want you to get out at all unless the roads are clear."

She was thankful for the full box of firewood on the porch and the huge stack at the side of the schoolhouse, but she did not want to get snowed in. After the last child headed out the door, she checked the fire in the stove and prepared to leave. She locked the door behind her, sorry that the children had to walk home under uncertain conditions.

One of the big boys had hitched Prince to the buggy for her; the little horse seemed anxious to get back to his own warm stall. "I'll ask Mr. Reuben if we can get a little shed built for you here at the school," Rainie said to the shivering animal. "Never thought about it before now, but I guess I should have."

The buggy lurched forward, its wheels jostling from side to side. Deep tracks from previous rains made progress slow. It was all Prince could do to climb the first hill. "Only two more to go," Rainie said encouragingly, but she finally had to get out and lead the horse the last two miles. A fine sleet showered little cold needles all over them. Rainie's boots were a lost cause by the time they turned off the road onto the Samuel property.

Jasper ran out to take care of Prince and put the buggy away. "I'll get him some oats and a blanket," he called out to Rainie who was making her way to the back porch.

Rainie saw herself, a bedraggled mud hen, full length in the oval glass of the door. Helga opened it wide with a disapproving look on her face and a cup of hot coffee in her hand. She spoke in such a rush of guttural grammar that Rainie only caught half what she said. The intent, however, was unmistakably a scolding. "Ach! And didn't I try to be telling you this morning not to go, and didn't I say the sleet and snow was coming soon? Here you look a sight for sure I'm thinking. Get down to the basement quick and out of them clothes. Your robe I got out 'cause I knowed for sure and for certain you'd be wanting it, Miss Truden. Ya, I got the sense what don't come with the books, common or not. And didn't I mop the floor, too, all the back-breaking vork of it coming to nothing and to naught!"

Rainie tried to hold the coffee cup still, but she couldn't control the shivering. She told Helga she was sorry for her boots tracking up the floor. It did no good. Helga kept stewing all the way down the basement stairs and never stopped till the hot water poured out of the faucet into the brass bathtub. Rainie stripped and stepped into the steaming tub, too cold to feel modest.

"Oh, thank you, Helga!" she said again and again. "It's awful out there. I should have listened to you this morning. You were so right, Helga, so right. Yes, you certainly did know how things were going to turn out."

Helga snorted triumphantly and nodded her blonde head furiously. Her cheeks were flushed a bright pink, and the ripples of fat danced over her plump arms and face as she shook Rainie's dress and cloak and petticoat and undergarments before putting them in another tub to soak.

"I be leaving you then to your privatecy," she said at last. "And no more's the words need to be said on the matter. May Dean will bring your other clothes directly."

Rainie enjoyed a long soak and washed her hair thoroughly. It had been a while since she'd had a whole bath. Her toilet usually consisted of sponge washing with warm water in a bowl. She was almost glad she'd been so muddy, to be able to indulge herself this way and in the middle of the day at that!

She heard steps on the basement stair and reached for a towel Helga had left there. "It's me, Miss Truden. May Dean." May came into the light carrying a fresh dress and other articles of clothing. "Helga said you'd be wanting these soon."

"Yes. Thank you, May." Rainie was always at a loss when trying to speak to her. It wasn't that she felt better than the housemaid. How could she, an orphan, feel superior? The fact was that Rainie was intimidated by May Dean's beauty. The young girl seemed to have developed perfectly in all the places depicted as ideal femininity so praised in books of art and sculpture. Miss Truden had seen a painting of the goddess Diana emerging from a great shell amidst other plainer beauties. She thought of May Dean as this Diana, herself but one of the lesser figures in the background. She kept the towel draped over her figure.

May stared at her with unabashed interest. "I wish I were slender like you, Miss Truden," she said admiringly. "You always look so fine and—what's the word? Mr. Samuel said it the other day. Like a lady."

Rainie was stunned. She never would have guessed that May even thought such a thing, much less that she would express her feelings so openly. "I don't know what to say," she answered softly. "But you're such a pretty girl, May. You must know that. Not like me. I have no shape at all." She blushed.

"I didn't mean to embarrass you none," May said. "I'll turn around now so you can dry off and get dressed, Miss Truden."

The water wasn't as warm as it had been, and she was ready to get out, but Rainie hesitated. "Isn't there something else you need to be doing?" she asked as kindly as possible, looking to make sure the girl had turned around. Rainie stood up in the bathtub and started drying herself with the towel. "I don't want to keep you."

May Dean shrugged. "I'm done with my work, most of it anyways. I wanted to ask you something, if you don't mind, I mean."

Rainie was glad May couldn't see the frown on her face. This wasn't how she'd wanted her afternoon to turn out in the first place, and she certainly didn't want to hear any confidences or gossip. "Tell you what," Rainie said, trying to control her voice so that she sounded more patient than she felt, "you go ahead and ask me whatever it is while I'm getting dressed. I've got schoolwork to take care of, papers to check, so I really don't have all that much time." She stepped out onto the thick rug and began to dress.

"How do you know when you're going to have a baby?" May asked.

The suddenness of the question, together with the tone in her voice and all its implications, set Rainie's mind reeling. She dressed hurriedly, her hands shaking. She sat on a chair by the bathtub and drew on her long stockings, thinking all the while.

"I don't know much about it except what I've read," she said at last, trying to sound objective and factual. "Women menstruate each month, but if conception occurs, why then the menstruation ceases for the duration of the pregnancy, and, well, that lasts for nine months or so. Hasn't your mother ever talked to you about these things?" Rainie's throat was dry, and she needed a drink of water badly. "I guess you can turn around now."

When May faced her, Rainie saw that the girl's eyes were filled with tears that now poured forth as she started crying in earnest, choking out between sobs, "Oh, no. Oh, no. He'll kill me. He'll kill us both, and then he'll hang, and what will become of Ma? Oh, God! Oh, no!"

Rainie went to her and put her hands on May's shoulders as tenderly as she could. She was not demonstrative, had never been, and it was hard for her to bring herself to touch another person except for a polite handshake. "It seems you have reason to suspect that you are pregnant. But stop for a minute and think. First, there has to be conception."

May nodded her head. "I know that," she said. "I done that already. I done that lots of times, if you want to know . . ."

"I don't!" Rainie insisted. "I don't need to know."

"But I have done it anyway," May cried, "and it's too late now!"

"Who's the father?" Rainie asked angrily.

"Jasper," May whispered. "You know, Jasper Knight. He works here."

"I see," Rainie said. "You don't have to say any more."

The weeping girl dried her eyes with the back of her hand. "So that's how it is," she said. "I guess Jasper will marry me now." May hardly moved—she sat so still, like a great wind had passed over her and taken everything away that could be taken, leaving a dread calm in its wake.

Rainie shook her head slowly. "It does no good to go on about what might or might not happen. You've gotten yourself into trouble, May Dean, and you won't be able to get yourself out. This is a work for one and one alone, and that one is our Almighty God."

The young girl lowered her gaze. "He'll send me to hell," she said. "I'm no good. This here sets it."

"God sends no one to hell," Rainie said. "People choose that for themselves. Everyone sins at one time or another, and some of them all the time. It's human nature, May. But it's when people sin and refuse to repent and change that they wind up lost. It isn't God's fault, not when He gives us every chance there is to believe in His Son and try to live for His glory."

May's eyes looked soft and sad. "I want to change, Miss Truden. I really do want to change, but how can I if I'm going to have a baby? I can't do nothing about that, and I don't want to try to hurt myself like some girls do to get rid of their baby. People will see when I start to get big, and they'll laugh and make fun of me and call me bad names because I've been bad, plain to see, plain as day, when your stomach sticks out to here." She held her hands out in front of her flat, little stomach.

Rainie towel-dried her hair as May spoke, but she was listening carefully to everything the girl said and to what she did not say. "You haven't mentioned the father except to name him," she said at last. "He has to bear the responsibility with you, May Dean. Don't you remember what happened to Hester in the book *The Scarlet Letter?* She had to wear that red letter *A* sewed onto her dress for all the world to see, and the people didn't know who the father was until the very end of the story. The truth came out about the preacher, about Arthur Dimmesdale, in a sad and brutal way, but God's redemption is what Nathaniel Hawthorne was writing about." Rainie felt that she had gotten carried away and that maybe the story in question wasn't quite the point she wanted to make. "Have you read that book?"

May shook her head no.

"Well, it's a classic," Rainie said. "You should read it. Mr. Samuel has a copy, and I know he won't care if you read it. You should read it and know that mistakes can be redeemed. But we have to respond to God when He calls us."

"You sound like you don't blame me for doing sin," May said. "You sound like it don't matter."

"It does matter, but how can I point a finger at you when the Lord Jesus said that only one without sin could cast a stone at a sinner. He meant that everyone sins, May Dean. None of us is pure."

"But my sin is so bad," the girl said, hanging her head.

Rainie sat quietly for a moment. "Yes," she agreed, "it is bad, and you can't get away from that. But the Bible says when we tell God we're sorry and go and sin no more, He removes our sins and forgets about them. It's like we get a chance to start all over, like nothing ever happened."

"But I'll still remember," May said, "especially with a baby there to remind me."

"That's because we still live in the here and now," Rainie explained. "God is present with us through His Spirit; yet He's also beyond time. At His right hand is the Lord Jesus Christ who died for our sins and was raised again from the dead. In the book of Hebrews we're told that Jesus ever lives and prays for us. He has the power to forgive us and to remove our sins as far as the east is from the west. If we believe in Him, confessing our sins and repenting of them, He has promised to forgive us and to give us a new life." Rainie lowered her head and waited for a moment. "Do you want a new life, May?"

"I don't understand," May answered. "I hear what you say,

the words, I mean, but I don't understand. I don't think I'm any worse than anyone else."

Rainie prayed silently for guidance before speaking. "You aren't any worse than anyone else. And you're not any better either, because none of us is good enough. The Bible teaches that all our righteousness, that means even the good things we do, all of this is just like dirty rags compared to God's holiness. Jesus told a rich, young ruler that there was only one who was good, and that's God. Since Jesus is also God, it means that He alone was good enough to die for our sins."

"But why did He have to?" May asked. "I've always heard people talk about this, and I don't know why He had to be nailed to a cross. It's horrible!"

"It is horrible," Rainie said. "It was a terrible thing, but it had to be. When God created the world, He made the first man and woman to be perfect. They lived in the Garden of Eden, and they were so good they were naked and didn't even know it. You know this story, don't you?"

"About Eve eating the apple? Yes, I heard it from Mrs. Reuben. She was always telling stories from the Bible and talking like you are."

"Then she was a believer," Rainie said. "And a faithful witness about what God did in her life. What happened, May, is that Eve disobeyed God's command. Not only that, but she gave the fruit to Adam, and he ate it, too. We don't know if it was an apple because the Bible doesn't say specifically. We do know that they both disobeyed God."

"But the snake told them it was all right," May said. "I remember a snake in there. Mrs. Reuben said it was the devil dressed up like a snake, only that the snakes back then were beautiful and not scary or nothing."

"The serpent did tempt Eve, but she didn't have to do what

he said. She chose to," Rainie said. "She saw that the fruit was pleasant and that it was good to make one wise, and she ate it. This brought sin into God's perfect world, and sin had to be dealt with. Sin causes death. God told them it would, and it's true. Everyone dies."

"Everyone dies," May repeated. "Yes, it's true. Even little babies that don't do nothing bad at all."

"But they are born into a sinful world, and they inherit the nature of sin," Rainie said. "The Bible tells us that the soul that sins will die and that every soul sins. What can we do?"

May shook her head. "I don't know. It seems hopeless."

"It would be," Rainie answered, "if Jesus had not come to die for our sins. We still have to die a physical death. But Jesus died for our sins so that when we do die, we don't have to be separated from God. God looks at the death of Jesus as the sacrifice that takes away our sins. He looks at us through Jesus, like Jesus is standing right in front of us and becoming righteousness for us. He does what we cannot do. God asks us to believe that Jesus did this. And then He wants us to be baptized to symbolize that we are joined with Christ in His death, burial, and resurrection."

May's eyes filled with tears. "Why'd He do it, Miss Truden? Why'd Jesus die for us? He didn't have to if He was God's son."

Rainie touched May's arm gently. "I know how you feel because I've wondered so many times myself. I've come to see that He did it for love, May. He loves us more than we can possibly know. He died to prove His great love for men and women, for boys and girls, for little babies. It made Him sad that we sin, and He died for us so we wouldn't have to be separated from Him when we die."

"You mean go to hell, don't you? I heard a preacher preach on that last summer, and it scared me to death. All those flames and fire forever and ever!"

"To be lost is to be forever separated from God, and the Bible does say that the lost are in a lake of fire," Rainie said. "But it doesn't have to happen if we turn to Jesus. He's done everything possible to save us from our sins. Think of that, May. He saves us and gives us the power to live the way we're supposed to. And we have the holy Scriptures to read to help us."

"Do you read them every day?" May asked.

Rainie nodded. "Every day."

"And do you pray every day, too?"

"Yes, May. I pray for God's grace to reach everyone I know through my example and through His Word."

"Have you prayed for me?"

"Yes, I have. But I didn't know about all your troubles. I just felt that I was supposed to ask God to help you."

May wept. "I've been so bad, Miss Truden, but you say that if I'm sorry and believe in Jesus, He'll take away my sins and help me be good. If that's true, I want to do it. I want to."

Rainie went to the young girl and put her arm around her shoulders. "Tell Him," she said. "Tell Jesus."

May wiped her eyes and then folded her hands in prayer. "Jesus, You know all about me 'cause You're the Son of God. Miss Truden says You died for sin, and that means mine, too, I guess. Please take my sins away and make me good. I don't hardly know how I'm going to do what has to be done now, but I want You to help 'cause I don't know who else to ask anyway. If You would just forgive me for flirting and kissing and sinning, I'll try to do right by You. Thank You then. And please tell Jasper so our baby won't be no bastard. Amen."

Rainie sat quietly for several moments before she, too, prayed. "Dear Lord," she began, "thank You for creating us and for saving us from sin. Thank You for touching May Dean's heart with the truth that You are our Savior. Please teach her now to forgive anyone who has hurt her in the past, and please show her the narrow gate and help her go through it to eternal life. Please touch Jasper's heart and redeem these lives for Your purposes. In Jesus' name, amen."

Rainie smiled at May and hugged her. "You're a child of God," she said. "Have you heard the story of the Ethiopian eunuch?"

May shook her head. "What's a eunuch?"

"A eunuch is a man who is castrated. They used to do that a long time ago to certain servants of kings and queens. Anyway, this Ethiopian eunuch was riding home from Jerusalem in a chariot, and he was reading a passage from Isaiah."

"Who's that?"

"Isaiah was one of the prophets of Israel who wrote a book of the Bible. In it he tells about the coming Messiah. Jesus is the Messiah Isaiah was writing about. Now the eunuch was reading a passage in Isaiah that he didn't understand, and God's Holy Spirit told one of Jesus' disciples named Philip to go talk to the eunuch. Philip obeyed and got into the chariot with the man and explained that the passage was about the Messiah—about Jesus. As a result, the eunuch decided to follow Jesus. Well, pretty soon the chariot came to some water, and the eunuch asked Philip if he could be baptized. So the eunuch was baptized right there."

"I saw some people go under at the revival last summer," May said. "They acted pretty happy when they came up, but some said it was 'cause they had to hold their breath such a long time and were glad to be able to breathe again. It's pretty cold to go outside and get baptized now."

Rainie looked at the girl. "Do you want to be? We have a bathtub right here."

"You mean we could do it here? You could baptize me in the tub?"

"I believe so," Rainie said. "In the name of the Father and the Son and the Holy Spirit, the same as if you were in a river."

May removed her shoes and went over to the tub. "I want to," she said. "I believe in Jesus, and I want to do what the Ethiopian eunuch did."

They dumped out the bath water and filled the tub with clean, warm water. Then Rainie prayed for God's blessing and baptized the girl, marveling that the Gospel had come alive here, that God had ordered every event to bring them both to such a place and time. There were practical matters still to attend to, but the most important step in May Dean's life had already occurred.

FIFTEEN

A UNT ADDIE'S FINGER would not heal. Ben pounded the bottom of the offending washtub so no one else would get hurt doing the laundry. Although Addie and Hannah cleaned and bandaged the gaping wound as well as they could, it flared angrily for several days. Addie took a fever and had to go to bed. She complained of stiffness in her neck and arms, and her appetite, always healthy and varied, fell off considerably. "It hurts to open my mouth," she said. She didn't do much talking either.

Doc Pierson was sent for and spent a long time determining his diagnosis. Saying nothing to Addie, he cleaned the wound again and gave her medicine for the fever. Outside her room, however, he looked gravely at Ben. "Tetanus," he said in an emotionless voice. "I'm afraid she's in the first stages of lockjaw."

Ben knew that lockjaw was fatal. He had heard stories of the agonies of the dying victims, of convulsions, sweating, and intense pain. He hung his head and motioned for the doctor to follow him downstairs.

They went into the kitchen where Hannah was pouring two cups of coffee. When she saw their faces, she held her apron to her face and wept. "I knew it was bad," she said. "I knew it was lockjaw all the time, only I didn't want to say anything to upset Addie or scare the children. Why didn't I fix that washtub before something like this could happen?"

Ben put a hand on her shoulder. "Won't do any good to go blaming yourself or anyone else for what's happened," he said. "If it wasn't the washtub, it could be a nail. If it wasn't a nail, it could be a knife. Nothing's sure and certain, Hannah, nothing but death."

He looked at Doc Pierson. "What can we do for her?" He was thinking of Lillie's death, of the funeral last April, of Aunt Addie reading about the virtuous woman. He felt incredibly weary.

Doc Pierson set down his cup, took off his eyeglasses, and rubbed his eyes. They were a cobalt blue, a startling feature in such an old face, and had seen much sickness and suffering. "I've seen this before," he said sadly. "There's nothing we can do but make her feel more comfortable. You can pray. I know I will. It's a brutal death."

Ben stared out the window. It was the last week of January, 1901, and the new century was underway. From the warmth of the kitchen, the outside air looked frigid, the sky a cold slate with no wind and no clouds. Several cattle stood by the barn, exploding little gusts of steam through their nostrils. One or two went into the barn.

The girls had left for school all bundled up and complaining about having to go out into the cold morning, worrying about Aunt Addie and what the doctor might do to her. "We should stay home today and help," Grace had said. But Aunt Hannah wanted them out of the way, fearing what was coming.

"'Course we can work to get her temperature under control," Doc Pierson said suddenly. "I want you to use cold cloths and try to break that fever, Hannah. And try to get some soup down her throat. She'll be thirsty, too."

Ben stood up abruptly. "What good will any of this do?" he asked hopelessly. "She's going to die the worst possible death, except maybe for rabies!"

Doc Pierson sighed. "I won't argue with you, Ben. But I won't have a bad conscience either about starving the poor woman to death or letting her suffer without even the respite of water on her lips. You can't just put a bullet through her head. I deal with misery every blessed day of my life, and so far the only answer I've got from the Almighty on why these things happen is so we can learn something from each other by doing the right thing, doing the right thing all the time!"

Ben and Hannah looked at one another and nodded their heads. "'Course we'll do the right thing, Doc," Ben said.

"And we'll pray," Hannah added. "Especially hard. Poor Addie—poor, sweet Addie. God rest her soul."

"God rest us all," Doc Pierson said. "And now I've got to get over to the Samuel household and see about May Dean. I'm told she's feeling poorly, though Miss Truden did not elaborate when I saw her at church last Sunday. It's always something, and some-day it'll be something my old, worn-out body has to face, too."

Ben helped the elderly man with his coat and hat and walked him out to his buggy. "We can be thankful it's not raining," Ben said. He reached for Doc Pierson's hand and slipped some money into it.

Doc looked at him with a startled expression. "It isn't nec-essary to pay me now," he said and tried to give the money back.

"Nope. It's yours, Doc. You keep it. Put it to good use," Ben said.

"I'll be back to see Addie tomorrow. Oh, God help us, Ben Reuben! There's such sadness in this old world."

Ben watched the buggy drive off, shaking his head at how much religion had changed the doctor—in less than a year, too. He didn't even drink anymore. *Anything can happen*, Ben thought, *anything*.

———◆———

GRACE SAT AT HER SCHOOL DESK and tried to pay attention to the lesson. Her thoughts were many places, but none of them here. What was it Miss Truden was reading? Oh, yes. *Evangeline*, Longfellow's epic poem, the one that made Grace cry. She had already heard it twice, all the way through—once when her mother read it aloud. That had been the year before when the baby growing inside Lillie's body made its presence known to the children's expectant hands with little kicks and jabs. Evangeline had played second fiddle to the unseen baby's movements. Grace looked at her hands, at the same palms that had touched the apron pulled over her mother's round stomach. Her palms remembered.

"Grace." Miss Truden's voice brought her back reluctantly to the present. There was the potbellied stove in the center of the room; there were the kids huddled around it, trying to keep warm. There were Grace's own hands held out toward the fire. "Grace, please pay attention. I want you to take up reading the next page. Here, I've marked it for you." Miss Truden handed her the little green book.

Grace looked at the words and knew that they were about the Acadian lovers trying beyond hope to be reunited, that the passage before her illustrated one more heartbreak in two lives of abject sorrow, but the print was a blur. "I can't, Miss Truden," she heard herself say. It surprised her that any sound came out at all, her throat felt so full, so constricted.

"Why, what is it, Grace? Are you feeling ill? Children, return to your desks for a while. I want to talk to Grace. You do feel warm," she said, touching the girl's cheek with her hand. "The rest of you please write in your own words what I read to you up to our present passage. *In your own words*," she emphasized.

Miss Truden turned a concerned face to Grace. "Now tell me where you hurt, Grace. I can send one of the boys for your father if need be." The young schoolmistress had seen a great deal of sickness that winter. One of the Coonrod children had died of the whooping cough, and she didn't want to take any chances with any of her students.

Grace covered her face with her hands. "Please, Miss Truden," she said, trying to control her tears, "I don't want anyone to see me cry."

"It's all right, Grace," Miss Truden said, patting the girl's arm. "No one's going to say anything amiss about what happens here. If they do, they'll answer to me for it. Now tell me what's wrong so I'll know what to do."

Grace shuddered, forcing control, and her words came out all in a rush. "It's Aunt Addie, Miss Truden. She's most dreadfully sick, and Doc Pierson came, and he told Pa and Aunt Hannah that she's got the lockjaw and that there's no cure for it and that he's seen it before, and people always do die from it, and we've already had Mama die and the baby, and I don't know what I'll do if Aunt Addie dies, too. She looks so bad lying in her bed, and she can't say a word, and she can hardly get anything down, and Doc says it'll only get worse. I can't stop thinking about it and how she's suffering so, and I'm here . . ."

Miss Truden put her arm around Grace's shoulder. "You're here and feel powerless to help her. I know. Listen to me, Grace. If Doc Pierson says Aunt Addie has tetanus, then she does, and if she dies, there's not a thing you can do to bring her back. But we can do something now. We can get on our knees and pray to our heavenly Father to spare Aunt Addie and to let her die in a more peaceful way at an older age. For you must surely know, Grace, that we are all of us born to die, and there's no escaping that valley. You do know that, don't you?"

Grace nodded slowly. "I know it like I know some of my lessons," she said, "but it doesn't seem real to me because I'm alive, and I don't know what it's like not to be. I know that Mama died and baby Elizabeth and little Dusty Coonrod, and it makes me sad, but it doesn't seem like it will happen to me somehow. I don't mean to be sounding like I'm not believing God or anything like that. It's just hard to understand. But, oh, Miss Truden, I don't want Aunt Addie to die, not like this, not this horrible way."

Miss Truden stood up and called the class to order. A soft undercurrent flowed through the room, for everyone had turned their full attention to the conversation by the stove.

"Class, class!" Miss Truden clapped her hands. "Grace and Gertie's Aunt Addie is very ill, and she needs our prayers. You don't have to be in your church to pray. You don't have to be in any special place at all. Our Lord Jesus said that the time would come and was now here when true worshipers would worship God in spirit and in truth. I want you all to think of this and to pray now with me for Aunt Addie, for God's will to be done. She has the lockjaw, and that's serious indeed. It causes death, and I'll make no bones about that. It surely does. But we can still pray. Remember, God hears every prayer, and He answers every prayer—not always the way we want, but He does answer according to His will."

Miss Truden looked at each child in turn and then knelt on the floor in front of the class. The boys and girls followed her example, kneeling at their desks, some not knowing what to do, some entering into the prayer she prayed out loud with murmurs of agreement.

Grace and Gertie prayed especially hard. Now they were sorry for all the times they had made fun of Aunt Addie's quaint expressions of belief, for the scarf she wore to show respect to the angels, for the peculiar way she had of walking across a room—slightly skipping, and unaware that she did so. They remembered the times when they had disobeyed her. They asked God to forgive them through fervent tears as Miss Truden had each child pray out loud in turn.

Grace felt a burden lift. She felt a lightness, an assurance that whatever would happen would happen, and it would be all right because God knew, and His knowing had Grace in it somewhere. She was anxious to be home and taking care of her aunt, anxious to tell her about how they prayed for her. And when she looked at Gertie, it seemed to her that she, too, had been similarly affected.

By the end of the school day, Gertie was humming to herself and drawing again, a picture of children kneeling in prayer in a schoolroom. "It's for Aunt Addie," she said, "to show her that we prayed for her today."

ISAAC SAT AT HIS DESK and waited for Jasper to answer his summons. The young man was a fair worker, not too lazy and more serious about completing jobs than some others. He had a good report from the other men he lived with on the property; he had a good report from Primus. He even had a good report from Helga, and it was hard to get Helga to say anything nice about anyone. What Isaac had to discuss with Jasper Knight was not a good report, however.

When Isaac had learned the facts from Rainie and May Dean, he was sick at heart. The two women had come to him the week before when he was alone in his library. They had spoken in quiet tones, with expressionless faces. All he could grasp from Miss Truden was that May had come to spiritual terms with her situation and had been baptized. It seemed incredible to him that she would request what he called a *mikvah*, or ritual cleansing, under such circumstances. He told Rainie that such an act, however prompted, didn't alter the facts.

Isaac wished May had thought about such consequences sooner. He had hoped for so much more from her and feared that his profound disappointment was not lost on the perceptive Miss Truden. She seemed to have the uncanny ability of being able to look right into his soul even though he had not invited her to do so!

As for his own feelings toward May Dean, Isaac knew they must be put aside. The only course of action was for the reckless young lovers to marry as soon as possible and take up responsibilities for which neither, to Isaac's discerning mind at least, were prepared. He couldn't judge their inclinations, but he doubted those as well.

Jasper was shown into the library by Primus. The young man stood awkwardly, rolling the rim of his hat around his nervous fingers and brushing back an unruly lock of hair from his forehead.

"You sent for me, sir?" he asked. It was obvious that Jasper had no idea why his master had called him.

"Be seated, please," Isaac answered. His voice sounded stiff and unnatural when he had wanted to communicate more of a serious concern. Jasper obeyed, though he had to push his chair back to keep his long legs from bumping the side of Isaac's desk.

"'Scuse me, sir," he said, turning expectant eyes toward his employer.

Isaac cleared his throat and folded his hands on top of the desk. "Jasper, I'm not going to beat around the bush with what I have to say here. And, no, it's not about your work. You're a fine hand. Everyone says so, and your work proves it anyway. You're honest, they say, and pull your own weight."

Jasper smiled uneasily as Isaac focused his stare on something behind and a little above Jasper's head. When the young man turned his head, he saw an unsmiling May Dean pass by in the hallway on the other side of the sliding glass doors. Isaac waited until she was gone.

"Still, I fervently wish that you had demonstrated more discipline and restraint with regard to one thing, Jasper, and that is your passion. Yes, you heard me speak rightly. Your passion. It has come to my attention that May Dean is with child—further, that she is with child, according to her solemn testimony before me and Miss Truden, through complicity in carnal knowledge with you, Jasper Knight. What I want to know and why I have called you in to discuss the matter with me man to man, in absolute confidence and privacy, is what you have to add to this revelation, and, if you do not deny it, I demand to know what you propose or intend to do about May Dean's situation. I will not have her disgraced. You must know that from the outset."

From the beginning of Isaac's pronouncement, Jasper's body had assumed a rigid position, his eyes locked on the space occupied by his booted foot. It was some moments before he was even able to raise his head, and when he did, Isaac saw that the young man's eyes were moist with tears. Jasper drew a deep breath and seemed to call upon some internal reservoir of strength. His voice was filled with humility.

"Mr. Samuel, I got to say how sorry I am that I lost your confidence in me. It's a hard thing to restore someone's good feelings toward you once they're gone. I hope it ain't too late. I will confess to you, sir, that I have loved May Dean for going onto two years now and that I proposed marriage to her just this last summer, though she laughed and treated me like I wasn't being serious, which I was, sir. I most certainly was serious. Maybe I should be sad that she's in the family way and that it happened because of our passion, but I love her, Mr. Samuel, and I'm glad she's going to have a baby and that it's ours, because now maybe she will know the depth of my regard for her. I would be only too honored and plumb pleased to marry her and be her husband and to provide for her and our baby. I would hope, sir, that in this you would help us and forgive us for offending you and this good house by letting us work for you as we do now till I can set by enough to build us our own place, that is. My folks has got some land, and forty acres of it is promised to me upon my marriage and settling down. Mr. Samuel, I am most ready and willing and able to settle down with May Dean."

Isaac listened intently to Jasper's torrent of anguish and earnest hope. It was evident to him that the young man was deeply in love. The knowledge was a revelation and a pain to him. When Rainie and May had come to him with the confession, Isaac gave up hope for his own love. This was, he told himself, confirmed by the fact that May wept and could not look him in the eye. At the same time, it appeared that the young girl was undergoing a profound change unrelated to her pregnancy, something on the order of a spiritual awakening that was foreign to him. Her very countenance was altered. All conceit had fled; a sweet meekness had taken its place. Never had she been more beautiful, he thought.

And here was her lover, himself contrite and wanting to follow the honorable course. The young man's seed was growing in her body these past months, and no one had even suspected. And what of May Dean's parents?

Isaac determined to put a good face on the whole situation. "What will you tell her parents?" he asked. "They'll have to know sooner or later, Jasper, and I must tell you frankly that I'm concerned about their reaction."

Jasper lowered his head. "I been thinking about it ever since you told me," he said, "and I'm the one that's got to do it, to tell them, I mean. I been suspecting this for some time, Mr. Samuel. Can't say why, but I been thinking for a while that May was in the family way, only neither of us had the guts to talk about it. I been studying what to do, though. I saw clear that I had to tell her folks. Guess I been waiting for a kick in the pants to do it is all, and now it's here, and I know and she knows, and so there we are."

"Will she marry you, Jasper? There's that to consider."

"I don't see how she won't, though she's never said she would. Said she wouldn't last summer, I know that, but we was younger then. I don't hardly know, but I think she will now, now that it's out in the open, and I'm glad. Sure does take a load off."

"Still, I think you need to talk it over with May Dean and get a proper answer." Isaac saw that Jasper had about reached his limit on the conversation. "But whether she consents or not," he said, going to the library doors and opening them, "you can't put off telling Roy Dean. Plans have to be made, wedding arrangements attended to. You may have the ceremony here if you wish, and, yes, I will let you both stay on. I wouldn't be throwing a young family out."

Jasper stood and bowed awkwardly at the door. "I'm obliged, Mr. Samuel. Can I talk to her now?"

Isaac nodded. "I think that is most advisable. And, Jasper, I expect to be kept informed. We need to get this matter settled at once."

THE MATTER WAS SETTLED in May Dean's mind. She accepted the fact that she was to marry Jasper and become May Knight. She determined to love the father of her child. Since her profession of faith to Miss Truden, she had felt weights of guilt and condemnation falling from her. For the first time, she believed that her life was a gift from God, significant to Him, and that she was expected to live according to His will.

The two women had received permission to use Isaac's library each evening for their devotions. Helga sat in with them on occasion, but she declared that she herself had been raised a good Lutheran, and that was all she needed, if only she could find a church to go to.

"It's right there in *Pilgrim's Progress*," Rainie told May one evening when the two met alone to pray and read the Bible together. May listened intently as her beloved friend and teacher told her about John Bunyan's faith and the classic book he wrote way back in the 1600s.

Rainie opened the book to a much-read passage. "'If a man would live well, let him fetch his last day to him and make it always his company-keeper.' This means that if we hold the day of our death ever before us, we'll be encouraged to live godly lives and to let our faith mature into increased obedience to what God wants us to do."

"Like me and Jasper getting married and starting a family?"

"Yes, and many more acts besides. Our lives are not our own any longer, not when we come to the Lord. We give up our life, and He comes into us to help us do His will. The good works are part of our faith. We have to believe and be led into them. We learn more from the Holy Spirit as we continue to pray and read the Word of God."

"We never read the Bible at my house," May said. "We had one, but it was kept inside a box. Must have been like that since my folks got married. They never even opened it."

"I know it makes you feel sad for your parents, May, but this is a good sadness. It will help you pray for them better. Which reminds me, has Jasper talked to them yet?"

"He's going tomorrow," May said. "Mr. Samuel gave him the afternoon off to do it. I offered to go with him, but he said that it was up to the man of the house to take care of such things and that he might as well be getting used to it. I had to laugh, though. He hardly seems like a man, that Jasper. He's sure not like Mr. Samuel."

"He is a man, though," Rainie said sternly, "and he has to deal with God, too, May."

May nodded her head. "I know that, Miss Truden." She could not get used to the idea of calling Rainie by her first name even though Rainie urged her to do so. "I tried to talk to him about the Lord, but he just laughed at me and said that a simple woman might believe in such, but no man could take it seriously. He said men, himself included, were too strong to need God or anyone else telling them what to do."

"Yet he listened to Mr. Samuel," Rainie said, "and was eager enough to do what he told him."

May looked up quickly. "That's only 'cause he does want to marry me, Miss Truden. Of course he'd do what Mr. Samuel told him if it has to do with me."

Rainie sat quietly. "I'm concerned now. I don't know if you should marry Jasper Knight if he doesn't intend to follow the Lord. You were so ready, May. Your repentance was heartfelt and immediate. The Bible says that believers shouldn't be unequally yoked with unbelievers, that light has no fellowship with darkness."

"I don't understand that," May said. "What do you mean 'yoked'?"

"It means that if you, a believer in Jesus Christ, marry a man who is not a believer, it will be most difficult for you to do God's will effectively. You'll be wearing the yoke of marriage with Jasper, and each one of you will be pulling in a different direction—you, toward God's purposes, and Jasper, toward his own way."

"I've seen animals do that," May said thoughtfully. "You have to change them. There's no other way but to get two that will pull together. But I got to be married, Miss Truden, or my baby will be a bastard."

Rainie closed her book and set it on the table. "We'll keep praying for Jasper to have a repenting heart, and while we're at that prayer, we must remember Aunt Addie, too. Ben Reuben was over this morning and told us she was truly suffering with the lockjaw. Doc Pierson doesn't expect her to make it through another day."

Tears welled up in May's eyes. "It's a terrible death," she said. "Pa told us once of a boy he knew who got it and died. Let's do pray, Miss Truden. I believe that God can make it go away and raise her up."

The two young women knelt and began to pray.

AUNT ADDIE'S SUFFERINGS WERE TERRIBLE. From the first sign of her stiffening jaw, she suspected the worst. Addie had nursed an old man many years before, a distant cousin of someone in the family, who had lockjaw. His resulted from a rusted nail piercing his foot. Fear of tetanus was so great that no one

wanted to have anything to do with him once the doctor's diagnosis was made. But Addie had come forward because she
believed the Lord told her to do this for the least of His brethren,
and if a man with lockjaw wasn't the least, then who was? Addie
was in her early thirties at the time, enough of a spinster to know
that she was destined for old maidhood and peacefully resigned
to the fact. She took up home nursing like it was a second skin
and stayed with the man until his death. It didn't take long.

Now *she* had lockjaw and knew for a solid fact what she was
in for. She communicated through tightening jaws at first, then
through clenched teeth. Finally, it was too difficult to do anything more than write notes to her family. "PLEASE PRAY FOR
ME," they said in crooked letters.

Grace and Gertie tiptoed in to see her every morning before
school. The girls took turns wiping her forehead with a damp
cloth and brushing her long hair. Since the first day of her infir-
mity, Addie's hair remained free of tortoise-shell combs and pins,
its rich whiteness blending into the pillow on which she lay.

Hannah read to her through the day, favorite passages that
Addie had marked in her Bible with stars or crowns inked in the
margins. Ben read to her at night. They took turns placing drops
of water on her dry lips until it was impossible for her to swallow anything at all. She was steadily weakening, and then the
convulsions started.

They were small spasms at first, which became increasingly
violent. Addie's eyes stared at the family through layers of pain.
She was sweating profusely so that Hannah had to change her
night dress several times every night to keep her from getting
chilled.

"Prepare for the worst," Doc Pierson told Ben the evening
that Rainie and May prayed for Addie. "I fear she will become
unconscious at any moment, and if her chest gets any more rigid,

she won't be breathing long. It's like the whole body stops working, one part at a time." Doc Pierson turned away from his rigidly convulsing patient and wiped his eyes. "I hate it!" he said vehemently. "And I can't do a thing to help her!"

A lump rose in Ben's throat when he heard Doc's words and saw his grief. Addie's dying was probably the worst thing he'd ever seen, her fixed stare begging him for relief when there was no one to share her agony, no one to bear her pain. Lillie's dying had been hard enough to endure, but her crisis came in a short time. Addie had been convulsive for three days now.

Ben saw Addie's Bible on the table by the bed. A piece of paper stuck out of it, marking a passage to which he turned. It was where Jesus said that all things were possible to him that believed. The piece of paper bore Addie's feeble plea, "PLEASE PRAY FOR ME." Choking back his tears, the tall man fell to his knees by her bed and took her hands in his. They were on fire with the fever that possessed her.

"Oh, God," he cried from the depths of his heart, "You know how hard this is for Addie and for us who stand and watch in helpless fear and wonder. She only cut her finger, Lord. It was such a little cut, a little thing, but it's killing her. Please, dear God, have mercy on Addie and on me, a miserable sinner. I beg You to end her suffering. Please, Lord. She knows You. She's served You as long as I've known her, and that's a bit of time. She loves You. She's prayed for us, and we've not heeded as we ought. Put it on me, Lord, not on Addie, that we failed You and her. But spare her this agony. She's not afraid to die, dear God. She's ready. Oh, Lord, hear. Oh, Lord, come to us. Please. In Jesus' name, amen."

Ben's body shuddered with tears. He felt her hands become still and cool in his. He lifted his head and looked across the bedclothes at Doc Pierson. The old man was also kneeling on the other side, his head fallen on the quilt. Ben turned and saw his children, all four, standing in the door with Hannah behind them. He didn't know how long he stayed on the floor, on his knees. But after some period of time, Addie's convulsions ceased, and the bed was still.

Ben and Doc Pierson stood at the same time, looking first at each other and then at Addie. She was bathed in light from the kerosene lamp hanging over the bed. She was just opening her eyes as the children walked into the room quietly. Aunt Hannah followed, her eyes moist with glad surprise.

Addie looked at each in turn, her eyes bright with tears of relief and joy. She parted her lips in a wide smile as the girls, weeping softly, fell upon her neck with hugs and kisses. Herman and Hiram stood together, shyly patting her arm. "See what the Lord has done?" Addie's words hung in the air as wondrous declarations of faith made evidence and substance. "The Lord is my strength and my salvation," she declared.

A reverent circle of silence surrounded the bed, filling the room with the glory of God's provision. No one knew what to expect. Anything might happen with such a God. Ben shook his head in a slow and deliberate motion. Doc Pierson took out a handkerchief, wiped his forehead, and choked back a sob. Hannah held her hands clasped tightly in an attitude of prayer. The children kept repeating Addie's name, their voices filled with wonder.

"I think we should let Addie rest now," Doc Pierson said finally.

Ben led the children from the room, but Aunt Hannah insisted on sitting in the rocker by the bed. "All night long if need be," she said. "She might need a drink or something."

The doctor felt Addie's forehead with the back of his hand and found no trace of fever. He felt her pulse and patted her arm affectionately. "I'm telling you the truth, Miss Addie," he said, "no one is more surprised at what's happened here tonight than I am. Oh, I've seen what you might call run-of-the-mill miracles, though they all amaze me. Take a baby's birth now. That's a miracle if ever I saw one. Or take other examples of healings and folks getting well when they were expected to die any minute. But I declare before God and you that I never saw anything like this. I've never seen anyone healed of lockjaw. I never heard about anyone else ever seeing it healed either. I don't know quite what to make of it, but I vow before God to tell of it all the days of my life."

Doc fiddled with his stethoscope and scratched his head. "I'm most sincerely relieved that your suffering appears to be over. Oh, I don't know what I'm saying. Of course it's over. Any fool can plainly see that God Almighty has intervened." He wiped his eyes, and Addie reached for his hand.

"Thank you for your care," she said, giving it a gentle squeeze. "You should go downstairs and have a cup of coffee, Doc, and maybe some fresh air, too."

He nodded. "Don't you go opening any windows, though," he warned. "I want you to rest in bed and keep warm. Hannah, please make sure she drinks a lot of water through the night. We'll see what tomorrow brings."

The morning brought confirmation of Addie's healing. Ben was almost beside himself with amazement and a strong desire to tell the whole world. He saddled his horse early and rode at a good gallop to Isaac Samuel's house. He had to tell Rainie first because he knew how hard she had prayed for Aunt Addie. She would certainly want to know.

Rainie clasped her hands over her mouth when he told her. She wept with joy and said, "Thank You, thank You, Lord," over and over. She hugged Ben quickly and ran to bring May

Dean in to hear the news. "She's prayed with me every night this week," Rainie cried over her shoulder as she ran down the hall to the kitchen to tell Helga also.

Soon everyone gathered in amazement around Ben.

"Baruch Hashem!" Isaac exclaimed. Then seeing Ben's questioning gaze, he translated, "Praise the Lord!"

"I'll make a chocolate torte and take it over to dear Addie myself," Helga announced, wiping tears from her eyes.

Primus folded his hands and spoke reassuringly. "We must never doubt the Lord or His power to save."

May took Ben's hand in hers and looked at him with moist eyes. "I'm so glad, Mr. Reuben—so very glad." Her voice trembled with emotion.

"I'm deeply touched by the concern you've all shown for Aunt Addie," Ben said, turning to leave. "I knew you'd want to know. Doc Pierson said she can be up in a day or two, but Addie's raring to go right now. I tell you the truth, if I hadn't seen it with my own two eyes, I would never have believed it."

"Thank the Lord you were there to witness this great miracle," Rainie said. "There must surely be a great purpose in all this, far more than we realize. Please tell her that we'll continue to pray for her strengthening and that we'll pay a call real soon."

Ben thanked them all again and knew that he would ride to town on this particular Saturday and spread the word there and that the first house he must visit was that of his sister-in-law and her family.

———◆———

WORD OF ADDIE REUBEN'S HEALING spread throughout the community. Some rejoiced; others scoffed. "Well, you know how peculiar she is. She probably didn't even have lockjaw," the doubters said. But Doc Pierson silenced them all when he and Ben Reuben made an unexpected appearance in the Baptist Church that Sunday and proclaimed the miracle with their own lips and rededicated their lives to God.

"Ministers report that the Addie Reuben miracle touched many hearts and led a score of fence-walkers to church altars last week," the town newspaper said in a story on page 1. "Congregants reported that the sin and pain of many years were laid to rest by an infusion of rekindled faith. Those who experienced this grace explained that suddenly what had been so important no longer seemed so, that knowing the Lord and drawing closer to Him were all that mattered."

Addie sought no attention for herself throughout the weeks that followed. She told whoever dropped by to see her that what had happened was God's will, pure and simple. "It is the work of the Lord," she said, "and marvelous in our eyes."

SIXTEEN

———◆———

MAY DEAN'S PREGNANCY was not marvelous in the community's eyes, however. Whether the news spread due to Helga's careless speech or the talk of Isaac Samuel's hired men, everyone knew of her condition about the same time that Addie was healed. Jasper was as good as his word to his employer. He laid out the facts to Roy and Pearl Dean along with his offer to marry their daughter.

When the young man finished speaking, Roy Dean said nothing for several minutes. Then he spat a long stream of tobacco on the porch and cursed. "I ain't a bit surprised," he said. "When we sent her off to that fancy house, I knowed something like this would happen to her. Living around the wrong sort of folks more'n likely give her ideas. Going around putting on airs 'cause she lived in a fancy house, but she's nothing but a common whore what's got herself a bastard child to disgrace the name of Dean."

Jasper spoke excitedly. "But I told you it was my fault, Mr. Dean. May's not a bad girl, not the way you're saying. She and I done wrong, it's true enough, and we got to do the right thing now. I want to marry her and take care of her and our baby and give it a name so it won't be no bastard. Mr. Samuel, he said he would help us by and by . . ."

"Mr. Samuel! That meddler brought her to this, him with his fancy house and his, 'Here, Mr. Dean, is May's wages so you don't have to ride out and get them.' He never wanted me on the place at all! He wanted to take our precious one far from home, and now see what's come of it!" Roy clenched his teeth and his fists at the same time.

It seemed to Jasper that the man wasn't listening to a word he was saying, that Roy had made his mind up about what had happened, and he wasn't about to change it. Jasper said so to Isaac later.

"How was the matter finally settled?" Isaac asked. He dreaded a misunderstanding with Roy Dean and where it might lead.

"He didn't say nothing about me marrying May. It was like he didn't even hear me," Jasper answered, shaking his head. "He got a wild look in his eyes and said something about getting it all taken care of in the end and how he'd clear his name in this community once and for all. He cursed something awful, Mr. Samuel. Mrs. Dean looked right scared to hear him, though she never said a word and wouldn't hardly look at me neither."

Isaac pondered this. "I think you and May should go ahead with the wedding," he said. "I want you to ride out and let her folks know so they can decide whether to join you or not. I don't want them to accuse anyone of slighting them, and I don't want this to drag out any longer, Jasper. Do it tomorrow."

———

NEWS OF MAY'S PREGNANCY CAUSED Roy Dean to nurture his long grievance against the world with new intensity. His hatred found a solid form in the persons of a Jew and a black man. Isaac Samuel and Primus loomed in his imagination as symbols of all his misfortune. "People like them . . . ," he'd say under his breath and let fly a stream of cursing. That this was illogical and evil never occurred to the man, so solid were his habits of blaming others, so great his cruelty.

Roy sat, silent and stunned after Jasper left. A new desire was conceived that night and the next as he nursed his hatreds. Several bottles of rot-gut whiskey helped clarify his individual revelation. Sometime during the afternoon of that second day, he took it in his head to get his rifle down from where it hung on the wall by the front door. He started taking it apart and cleaning it with meticulous focus and attention. It seemed to possess him, this need to dissemble every mechanism, to linger over each separate part with his eyes and his hands. It was the first of many steps that must be taken to fulfill a gnawing need. What he wanted and therefore determined to do was to kill a Jew and a Negro, both at the same time or, failing that, on the same day.

Pearl watched him as he worked. She stared through eyes puffy with weeping. Her body was bloated, and her ankles ached whenever she stood. She watched her husband clean the inside of the rifle, work every part that could be worked, oil the wood butt, spit and wipe the sight. She shivered as he swilled his brew, avoided looking too long at his red and swollen eyes.

It was a Thursday, and there was work to do. There was always work to do, chores to finish, and here was this man of hers cleaning his rifle and drinking himself under the table. She was glad she'd put Nellie down to nap, but taking care of the little girl was the least of her troubles. She still had to wring a chicken's neck if the family was to eat that night, and she just didn't feel like doing that or the plucking and cleaning that had to follow sure as night followed day. It was times like these when she bitterly missed May.

As if reading her mind, Roy said, "Things don't get done 'round here like when May was still living with us. You noticed that, Pearl?"

Pearl's eyes darted about the room. "I do my best," she whined, "but these young'uns won't pitch in like May done."

Roy squinted an eye down the rifle barrel and then blew into it. "You complainin', Pearl? 'Cause if you are, you just might get more of a remedy than you was wanting. Know what I mean?" His tone was threatening.

"All's I want is my girl home again. Poor little May, going to have a baby now, a baby of her own." She said this and drew back, calculating Roy's ability to hit her from where he sat. She hadn't meant to say so much, but there was this feeling like a knot in her throat, and she just had to get rid of it. It had been stuck there ever since Jasper had come.

"You ain't complained 'bout the extra money she's been making, though, have you? And you ain't once gone over to pay her a visit neither. What kind of a mother are you, Pearl? Don't sound like a caring one for all your slobbering and whining," Roy said cruelly. He eyed the dismembered rifle lying on the filthy table and leaned back, rocking in his chair. "Fact is," he said, "none of this ought to have happened if you was a decent mother."

He stood up faster than she thought he could and brought the back of his hand hard against her jaw. Pearl gasped with pain.

"What'd I do, Roy?" she cried. "What could I have done? She's a willful one. You know that. And then . . ."

"Then what?" he snarled, weaving from side to side. He unbuckled his belt and drew it slowly through his pant loops. He folded the leather strap and slapped his palm with it.

"You was bad to her, Roy!" she cried, rising unsteadily and backing up all the way to the wall. "You drove her away! Go ahead and hit me! It won't change nothing! You put sinning into her. You're the one what did it!" Her words rose into an awful scream. The blow raised a red diagonal welt across her face. Pearl tried to shield herself from what followed. Her husband was too fast for her, though, his eyes red and crazed.

"Blame me, will you?" he screamed. "And whose child is she if not mine to do with what I will? I made her, Pearl! May is mine! You was always jealous! Always hated her!"

Pearl was no match for him, and she knew it. What was happening had happened so many times that it was no longer a surprise. There was a dull finality to the whole thing, a harsh ring of familiarity. Suddenly it didn't matter anymore. She felt herself falling backward, heard the thud when her head hit the corner of the iron stove, and that didn't matter either. Even when she saw the blood on the floor, she felt far removed, totally uninterested in the fact that it was her lifeblood there, flowing away from her. *Who will clean it up?* she wondered.

Thinking that now she might be free of Roy Dean once and for all, she lay still and died.

"Playin' possum, are you?" Roy yelled. "Won't work this time, Pearl, old girl! Get up! You'll wish you never . . ." His words trailed into silence as it dawned on him that his wife was not going to get up, not now, not ever. His eyes blinked rapid-fire. "Middle of the afternoon," he said to the quiet room. "Kids is all at school. Only Nellie here." He heard the two-year-old stirring in the next room, whimpering. He lifted his whiskey jug and swallowed the last of it before going in and picking up the terrified child. "Shush up, you! You're goin' over to Miz Coonrod's, you are," he said, lifting her roughly and carrying her outside under his arm. Roy told her not to so much as move while he saddled his horse. That done, he lifted her in front of his saddle and swung up behind her.

"Mama!" Nellie cried pathetically. "Mama!"

"Shut up that crying!" Roy shouted. "You're goin' to stay with the Coonrods a spell, and I aim to get you there right quick, too!"

Nellie choked on her fear, but seeing the look on her father's face, she kept quiet and hung on to the saddle horn all during the hard ride. Finally Roy let her down into the sour-smelling arms of Mrs. Coonrod.

"Pearl's sickly," Roy said, weaving in the saddle. "Where's that man of yours anyhow? We got business to attend to." He slurred the words, placing great emphasis on the word *business* and spitting out a long stream of tobacco juice.

"He's down to the south forty," Mrs. Coonrod answered, looking up at him suspiciously. "Least he was headed thataway at noon. You best watch that business of your'n, Roy Dean, whatever it is. Get you in trouble if you ain't careful! Get you both in trouble!"

Roy grinned. "Why, Joadie Coonrod! You know there's more than the two of us to tend to business round here!" He spun his horse around toward the road, kicking the animal savagely. He waited till he was well over the hill and out of sight before he turned back across country toward his own farm. It seemed to take him a long time to get there. His head was pounding.

Roy bumped his head riding into the barn and fell to cursing all over again. He slid off the horse's back and veered toward a wooden trunk in the corner where he knelt all in a slump before opening the dusty lid. Anyone watching would have seen what looked like a man of prayer in supplication to his god. Roy lifted a white sheet and hood with reverent motions and put them in his saddlebag. Grinning wildly, he ran across the yard to the house. It was late afternoon, getting on toward dusk. The kids would be home soon enough.

Pearl was right where he had left her. He sat at the table for a spell looking at her until she became a stranger in his mind. He put his rifle back together and consumed another bottle in the process. What he needed was to get rid of Pearl, and the best way would be to set the whole blame house afire. There were even dirty rags and kerosene on hand. Dirty rags! Why, those were his unwashed shirts and trousers! That lazy wife of his sure let things go. He would see to it no one found out about her!

"Get something from that Jew house and blame it on the Negro!" he said under his breath. "Nothing like a good fire to stir up a whole town. And if one's good, two's better still." The barn would go first. He'd put something incriminating there, too, something to place the blame on Isaac Samuel and his black butler. Roy cackled with delight and helped himself to some more Okie Territory rot-gut home brew. Hearing his children hooting outside sobered him up some. Roy shot up like a flare out of his chair and onto the front porch.

"Get away from here!" he screamed. "Get on off down to Coonrods' and don't tell no one you seen me neither!"

The three startled youngsters, knowing enough from long experience with their father's rages, backed off to where the fence met the road and ran full speed all the way to Coonrods'.

JASPER TOOK ISAAC'S ADVICE to marry May Dean quickly to heart. He asked May if she wanted to go with him to tell her folks the date.

"I'm not ready to face my folks yet," she said simply, and no amount of argument could change her mind. She seemed distracted and uneasy any time Jasper mentioned her parents. Still, she agreed that it was best for someone to tell them face to face. "They can't read anyhow. You go, Jasper."

Jasper saw a new facet of May's personality begin to emerge.

What had once seemed a charming stubbornness was turning to definite hardheadedness, and it wasn't restricted to this matter alone. She made him pray with her and Miss Truden at night and sit for Bible readings, too. She had turned modest since she got religion and even refused to sleep with him until they were married. All this and she wouldn't stop talking about how he needed to be saved so their family would belong to the Lord. He guessed he'd have to get religion, too.

But first her folks had to be told the wedding date. It was a task Jasper dreaded. As he rode over to their house that Thursday, he consoled himself thinking about the wedding. May said she wanted to be married on the first Sunday in April, what she called "true spring." The ceremony would take place in Mr. Samuel's backyard; Helga promised to do the wedding cake. There would be no honeymoon, of course. Jasper could barely afford a wedding band. But Mr. Samuel told them they could live in the gatehouse for a while, till they saved enough for their own place.

Twilight was coming on; the sky was shot through with signs of the day's demise. Shafts of golden light rose from one end of the horizon to the other, forming a great arch for the sun's descent. Lower, close at hand, Jasper saw a dark cloud, one that did not originate in the sky. A stiff breeze nearly took his hat as he stared, trying to make out where the fire was. Moments later he saw embers flying through the air and knew that the column of black smoke was over the Dean place.

"Whoa!" he said, reining in at the top of the hill. Below him he saw the barn engulfed in flames, its roof and sides solid sheets of fire. An eerie glow flooded the empty yard and the dark house. There was no sign of a soul on the place. "Giddap," Jasper cried, digging his heels into his horse's sides. Within seconds they were in the smoke-filled yard. The sound of falling timbers spooked his horse; it whirled so violently that Jasper was thrown to the ground.

He got to his feet shakily, yelling over the roaring confusion, "Hallo! Anybody home? Anybody here?"

"Whoa!" a loud voice cried behind him. Jasper turned and saw Ben Reuben and his hired man Si riding into the yard.

"Mr. Reuben! What are we going to do? There's no one here, not a blessed soul!" Jasper cried.

"Too late to save the barn!" Ben yelled, jumping off his horse. "Have you tried the house yet?"

"Only just got here!" Jasper said.

"Sure looks deserted," Ben said. "I wonder how it started. Never mind. Where's the family gone off to? Yet another blow for Roy Dean!"

"She's a goner!" Jasper said, staring at the barn and wiping his face with a kerchief. "Look at that, would you?" The barn's roof collapsed as the three men stood by helplessly.

"Wind'll carry them embers, Mr. Reuben," Si said. "Best wet the house or it'll go, too!"

"And every other blessed thing in sight," Ben said. "But all we've got is this one bucket at the pump!"

"And our hats!" Jasper cried.

"Best we can do," Ben said. "Let's wet 'er down, boys!" They filled their hats and the bucket and started throwing water against the side of the house facing the barn.

"Wasn't nobody in sight when I rode up!" Jasper exclaimed. "I can't make out what's happened! Didn't hear nothing either, nothing but the sound of a dog howling off in the distance. Gave me the creeps, it did! What's that there?" he asked suddenly, pointing inside the house. "Looks like a light, Mr. Reuben."

"Couldn't anybody be inside and not know what's going on out here," Ben said, turning away. "Must be a reflection. Si, I want you to ride for help. Looks like we'll be needing it before this night is over." Si mounted up and was gone in a moment.

Ben washed his face with a wet bandana. "What're you doing here anyway, Jasper Knight? I thought you were only keeping company with one Dean these days."

Jasper smiled sheepishly. "I come over here to invite May's parents to our wedding," he said. "I'd done asked their permission to marry coupla' days ago, but they didn't say hardly a word to me one way or the other. Roy just stared at me, not saying nothing, not hardly blinking. When May set the date this morning, Mr. Samuel, he told me to ride over here and let her folks know. When I cleared that hill yonder, I seen the barn all lit up. Whoops!" he exclaimed suddenly. "There *is* a light in the house, Mr. Reuben, more'n one. I seen them good."

Jasper ran to the back door.

"What the . . . ," Ben asked, confused. "Look at that smoke oozing from the eaves there! You want to watch yourself, son! Looks like there's another fire inside."

"Well, I'm bound to find out," Jasper said. He covered his mouth with his kerchief and kicked in the door.

Ben heard and saw two things simultaneously. One was a deafening roar from inside the house; the other was the terrified look on Jasper's face. A wall of fire engulfed him and drew him inside. Every window exploded with the influx of oxygen.

"Jasper!" Ben screamed. Intense heat held the house in an infernal circumference. He ripped off his jacket and ran toward the flames, beating them over and over. The searing pain of black smoke swept over his body, causing his eyes to smart, filling his lungs so that he coughed and choked and fell on the ground.

"Jasper!" he cried again, attacking the flames afresh. It was no good. Ben staggered to the well, drew up a bailer, and poured the water over his head. Fresh embers rose on hot currents of night wind as the sun sank out of sight.

Ben sat a long while, his mind focused on nothing and everything. The inferno at his back smoldered; the fresh one before him raged and spat, raged and lagged, until there was nothing left to consume. He stared into the white heat, the world around him like a mirage seen through a hazy lens. The first stars were out in full force. When he turned around, it was to the sound of approaching hooves.

"Too late!" he cried, pounding his fists into the ground. "Poor Jasper! Lord, have mercy, but it's just too late!"

Half a dozen riders dismounted, among them Si and the sheriff, all the way from town.

"What're you yelling about Jasper?" Si asked Ben.

The others stood to one side, shaking their heads and murmuring among themselves.

"Jasper's dead," Ben answered in a low voice. "He was kicking in the door of the house when the fire took him. Never saw anything like it and hope to God I never see it again. He was sucked inside, and the flames came down before I knew what was happening. Any of you seen hide or hair of the Deans?"

"Saw the young'uns over to Coonrods'. Tight-lipped bunch, too," Si said. "We stopped to get Had to come with us, only he was gone. Just the missus there with all them kids."

"Thank God they're safe!" Ben said. "But what about Pearl? Where's she at?"

The sheriff spat a stream of tobacco. "Can't say. She sure wasn't with Joadie Coonrod. Maybe she and Roy lit off somewheres alone."

"Had was with Roy," Si reminded the sheriff.

"That's so. Joadie never said nothing about Pearl being with them. 'Pears we got ourselves a mystery."

"Joadie didn't say a word about Pearl then?" Ben asked, standing to his feet. He felt weak and sick to his stomach.

"Said she hadn't seen Pearl all day, only that Roy rode over all in a dither and handed her little Nellie to take care of. Said Pearl was sickly. Later the other Dean children showed up saying their pa told them to go there."

"Well, I expect we all know what Had and Roy were up to," Ben said.

"Drinking, you mean?" Si asked.

"That and other things," Ben answered. "There's been a lot of talk lately about men taking matters into their own hands, doing mischief, scaring folks. There's been threats made, grievances uttered." He was thinking of what Isaac Samuel told him May Dean had said.

The sheriff spat again. "Men wearing the sheet don't generally go around setting fire to their own places," he said slowly. "Such speculation can land you in trouble more ways than one, Ben Reuben. Got to be on the right side in these here matters."

Ben put his hat on and swung into his saddle. "I thought I was on the right side. Come on, Si. We've done all we can here. You head on back to the house."

"What about you, Mr. Reuben?" Si asked.

"I'm going over to the Samuel place. Someone's got to tell May Dean about this fire, about Jasper. I'd rather it be now."

"Tell her we'll get Jasper's remains when everything settles down," the sheriff called after him.

Ben stopped his horse at the top of the hill and looked at his pocket watch. It seemed incredible that such a brief period of time could contain so much tragedy. What would happen to May Dean now? Where was Roy?

"Too much misery, Si!" Ben said. He turned his horse and rode hard all the way to Isaac's, straight as a rifle shot.

MAY DEAN WAS SENT FOR after Ben broke the news to Isaac. When she came into the parlor and saw the expression on both men's faces, she turned pale. When she heard the story, she fainted. Isaac stood by the fire, staring at the flames while Rainie waved smelling salts under May's nose as the girl lay on the sofa. Helga and Primus, both looking extremely anxious, were excused from the room.

"How terrible for May Dean!" Rainie said.

"It was pretty terrible for Jasper Knight," Ben said. "But it's over for him now."

"What's to become of her and the baby?" Rainie asked.

"I don't know," Ben said. "Is May coming around, Rainie? Can you tell?"

May grimaced and pushed the bottle with its pungent odor away from her. As soon as she was fully conscious, she cried Jasper's name and started weeping uncontrollably.

"Rainie," Ben said, "I think you'd best get her up to bed. There'll be enough for her to face tomorrow."

"Jasper!" May cried. "Oh, my poor, sweet Jasper."

"Help me," Rainie said to Isaac and Ben. "You both carry her while I go ahead and get her covers turned down."

The two men supported May between them and lifted her easily. "It'll be all right, May," Ben said. They made their way up the stairs to her bedroom and eased her to the bed, May sobbing all the while.

"You can leave us now," Rainie said. "I'll sit up with her." Rainie sat on a chair by the bed, never taking her eyes off the weeping girl.

"There's more," Ben said to Isaac once they were alone downstairs.

"Yes?"

"I didn't want to worry May with more bad news. Her mother seems to have disappeared."

"What do you mean?" Isaac asked.

"I mean there was no sign of her tonight. Jasper rode over like you told him to do. He was there when Si and I rode up. We had seen the smoke over to my place and set out to see what it was. Dry as it's been, it's a heap to worry over. Jasper said no one was there when he arrived, only the barn a-burning."

"And afterwards the house went up?"

"Exploded more like, exploded into flames when Jasper kicked open the back door."

"You have any idea how the fires started?" Isaac asked.

"None whatsoever. But I've been putting something else together, Isaac. When Si came back with the sheriff and some other men, they stopped at the Coonrod place to see if Had would come with them. Mrs. Coonrod told them that Had was off with Roy, that Roy had brought Nellie, the youngest one, over earlier, and then the other three Dean children showed up. She said Roy told her Pearl was feeling poorly. Later the two men rode off together."

"What's so unusual about all this?" Isaac asked. "Roy and Had were drinking at the school the night of the harvest program. You said they keep company."

"They do," Ben said. "They keep company with some others like 'em, too. You hear about things from time to time, about some Negro or Indian being set upon by surprise and beat up, even run out of the county, or a house being burned. No one ever does anything about it. Even the sheriff looks the other way most of the time unless there's a killing."

"I'm familiar with such activities," Isaac said. "They happened in Missouri from time to time, not so much in St. Louis but in the smaller towns. Men dressed up in white sheets and masks and terrorized their victims."

"That's what I'm talking about," Ben said. "It's why I don't belong to any secret fraternities anymore. You never know who's doing what, and I never have cottoned to being around bullies."

"But Roy wouldn't set fire to his own place!" Isaac said.

"Not unless he was roaring drunk and got careless," Ben said. "The fire part could have been an accident. But Had and Roy being out tonight may not be. There's been threats."

"I've been concerned about this since May told me, but I didn't think Roy would do anything."

"You and Primus are the only ones this side of anywhere who're what men like Roy and Had call different." Ben stood up and paced the room.

Isaac shook his head. "That still doesn't tell us where May's mother is."

"No, it doesn't."

"I don't think we're going to find out anything at this late hour," Isaac said. "You look like you could use some sleep. Want to wash up and stay over here? You're welcome to."

"I'm obliged," Ben said. "But I'd best be on home after washing up. Don't want my family to see my hair all singed. Where's that lavatory of yours?"

Ben felt a wave of weariness sweep over him as he walked down the hall. He closed the lavatory door and stared a long while in the mirror before washing his face and hands. He looked worse than he'd thought. There was a long cut across his chin; he hadn't even known it was there. Patches of the eyebrow over his left eye were scorched; his hair was peppered with ashes. After a thorough dousing with soap and water, he dried himself and went back to the foyer.

"I got to get to the bottom of this business," he told Isaac. "There's a man killed through either mischief or negligence, and someone's to blame. You might want to post a man close to the house tonight. Don't mean to alarm you or Miss Truden here, but with Roy drunk and all, you can't take any chances. Make sure your man's got a gun and knows how to use it."

Rainie followed him to the porch steps.

"Take care of May Dean," Ben said. "It'll take some time for her to get over a blow like this. Someone's going to have to tell Jasper's folks tomorrow, but I don't plan on it being me."

MAY LAY IN HER BED STARING at the ceiling. Her eyes were red and swollen, and her breath came in little shuddering gasps.

"I told Miss Truden to go on to bed," Isaac said upon entering her room. "I'll sit here till you go to sleep."

"Tell me about the fire," May said hoarsely. "I got to know it all before I can sleep. I just got to!"

He told May as much as he knew. "But this is all secondhand information," Isaac said. "Ben Reuben was there all right, but he may have left out something. It's easy to do when tragedy strikes."

"He told you none of my family was there, that no one was at the place but Jasper?"

Isaac nodded. "We know where your brothers and sisters are. We just don't know about your mother."

"Nellie's all right, though?"

"Mrs. Coonrod told the sheriff that your father brought Nellie to her in the late afternoon."

May looked confused. "Pa never takes Nellie anywhere, but he never watches her either. He'd unload her sure if she got in his way. Sounds like that's what happened."

"And then he went off somewhere with Had Coonrod," Isaac added. "That was the other thing Mrs. Coonrod said."

"Nellie has no business being at the Coonrods'," May said,

shaking her head vigorously. "And neither do Zeke or Abe or Molly. The Coonrods got ten kids of their own and a pig sty of a house!"

Isaac said nothing.

Raw emotion flickered over May's face as the enormity of her loss dawned on her again. "But I don't care about that, Mr. Samuel." Her voice teetered on the edge of hysteria. "Is it wicked of me to say that? I'll say it, though. I left them all behind to come to work here, didn't I? And I never went back to see them either—not once. It's Jasper! Oh, Jasper!" she cried.

Isaac picked up a talking tube and told Primus to come up immediately. "Bring something to calm Miss Dean," he instructed.

May went on expunging her grief and guilt. "If I'd married him when he asked me last summer, if I'd loved him more and been a real Christian, none of this would have happened, and he'd still be here. We'd be married, and I never would have come here. Do you hear me!" she screamed. "He'd be alive!"

Primus came in with a glass and handed it to Isaac.

"Drink this," Isaac said, helping May Dean to a sitting position. He resisted an impulse to linger. "There's nothing you can do for Jasper," he said softly. "You've got to think about your baby now and take care of yourself for the sake of the new life."

May drank the contents of the glass and turned away to sob into her pillow. "Leave me alone!" she cried. "I want to be left alone!"

Isaac asked Primus to sit up at the foot of the stairs. He himself prayed silently as he went to his own rooms, "*Baruch attah adonai elohenu melech ha-olam.* Blessed are You, O Lord our God, King of the universe, who hears us in our need and answers us quickly and soon."

BEN WAS DOG-TIRED WHEN HE FINISHED taking care of his horse and finally made his way back to his house. The clock in the parlor chimed twice when he came inside. He walked quietly to the bottom stair, sat down, and took off his boots. It was hard to believe that the new day had come. "Can't take many like this," he said to himself. "Horse can't either, for that matter. Poor old Penny was plumb stove-in when I put her in her stall." Too tired to move, he sat with his head in his hands, thinking of how Lillie would have been waiting up for him if she were still alive. She was once a living person in that quiet house. Had she been gone almost a year already? She would have been up, sitting in the rocker there with the kerosene lamp turned low, patiently waiting for him. There would have been hot coffee and a plate of biscuits and jam; they would have talked into the morning. That was what he missed the most, how they used to talk for hours on end. Lillie would have an opinion about everything—about Jasper's untimely death, about Roy Dean, about the fires. She would have spoken her mind freely and listened to his thoughts.

"Pearl will leave that man one day," Ben had once said to her. It was when he was helping Roy build their house and told Lillie about his drinking and rages.

Lillie had looked at him with her grave, sad eyes and answered that Pearl wasn't the sort to leave her man. "Some folks think the devil you know is better than the devil you don't," she'd said. "But beyond that, there's no place for her to go."

"He'll kill her then," Ben had said, blurting out the words without thinking. There had been no remonstrance from his wife, however. She had simply looked away.

Those idle words haunted him now. Did he really think that Roy would kill Pearl? "Dear Lord, I hope not," Ben said. His words were swallowed by the dark and silent room. It was too late to talk to anyone, much less to himself.

Right before he'd left Isaac's, Rainie Truden had spoken to him on the porch. "Do you want to stay and talk?"

And though a part of him longed to stay there, the rest of him was just too tired. "Another time," he'd said. He remembered that Rainie had put her hand on his arm when she said good night. It had been a long time since he'd touched a woman.

Ben made his way up the stairs in his stocking feet and opened his bedroom door quietly. He did not want to disturb Aunt Addie. She was still recuperating and needed plenty of rest, the doctor had said. Not bothering to remove his clothes, he sank into a deep sleep the moment his head hit the pillow.

THE COMMOTION BEGAN WITH the sounds of men on horseback riding into the yard and calling for him. Ben sat bolt upright, stunned that it was still dark and thinking it must be the next night surely. He jumped out of bed and opened a window to let them know that he'd heard them. The stars were frosty clear, the moon a far crescent of light. Eight men, two with lighted torches, looked up at him. Their horses snorted frosty air and stamped their feet.

"Ben Reuben!" It was Sheriff Dan Tate's voice.

"You want to wake my kids and scare them half to death?" Ben called down. "I'll be there directly."

When he came downstairs, Aunt Hannah stood in the kitchen door in her robe. Her nightcap sat askew on her head as she tucked loose strands of hair under the band and made a clicking noise with her teeth. "Tsk, tsk! All hours!" she said in a loud whisper. "Comes home at all hours and then off again! What I want to know is, when is this family going to get back to normal, Ben Reuben? You tell me that."

Ben held up a hand as if to ward her off. "Sorry, Aunt

Hannah. There's been some trouble tonight, and it looks like it's not over yet. I'll tell you about it later, but as for the rest, it's about time to get up anyway."

"What'll I tell Si and the men?" Hannah asked, peering out the window and frowning. "You tell them men out there to watch where their horses is a-stomping. I don't want my tulip bulbs disturbed nor the jonquils neither!"

"Tell them to start work without me," he answered. "It's nigh onto 4:30, so they'll be coming in soon for breakfast."

Aunt Hannah sighed heavily and went back to the kitchen mumbling to herself.

Ben stamped into his boots and grabbed his coat and hat. The morning air hit his lungs like a cold knife. The riders leaned forward in their saddles, anxious to be on their way.

"We done saddled your horse already," one of them said.

"I'd like to know where we're headed first," Ben said, tucking his shirt into his trousers with one hand and taking Penny's reins in the other.

"We found something," Dan Tate responded. The florid-faced little man had been elected sheriff two years before. Ben had always found him to be a master at stating the obvious.

"Well, I guess you wouldn't be clamoring for me to go with you wherever it is we're going if you didn't have a pretty good reason," Ben said. "What'd you find?"

Dan rubbed his face with a gloved hand and spoke with sober authority. "We was poking through the ashes and come across the remains of Jasper Knight."

"I thought you would." Ben mounted his horse, and the party moved as a single unit toward the road.

"Found something else," Dan said. "There was another body inside that house."

Ben felt his insides turn over as the sheriff continued. "Had

Coonrod come over to the Dean place while we was still there. I asked him where was Roy Dean, and he said he didn't know. Said Roy was plumb crazy, and he didn't want no part of it. We showed old Had what we'd found in the fire, and he turned sick right off—threw up all over the place."

"We're headed the wrong way," Ben said. "Aren't we going to the Deans'?"

"Been there enough to last me a lifetime," Dan said. "Our business is over to the Samuel mansion. That's where Had said Roy was bound for. Said Roy told him Isaac Samuel burned his house and barn—him and his Negro butler."

"It's a lie!" Ben cried. "Surely you don't believe it!"

"Can't say I do," Dan replied. "But there was bad blood between Roy and Isaac all on account of May Dean living there and getting in the family way under Samuel's roof and Jasper all fired up wanting to marry her. Seems downright odd, don't it? And now Jasper's dead and someone else besides."

"Well, I know Jasper's death was an accident pure and simple," Ben said, still trying to grasp what had happened. "I was there and saw it with my own eyes!"

"He walked into a house of death," Dan said. "How else could that body have been there and you not know it?"

"It's Pearl, isn't it?" Ben asked.

No one answered. The riders' torches were extinguished one by one in the dirt road as the sun rose behind them; the reddish ball cast a net of pearly light over the frost-tipped fields and trees. The sound of birdsong filtered through the air as three deer leaped at once, their elongated limbs silhouetted against the horizon. As the brightness of the morning star melted into the morning light, Ben wondered how evil could exist with such beauty all around. Then he remembered how cruel Roy was under the influence of strong drink. Sickened, he tried not to think of the dead.

"We'd best cut across country," he said to the others. "Save us some time."

"You go on with Hank and Rufus," Dan said. "The rest of us will stick to the road. Cover more ground that way."

The three men urged their horses to jump a low place in the sagging fence by the road and galloped on. They cut across furrowed fields and past a stand of trees on the other side. They forded a wide creek and made two more hills before hearing the sharp blast of a train whistle followed by five more shrieks.

"Strange," Ben said. "Rufus, you work for the railroad. Isn't this a mite early for the morning train to be running?"

"Railroad added a new arrival and departure about a week ago," Rufus said. "We put a notice in the newspaper to let folks know."

"'Course those of us who live out this way might not read a paper for a spell," Ben said. "Could be dangerous not knowing something like that."

"Always a danger with trains," Rufus answered.

The whistle was still blowing as the men cleared a third and fourth hill. The train's cars jostled and lurched as its huge wheels shrieked against the iron rails, braking to an unscheduled stop. Passengers piled out on both sides, shouting up and down the line and gesturing wildly. The engineer was climbing down a ladder as the men rode up, the expression on his face a mixture of fear and dread.

"Couldn't do nothing about it!" he shouted over the hissing steam, speaking to no one in particular.

"What is it?" Ben asked. "What happened?"

"Blamedest thing I ever did see!" the engineer said, shaking his head. "Man in a sheet rode onto the tracks—that's what happened! Yelling and carrying on like someone crazed! What fool would be out on a track this time of day?"

The conductor joined him at the front of the train. "Never had anything like this happen on this line! Lord, have mercy!" he cried.

Ben and his companions hurriedly dismounted and ran to join the throng already gathered at the front of the train. In a shallow ditch on the other side lay a riderless horse, its body thrashing in agony.

"Oh, no, no!" a woman in the crowd sobbed. "Do something someone! Put that poor creature out of its misery!"

Hank drew a pistol from his holster and fired two bullets into the animal's forehead.

"Where's the rider?" Ben asked. "I know this horse." He turned from the awful sight and looked around. There some fifty feet away was something wrapped in a dirty sheet. So many passengers were gathered around the dying man that Ben had to push his way through.

"What?" Ben asked, bending closer when Roy made a sound. Tears and nausea threatened to overcome him.

Hank and Rufus stood nearby. "He said something about it being nothing but lies and deceit," Hank offered.

"He's dead now!" several voices in the crowd exclaimed.

"Anyone know this man?" the conductor asked.

Ben nodded as he and his companions carried Roy's body to one of the freight cars. They laid it gently on a pile of hay and closed the door. "Take him to the undertaker in town," Ben told the conductor. "That'll be Doc Pierson. Have Doc send whatever it costs to Ben Reuben. We'll come back for the saddle and bridle."

"One last question," the conductor said. "You know where we are? Whose land is this?"

Ben climbed on his horse. "It's the Samuel place," he answered dully. He rode off long before the train finally pulled away, resuming its journey with an unexpected passenger.

SEVENTEEN

M AY DEAN SAT in front of the bay window in the parlor of Isaac Samuel's house, her legs covered by a
quilt. Her chair had been brought close enough for
her to rest her feet on the cushions in the window seat. The window itself arched to a height of ten feet. Damask drapes and
sheer panels were pulled open to admit the light of day, such as
it was. She could see the fireplace by turning her head slightly;
the fiery coals formed a warm contrast with the winter scene
before her. Snow had fallen through the night and was still coming down, huge flakes rotating through the air like filigreed
wheels forged in some fairy world. The snow and wind conspired
to turn everything into a different version of itself. The trees were
shrouded by magnetic sheets of snow that stuck and held fast.
Every branch was topped by layers of smooth icing. Silent tufts
of wind sent wild flurries whirling as thunder echoed in the
higher atmosphere.

May felt herself being drawn into the snowy scene from a
warm cocoon, like a spell was cast to draw her away to become
one with the snow, with the cold beauty of its falling.

Three days had passed since the funerals for Jasper and her

parents, days marked by storms and rain and now the snow. Late March was not kind to the country cemetery; its stark desolation broke over the sad, strange ceremony of death with a sign and a warning for all. Rainie told her she would one day forgive her father, that such grace was a gift from God, that He alone could supply what May lacked.

May stared out the window and thought about what Rainie had said. The snow covered every particle of land, hid every blemish of an imperfect world. She remembered a verse in the Bible. It said that even if your sins were as scarlet, they would be as white as snow; though red as crimson, they would be as wool. She'd asked God to forgive her many times. Now she saw that there was no reason to beg or plead with Him. It was already done. Everything was covered, every blot and stain. She had an imparted life that no more originated with her than the ability to forgive. Her very life was hidden in Christ because He was her life and none other.

She had grieved as she never thought she could, had wept till there were no tears left, and then wept some more. She would think that her sorrow was finally exhausted, and then a memory sharper than a sword would pierce her heart with visions of things past. Isaac encouraged her to think of the living—her brothers and sisters now staying in the mansion with them—and of the baby to be born.

Isaac was so good. He brought all the Dean children into his house without a word being spoken. Oh, there were rooms enough, and he could afford it. But to take them on for as long as they needed a home? It was beyond generous; it was godly. He even moved May into a room on the second floor with a door between her and Nellie's nursery. He bought clothes and toys for Zeke and Abe and Molly, and he set about helping them with things like speech and manners. He was patient, too. The children thrived. It did May's heart good to see how he smiled when Nellie held out her chubby arms to him!

Isaac paid for the funerals, too, and ordered tombstones as well. When May Dean told him they could never repay him even if they each and every one worked for him the rest of their lives, he told her it was nothing. Nothing! Then he hired an older woman from town to move in and take over the household tasks.

"Let me take care of you and the others," he told May. Who was she to refuse?

She watched the snow, turning her head now and then to the one who sat by the fireplace. Isaac was absorbed by a passage he was reading from a book in the New Testament. A new copy of Ben Reuben's prophetic book was on the ottoman by his feet. There were many books in the house, many avenues of study. May had determined to read everything she could. *A Tale of Two Cities* lay on her lap now, its second chapter held in place by her finger and thumb. She knew such efforts pleased Isaac and improved her mind; both considerations were important to her.

She watched Isaac until he finished the line he was reading. Their eyes met and held. May felt the quickening of the baby she carried within her womb. She would tell Isaac the next time it happened. This first time would be hers to ponder and cherish.

The snow continued to fall, its soft descent whispering over the yard and porch. It was a late snow, unexpected but not unwelcome. And when its frigid glory would finally melt away, disappearing into the treasuries from whence it came, the earth would rise renewed, shaking off its fitful sleep to bear fruit from the heavenly flow.

BEN REUBEN TETHERED HIS HORSE to the cemetery gate and walked the rest of the way to Lillie's grave. It was the ninth of April; all trace of the last snow had vanished more than a week before. Gone was the chill of winter, the piecemeal weather for which the country was known. Now the days were single-minded, warming with a will and straining toward the summer, which was still a good two months away. The cemetery was well tended these days; almost every family out that way had at least one loved one laid to rest there; some had many more. Flowers abounded, shooting up and around all four sides of the enclosed grounds. It was not yet a park, this cemetery, and perhaps never would be, but it boasted a proud vegetation noisy with color and variety. The rose was a favorite here; petals of every shade and hue would bloom in May. Tulips and jonquils held the stage for the present. The little peach tree Ben planted had taken hold; its sweet shade would expand to a full glory one day.

He walked around the yard, stopping at specific places for unspecified periods of time. He was in no hurry these days and didn't seem to worry about wasting time as he once had. He didn't worry about many things anymore.

There was much to be grateful for, and he was. His health might last another twenty years if he could keep feeling this good and not hurt himself in some farming accident or other. His family had survived the most difficult year of their collective lives. Aunt Addie was thoroughly recovered, and Aunt Hannah had been persuaded to stay on indefinitely. Ben was adding a bedroom downstairs, and he had plans to enlarge the parlor, too, as well as the front porch.

He wasn't as rich as Isaac Samuel, but then again, few people were. He had five thousand dollars in his brother-in-law's bank, a sum that astonished both his family and himself. His farms were prosperous; his horse trading, lucrative. There would be a good harvest if it was God's will, cattle to breed and sell, wells to prospect and drill.

Ben stood at Lillie's grave and found that for the first time, the old pain was fading. He knew she wasn't there, not the soul and spirit of her. He knew that if he lingered, the aching void would rise again, the numb wonder that she was gone. The new thing happening was that he was learning to endure his loss. He knew that she would not come to him. He hoped that in God's own time he would go to her.

"It's a beautiful place, isn't it?" Rainie Truden had come in behind him. He turned and saw her walking toward him, her horse and buggy waiting at the foot of the hill. She carried an armful of freshly cut flowers, and he knew whose garden had provided such bounty.

"I didn't hear you coming down the road," he said.

"The ground is still soft," Rainie answered. "I hope I'm not disturbing you. May asked me to bring flowers for her."

"She's getting around better now, isn't she?"

"Much better. And has her hands full, too. Those children keep Mr. Samuel's house pretty busy, I can tell you that."

Ben shook his head. "I never have seen such generosity. Taking in all the Deans! It's a wonder and an example to us all."

Rainie laid some of the flowers on Lillie's grave. "The daffodils are perfect right now. There are tulips coming on, too. You'll have to come over and sit in the garden soon before the blooms fade." She walked over to the new mounds.

"I'd like that fine," Ben said. "It's hard, that first time I mean, when you visit a grave alone."

Rainie nodded. "We read Scriptures this morning, all of us together. Even Isaac. We read that we're not to grieve as those who have no hope. May observed that Jesus was a man of sorrows and acquainted with grief and that because of Him our grief is covered by hope. She said that when others see this, they ask us to explain the hope we have within us, and we can tell them."

"She's come a long way," Ben said. "We've got to give grief full play before we can get on with life. I couldn't have stood here a year ago and talked like this to anyone. What most folks fail to understand, though, who haven't been through a loss themselves, is that the grieving part is different for every blessed soul. Everyone does it his own way, and I can't believe God worries or is the least bit surprised at how we do what we do. What I do know firsthand is that He gives strength to the weary. I know because of what He's given to me."

"He's certainly giving strength to May Dean," Rainie said, "and grace to Mr. Samuel. I've never seen such changes come over two people in such a short period of time. It does the soul good to see it."

"I've only known Isaac a short while, and yet it appears to me that he's found a deep peace and happiness here. It's inspir- that's what it is."

"His parents are coming to visit next month," Rainie said. hink they'll be hearing an announcement when they get ."

Ben whistled. "It occurred to me last time I was over and saw the way May and Isaac looked at each other that there just might be a wedding before the fall of the year. Hope his folks are broad-minded, as they say. Isaac says they aren't too serious about their religion."

"We've been praying about it, May and I. God's will is what we seek, and that's all that matters." She looked down. "It's hard to believe that May's parents and Jasper were all alive a few weeks ago. It makes you appreciate the brevity of life."

"It does for a fact."

"I've been trying to teach this lesson to my children at school, to urge them to be serious and earnest and to know that all our actions have consequences. Sowing and reaping is what it's all about when you get right down to it."

Ben looked at the sky, thinking that the country was about to reap some more rain. A thin skein of gray clouds filtered out the sunlight; rain clouds still some distance away were making a steady advance from the southwest. The breeze picked up, riffling the grass with a light tripping sound and making the flowers dip and sway.

"We've seen enough examples of bad sowing and reaping to last us a lifetime," he said. "Only I don't know if we really ever learn it for good, not till we finally come to the end of life—and a new beginning. That's why I come up here, to keep reminding myself."

Ben glanced admiringly at Rainie as she stood in the wind. He looked down at his hands; the contrast between their roughly callused size and her own quite delicate fingers was marked. He longed to hold her hands, so small and trim in their black leather gloves. She wore a long cape and a black hat with a wide brim. The breeze blew the cape open, revealing a yellow dress skirt that fell over the toes of her polished boots. The wind played havoc with her hat; loose strands of dark hair danced across her lips. The expression on her face was pleasant and unflustered in spite of the threatening weather.

"It's getting right chilly," he said, drawing closer to her.

Rainie shivered slightly and turned to face him. "It's been chilly at the school, too. After that late snow we had, I wondered if it would ever be warm again. We've about used up all the firewood. 'Course we don't have but two more months to go."

"You'll need more firewood all the same," Ben said, "and I'll see to it that you get some. We've got a few more wood-stoking days ahead of us yet." He paused, hating his shyness. "Miss Truden . . ."

"Yes, Mr. Reuben?" Her eyes skipped over his expectant features as if searching for something.

He laughed nervously. "It's funny, me getting all tongue-tied like this. What I want to say is that I want to get to know you better." Flustered by the surprised look on her face, he went on hurriedly. "It's not that we don't know each other. We've certainly been through a lot the past few months, enough for us each to see how the other one acts during good times and bad. I can only hope that you have as favorable an impression of me as I have of you. You've been an inspiration to me and my family from the first."

Rainie started to speak. "Let me finish," he said softly, encouraged by her smile, "or I'll never get this all said. I know you're a woman of prayer and action, that you live your faith. My wife was that way. You know that I loved her with all my heart, Miss Truden, and I still do in that part of me that goes on and on. But that isn't what I'm driving at. We had a good marriage, and now she's gone. She's been gone almost a year. My children and I will miss her always, but we've worked hard to get over it. 'Course you never do. We brought Aunt Hannah into our family circle, and then when we thought we would lose Aunt Addie, God was merciful and spared her. All these things have happened for a reason, most of which we can hardly grasp. God is taking what was bad and making life good again, in spite of our fear and loneliness."

Rainie put a hand on his arm. "Ben, if this is painful for you . . ."

He shook his head and cleared his throat. "It's been quite a year, but that's still not what I wanted to say. To be brief, Miss Truden, please don't mistake my words, for they rest on far more than a casual foundation, I assure you. They rest on my firm intent, which is this: I want to call on you. I want to call on you as a suitor. There now. I've said it, and it can't be unsaid." He coughed with embarrassment and relief. "I was afraid that if I said the wrong thing, you might misunderstand me or be offended."

The young schoolteacher stared at him a long time, apparently thinking over his words as well as the supreme effort put forth. Her face was a study of reflection and poise. "Apparently it's not occurred to you that I've been waiting, too," she said, "for at least as long as you."

Ben's heart beat faster. "So here we are, both standing about like a couple of kids wondering what to say or do when all I want at this particular moment is to hold you, Rainie Truden. Such a simple thing." He was amazed at himself, at the torrent that was already starting to flow from his heart and mind. Long-held emotions were finding both expression and a kindred spirit.

Rainie sighed deeply. "It is a simple thing," she said, "yet difficult to put into words. And I think it fitting, too, that this is all happening right here. Think of what we've said about the brevity of life, the certainty of death. What better place to confront one's feelings than in a cemetery! I confess that I was hoping you'd be here when I set out this morning. You've no idea how glad I am whenever I see you, Ben Reuben. So you see, I'm hardly the one to say it's improper for you to express your feelings or to act upon them, not when I want the same."

Ben felt all of her waiting for him in that moment. When he put his arm around her shoulders, she relaxed against him in response to their yet unspoken words and needs. The embrace that followed was tender and slow, the gentle yearning of friends becoming lovers. They knew that there was all the time in the world, for all their times were appointed by God.

"Rainie," he said, burying his face in her hair. It seemed that he inhaled the very life and soul of her. When they reached the gate in the early morning rain, their arms were still entwined.